WALKING RED FLAG

OCEAN VIEW SERIES BOOK 2

MORGAN ELIZABETH

Copyright © 2022 by Morgan Elizabeth

All rights reserved.

No part of this book may be reproduced in any form or by any electronic or mechanical means, including information storage and retrieval systems, without written permission from the author, except for the use of brief quotations in a book review.

❀ Created with Vellum

For all of the girls locked in their head with no way out.

I wrote this for us.

And for Alex. You were right. A watermelon would make a terrible house.

A NOTE FROM THE AUTHOR

Hey Reader!

Thank you so much for choosing to read Walking Red Flag! Ever since Gabi was revealed in Cassie's story, The Ex Files, I've had readers non stop asking me when we would meet Gabi.

I'm so excited to share this new character who is near and dear to my heart with you all.

Walking Red Flag features conversations about virginity, purity culture, neurodivergency, and ADHD. There is also a scene in a hospital featuring a broken bone. Always keep your mental health in reading - it's meant to be our safe space!

I love you all with my whole being.

-Morgan Elizabeth.

PLAYLIST

Follow You - Imagine Dragons
Cardigan - Taylor Swift
Overwhelmed - Royal and the Serpent
Nonsense - Sabrina Carpenter

PROLOGUE

-Gabi-

I should have stopped with my toothbrush.

When it fell into the toilet this morning, that should have been the sign any and all bathroom activities were off-limits for at least a whole day.

But I've never been good at reading the signs.

ONE

-Gabi-

Bridal showers are kind of weird, if you ask me.

I've only ever been to one other, my older sister Gianna's, but it was a lot of the same: weird games to decide if the guy you're marrying knows enough about you, followed by opening gifts in front of a mix of people in your life, from your best friend to your future mother-in-law. Oh, and these gifts can include both silverware and appliances, lingerie and vibrators.

The mere fact that no one finds the juxtaposition strange makes it more strange to me.

"What is that?" I say, eyes wide on the incredibly large phallic-looking pink thing my boss and best friend Cassie is holding, the box not discreet in even the slightest way. All eyes go to me, including Kerry Dawson's, Cassie's mother-in-law-to-be.

See what I mean? Why is she here, and why is Cassie getting... *that* in front of her? "I mean... I know what it is... but—" My eyes shift from it to Cassie and back. "—it's giant." I blame my family for the lack of filter I've always had. It's cursed genetics that somehow affect my speech. I gulp the wine I'm holding.

"That's the point, girl," Jordan says. Since Cassie met her now-fiancé, Luke, her circle of friends has grown in the past two years. Luke completely changed her life and was why she finally opened up and let me in. Now she's my best friend here in New Jersey since my childhood best friend Paige moved away to Cali not long before I started at the Ex Files.

"Okay, but like... that would not fit." Again, eyes on me, and again, I take a big sip of my wine. Again, I curse my stupid, *stupid* genetics and the fact that of my six siblings, I got more than my fair share of the trait. I also curse the inconvenient way my brain is hardwired to always have strange, unnecessary thoughts and commentary on literally everything happening around me.

"It fits, Gabs. It *always* fits." My eyes widen with Cassie's words.

"Always?" I say with a whisper, the wine working its magic and making me feel warm all over. She nods and laughs. Everyone else looks rightfully confused at our conversation.

"Have all of your exes been like, really small?" Sadie, another friend of Cassie's by way of Luke, asks.

"Oh my god, that's so fucked. My ex was small, but technically I have an NDA which means I'm not allowed to talk about that," Jordan says of her ex, country music star turned industry pariah after it leaked that he was abusive emotionally, financially, and physically with his long-time girlfriend before she ran off.

"All assholes have small dicks. It's like a rule or something," Sadie says, her face full of wisdom as if she's done some kind of accredited, peer-reviewed study on the topic. But, honestly, knowing this group, I wouldn't put it past them.

Cassie nods, agreeing with Sadie's words. My mind drifts off to another universe where I'm contemplating a research lab run by Cassie and Sadie. They would be the leading scientists, pioneering studies on men. Creating equations to compute the probability of red flags leading to heartbreak and the inverse relationship between the size of dick and the level of assholery. With my mind on this hilarious and fun topic, and because I'm just buzzed enough to lose the edge of embarrassment, I look around the room and spill.

"I'm a virgin," my mouth says without permission from my brain. My brain is still thinking about female-run research labs and drifting toward wondering if I could convince my brother Dom to send Sammy to a STEM camp this summer. Start a legacy of women who research dumb men, the true disease of humankind.

With my words, as one would expect, eyes widen. Eyes of women I know, but not necessarily well enough to tell them I'm a 28-year-old virgin. Women like Luke Dawson's two older sisters, his mom, and the crew of fun and hilarious women Cassie's met through Luke's childhood friend, Chris.

Blinks occur. Many.

This, too, happens when I reveal my secret.

It's not one I'm ashamed of. Not really, at least. And honestly, it's not even a *secret* unless by secret you mean it's something I don't tell random strangers. Because being a virgin at any age, 15 or 28 or 52 or 79, is nothing to *be* ashamed of. Regardless of what church and society and the freaking universe seem to tell us, virginity isn't even a big deal. At least not in the way we make it out to be. But when you go from a 16-year-old virgin to an 18-year-old virgin and then a college virgin and then a *college graduate* virgin, it becomes shockingly challenging to lose that status.

Here's the thing—I never *intended* to be a 28-year-old virgin. As a young girl, I never made some vow to stay pure for some fictional man who would sweep me off my feet. I never imagined losing it on my wedding day, surrounded by a puddle of a cupcake topper dress. It just... happened. When everyone was experimenting and losing "it" in high school, I was awkward and nerdy. I developed late, spending my golden high school years as a skinny thing with no hips and no boobs to speak of and five—yes, five—older brothers breathing down the neck of any boy who even deemed to look my way.

When I went to college at 19, doing online school for a year to help my brother out, I finally caught up with the other girls physically, and I was free of my brothers, if only temporarily. But it never seemed to be the right time. My virginity was something I'd been told my whole life was precious until that point. So losing it as a random hookup at a frat party seemed... like a disappointment.

So I waited.

I dated boys, of course.

Plenty.

Boys I kissed and boys I touched. Boys who touched me... But none stuck around long enough to do much more.

And then I was 23, graduated from college, and I was somehow still a virgin.

So I changed my mindset. I wasn't going to look for commitment or love to lose what I now realized with time was a not-so-precious v-card. I just wanted to find a guy who could prove he was worth it. I've heard all about first times being terrible, painful even, so I made it a rule that I'll have sex with a man if he could prove he'd make it good for me.

That, too, has turned into an... issue.

The first try was by a guy named Jason. He was nice enough, cute enough. I was 24 and out with my best friend, Paige, celebrating her new job, and he caught my eye. We danced the entire night before he said those cliche words: "Do you want to come home with me?" And I did. And it turned out he couldn't even find my clit.

No way was I losing my virginity to a guy who couldn't even find the clit.

The next try was a few months later with a guy named Peter. He could find it just fine, but... nothing. I felt nothing. Barely even a flutter. We both ended that night incredibly unsatisfied.

I figured both were a fluke. They had to be. I've heard horror stories from friends about how bad men can be at giving pleasure. Sometimes you have to suck it up; sometimes, you have to teach them. So I figured maybe it was time to learn myself, you know?

Yes, you read that right—I also had never tried to "do it myself."

But it turns out that part is *also* a lot harder than advertised.

So now I'm a virgin who has never been able to make myself, ahem, arrive.

I've heard the talk. I've read the books. I've searched the internet and read all of the *Cosmo* articles, but no matter how hard I try, how close I get—and sometimes I do get close—I can't seem to make myself come. It's to the point I'm thinking it's just not possible for me.

In fact, in one of the many articles I've read on the subject, I saw nearly ten percent of women genuinely *never orgasm.* Isn't that just crazy? Going your entire life knowing there's this insane, life-changing experience everyone talks about but you'll never get?

That's where I'm at now—wondering if maybe I'm broken, if perhaps I'm part of the unlucky ten percent.

And staring at that... *thing*... I'm wondering if I even want to. It looks more like a torture device than one of pleasure.

"And she's never had an orgasm," Cassie says, her eyes glassy with joy and excitement and the three glasses of champagne she's already had. I glare at her. "If anyone can help you, it's the women in this room, Gabs." I glare some more. "There's nothing to be embarrassed about!"

"I'm sorry, what?" Tara says. "But... you're gorgeous. You're practically a man's wet dream, Gabi." She looks me up and down, clearly confused. "Teeny tiny and all curves? Jesus, I'd ditch Jason for you." Heads nod, and I down the rest of my drink. But if I've gotten this far...

The mental filter fails completely, and the words spill out.

"I think I'm broken."

"You're definitely not broken, Gabi," Cassie says. "She reads smutty books on her lunch every day and blushes to high heaven. Trust me, she has a sex drive. It's just dormant. Plus, she always wants all the gritty details of *my* sex life."

All three Dawson women cover their ears.

"No, no, no. No! I've told you Cassie, no Luke sexy talk!" Quinn yells into the quiet room, fingers in her ears. We all laugh before Cassie leans over and tugs her hand.

"You're good. I'm not going into details now."

"I would like details at a later date," Sadie says, her hand raised, a devious smile on her face.

"Trust me, you want details," Jordan says, looking from Sadie to Cassie. Cassie, who, pre-Luke, would bury her face in shame at the mere thought of sharing details of her sex life. But now? She's smiling, a happy, satisfied look there.

Is that what it's like to have regular orgasms? Do you just slip into a state of blissed-out happiness?

My own buzz doesn't stop me from asking, "Has she told you about the time she recreated how they first met?" Hey, if she can embarrass me, I can embarrass her, right? I think that's how it works.

"Oh, my god, no!" Quinn yells, putting her hands back to her ears. Tears are now rolling down Sadie's face as she laughs at the exchange. This whole moment is too much.

See? Bridal showers are *weird*.

"Okay, okay, let's get back to the topic at hand," Tara, the level-headed of the Dawson sisters, says. My eyes go to the pile of gifts, the "toy" sitting happily on top. "You're not broken. You just need some... help." She smiles and I'm pretty sure she read my mind. "Do you have a vibrator?"

I'm sure my whole body turns red with an embarrassed burn. I look at the ground to make sure there's not a scorch mark.

Nope, all good.

Just a fictional puddle of embarrassed shame.

"No?"

"Let's go shopping!" Jordan says, clapping her hands, and Sadie instantly jumps up as if she's ready to go already, reaching for her bag.

"Stop. You're going to scare her," Quinn says. "She needs to start easy! I'm assuming you've tried all of the normal things? Fingers, etc?" Oh my god, kill me now. How did this go from Cassie's bridal shower to her fiancé's older sister coaching me through how to make myself come while his mom watched? I steal Cassie's half-full glass and down it before nodding. Isn't she supposed to be the one in the spotlight today? Not her maid of honor?

"No reason to be embarrassed, honey. All girls here. We've all been there," Mrs. Dawson says, and never in my life have I wished I had the power to evaporate more than this exact moment. "Have you tried the shower?"

"The... what?"

"Oh my god, yes!" Cassie says with a shout. Her happy buzz is set on high. "The shower!!"

"What is the shower?"

"Do you have a detachable showerhead?" Tara asks. I like Tara. Her kids are cute and she's less in your face than Quinn. She has a sweet motherly way, reminding me of my mother, except I would never in a million years talk in front of my mom about... this.

"Uh, yes?"

"So get into the shower, right? Then grab the showerhead and... ya know." Her hand makes a circling movement around her lower regions.

Kill me now.

Oh my god, kill me now. "The warm water plus the pressure..." Her fingers make an okay sign like she thinks it's the perfect solution. "It's an old trick. I'm shocked you've never tried it!"

The only thing I've ever "tried" was "hand stuff," and has gone terribly each time I attempted it. I felt silly, my mind wandering off to think about very unsexy things like the beeping of my fire alarms that needed new batteries. Once Cassie and I searched vibrators for virgins, but they all looked like crazy torture devices and scared the shit out of me. Instead of actually ordering anything, we spent the entire night laughing hysterically at the reviews.

A vibrator was out.
But a shower?
I think I could manage that.
What's the worst that could happen?

TWO

-Gabi-

I TAKE a cab back from Cassie's shower to my apartment. I'm glad I made the choice not to drive there because the champagne and shots —Sadie's idea and, at this moment, I can't decide if I adore her or not —have definitely gotten to my head.

The drive is nearly 10 minutes, most of which I spend on my phone reading. Cassie calls me a conundrum. Although I spend most of my time reading what my mom calls "trashy romance novels" and I work at a business specializing in finding true love for people, I have absolutely zero love in my life.

I usually just smile and say that my book boyfriends more than fulfill me. And, I mean, I'm not wrong. Most of them pass the list of "Cassie's Dating Rules," meaning if they were alive and willing to date me, they wouldn't destroy me, mind, body, and soul.

But the one thing that neither they nor I apparently can do is get me over the edge. Sure, reading gives me all the butterflies, but anytime I try a little self-love, it just ends up disappointing.

The driver turns around in his seat right as I'm getting to a particular saucy spot when the hero is talking incredibly dirty to his heroine, shocking me out of my daze.

"This you?" he asks, tipping his head to my apartment building that we're stopped in front of, and it takes everything in me not to burn to a crisp right here. I scramble out, nearly tripping as I press the button on my phone to leave him a tip before walking in the main doors of my apartment. I read more, getting into the hot scene that is definitely making me feel things. I continue scrolling and reading on my ride up the elevator until it dings on my floor.

As I unlock the front door, I make my decision.

I'm going to give it a go.

I'm perfectly tipsy, my inhibitions melted away.

This book has gotten me all kinds of hot and bothered.

I have a new plan of attack to make the big "o" happen.

Shower it is.

I throw my bag and phone onto the couch, walking straight to the bathroom to get undressed, champagne buzz making me feel maybe more confident than I should be, but fuck it.

I deserve a damn orgasm, you know?

Once I'm undressed, I start the shower, making sure it's nice and warm but not too hot. I think hot would probably be bad, right? I don't want to scald my vagina. That would be hard to explain to a doctor. I blush just thinking about it.

While the shower heats, I stare at myself in the mirror, wondering if this will be it. Everyone at Cassie's shower made it seem like this was the magic ticket, how everyone did it the "first time." Why didn't I try this years ago? As I look over myself, I can't help but wonder in some strange way if I'll look different after, if something in my face will scream, "Hey! I've had an orgasm! I'm not totally broken!" But soon, my face can no longer be seen as the steam builds, fogging up the mirror.

It's now or never. Let's go.

Stepping into the shower, there's a moment of panic as I try to figure out how to stand. What's the best way to do this? Sitting?

Standing? Lying down? I guess the name of the game is to get the water where you want it but not drown. That would be distracting, I'd think. I reach up, grab the handle of the handheld showerhead, and decide standing is probably best. Eyeing the lip of the tub, I shrug before I put a leg up, leaving myself wide open. Okay. This makes sense, a good angle.

Perfect. Now, I just...

I breathe in deep to prepare myself, strangely nervous as I move the showerhead in my hand to find the right angle. And then I say screw it and move so the water is right at ground zero.

The water is warm on my center as it hits and the feeling is... nice. A gentle beating on my clit, which from my extensive research and, ahem, self-exploration is the spot that needs the most attention. I tip my hips and move the showerhead closer, and that feels even nicer.

Huh. This is interesting.

I move the showerhead in small circles, so that spot gets a mix of high and low pressure. A low sound falls from my lips—a moan!

I moaned!

Don't get too excited, Gabi. We've been here before, I tell myself as I remember the many times I've read an exceptionally hot scene in one of my books and crept my fingers down between my legs.

But I never seem to be able to finish the job.

I take a deep breath, moving the showerhead in just a bit closer, increasing the pressure. *Wow, this feels really nice.* Another soft moan falls from my lips.

Holy shit! Okay, this is good. This is a good sign, right? Right path?

I think it's going to happen! There's a warmth in my belly, a clawing at my lower back that seems to be building with each pass of the water.

But that's when I make the fatal decision.

I decide I need more on my clit, more focused energy in one spot. I eye the little lever you can move left and right to increase or decrease the pressure and stream size, slowly moving it to the left. The pressure increases as the size of the stream decreases, the focus on my clit becoming more and more intense. Oh my god, oh my *god!* This feels amazing. I'm starting to moan, a fluttering in my belly growing, a heat in my lower spine building, my hips rocking gently. *Oh my god! It's going to happen! I'm not broken!*

And then my foot slips.

And I fall.

And the euphoric feeling morphs from utter pleasure and joy to unbearable pain and disappointment.

THREE

-Vic-

I NEARLY IGNORE the call when it vibrates from the white table in the break room. The sound makes my teeth grind, something about the phone case on the Formica putting me into sensory overload.

Or maybe it's just the name on the caller ID.

Mom calling.

I sigh, knowing what's coming.

My mom means well. She does; I know this. But my younger sister, Vivi, called this morning to warn me. It turns out, my mother told *her* that at tea with Mrs. Johansen, they were once again talking about setting me up with Mrs. Johansen's daughter.

Another blind date.

I have no *time* for blind dates.

Even more, I have no *desire* to go on these dates—especially the ones my mother secures for me.

Again, my mother means well. She can't quite understand how a doctor is single and not even looking. By her count, I should have a sweet, beautiful woman waiting for me at home, making me full three-course dinners and pregnant with our second child.

I'm not getting any younger, you know.

Occasionally I cave, accepting the date to stave off her insanity, her constant nagging, but it's always the same. Some nice young thing, too young for me, who wants to marry a doctor, have his children, and join the PTA.

They're nice enough. And they'll make some man perfectly happy, in the Stepford way, but they're all boring. They're all cut from the same cookie-cutter, with the same pristine, well-off background. Perfect for breeding more perfect specimens to continue on the family name. In my mother's mind, each is an ideal match, someone I can propose to in 9.2 months then allow my mother and future mother-in-law to plan an extravagant wedding. A too-expensive wedding where they can invite their hundreds of friends to. A spectacle to show off their successful children and, in turn, their successful parenting.

My perfect little wife will then become pregnant with the ideal 2.5 children and harass them to join all the extracurriculars and get perfect grades. Then, when they don't get 1600 on their SATs, she'll force them to retake it after countless hours of tutoring, spawning more perfection my mother can brag about.

Those children will each enter predetermined fields so that when she goes to mahjong on Thursdays, she'll have a variety of grandchildren in various professions to brag about, ensuring she remains on the top of the pyramid that is her incredibly competitive social circle.

I don't have the heart to tell her that's not my plan. It's not what I want by a long shot.

In fact, since I was a kid, I wanted unpredictable. I wanted adventure and excitement. The boring path which was laid out for me felt suffocating. So I spent weekends in high school pretending to go to science camps, working with my friends to make intricate flyers to trick my parents, and going to parties instead.

I spent so much time partying in college that I nearly had to drop out my first semester—the *ultimate shame*. After that, I had a friend who lived near my childhood home in Ocean View check the mail daily before my parents were home to intercept any reporting of grades that weren't up to standard. I knew if they found out, my days of independence were long gone and I would do whatever it took to keep that chaotic freedom.

Eventually, I got myself together, but I never lost the urge to find chaos in a predictable life.

Being a doctor was chosen for me, but an ER doctor? I chose that.

The chaos is strangely soothing to me. Not knowing what or who I'll see on any given day is a blessing. Can it be stressful? Of course. Can it be heartbreaking? Without a doubt.

But would I change that for something normal and "acceptable" in my parents' eyes?

No. Not in the least.

But with my sister's intel, I know this call will be painful.

I contemplate not answering. I get such a small amount of peace when I'm on call. There's nearly no time at all when I'm not rushing around, helping and healing. Do I really want to spend this time talking to my mother who is just going to try and shove another perfect woman down my throat?

Not in the least.

But if I ignore the call, there are two potential endings. One, she worries. My mother has an undeniable anxiety surrounding something tragic happening to my sister and me. It's beyond everyday stress that moms have, beyond the normal worries and anxieties. Her younger sister died in a car accident in her 20s, and that trauma still affects her daily. It's more prevalent with my sister, she needs to know where she is at all times, but my mom still worries about me. It's why she wants an easy, predictable life for me. And I know if I ignore this call, there's a chance that anxiety will manifest.

As annoying as my mother is, I don't want her worrying like that. When she has an episode, we all feel it.

But option two is almost worse—it results in her telling my father, who would do anything to keep his wife happy. Even call his grown-ass son in his early thirties and yell at him for not answering his mother's call.

Neither of those options is one I want to face right now.

So instead of hitting the "fuck you" button, as Ben calls it, I tap the green icon, putting the phone to my ear.

"Hello, Mother," I answer, fighting the sigh that already wants to break from my chest.

"Hello, Victor. Are you avoiding my calls again?" Always right to the point.

"Of course not, Mom. I had a patient this morning. So this is the first time I'm sitting down all day."

"Then why did I have to call you?"

"I just sat down. You beat me to it." She huffs and, as annoying as it is, I laugh. My mother is a tiny, gorgeous Indian woman who fits the description of my "future wife" perfectly. And although she's bossy and nosey, she's also sweet and kind and caring and... well... my mother.

"So, what do I owe this call to?"

"Beth—Mrs. Johansen—called me and wants to set up a time for you to go to dinner with her daughter." I sigh. There it is. Again, it's not unlike my mother to jump right into things, but that doesn't make it less trying.

"Mother..."

"She's a sweet girl. Volunteers at the school—"

"They're all sweet girls."

"Well, you never marry any of them."

"Maybe I just don't want to marry right now."

"You're a man. Men don't know what they want until it slaps them in their face."

"So wait until it slaps me, Mom."

"I'm the one doing the slapping here," she says, trying on her "tough" voice, which is about as tough as Tweety Bird. I try not to laugh, knowing it will make this process take longer and I don't want to somehow let it drag so long that I end up suckered into going.

"I don't want to go on a blind date."

"I just don't know why you won't at least meet her for coffee." The voice in my ear is a mix of disapproving and disappointed, the concoction that makes mothers so glorious at brewing guilt in their children.

But in this case, it doesn't work.

I'm tired of blind dates.

"Mom."

"What could it hurt?"

"I'm busy."

"Always so busy. Working all day and night, never even coming home to see me." I sigh. This conversation is not new either. "Are you avoiding me?"

"No, Mom. I'm just swamped."

"I thought once you were out of residency, it would be easier. You'd have more time for yourself and your family."

I do. I just choose not to spend my precious time in my childhood home being dogged about how I'm 34 and unmarried, with no prospects in my future. I don't want to hear my mother go on about how her children haven't made her a grandmother yet. How in her day, women were having children when they were 19 and I'm going to miss all the "good ones" if I don't stop messing around.

Do parents not realize this rhetoric is not only incredibly annoying and dated but doesn't help to get their children to enjoy being around them?

"If you'd chosen a more traditional field..." she starts, and this is part two of her fussing.

"Mother—"

"I'm just saying. Your cousin is in surgery and he's home for dinner every Sunday. I told you —"

"We're not doing this, Mom. I became a doctor because it's what you and Dad wanted. I chose the field." Emergency medicine was my choice. It's what I wanted. I love the chaos of it. I love the unpredictability, the excitement. After a life of being asked to be the opposite, when I started my residency, I fell in love with emergency medicine and helping people in the midst of trauma. Now I work on everything from urgent care to resetting broken bones to kids who shove things up their noses. I love never knowing what I'm going to be working on.

"There's still time—"

"Arjun is a plastic surgeon. I don't want to be tearing women down every day of my life, convincing them to spend thousands to fit some standard. Is that what you want from me?" After many tests, I've determined that this is the most effective way to get my mom off my ass when she takes her stance of telling me I should change my specialty.

"Well, no, but—" My pager goes off, the sound shrill, and relief washes through me. My quiet time and lunch might be cut short, but so is this hellish call.

"Sorry, Mom. Gotta go—there's an emergency."

"There's always an emergency," she says with a huff as I clean up my spot, heading back to the ER to find my next patient—a broken wrist. Potentially needs a pin.

"I'm an ER doctor. That's my job. Talk to you soon."

"I love you, Victor," she says, her voice soft, and it's the truth. My mom loves me. She just comes from a different generation with a much different focus. That focus contrasted with her other focus of getting me into some respectable job, and now that I'm here, she's at a loss for how to act.

"Love you too, Mom. See you soon." And then I'm hanging up and walking towards my next patient.

As I walk down the hall towards the room I was summoned to, a nurse meets me at the door and hands me a clipboard with the patient's information.

"Gabrielle Mancini. Slipped in the shower, and an ambulance came to her apartment. Says she landed on it and X-rays show a clean break. But it might need a pin." She hands me the X-ray film and I see what she means. From the incident description, I assume she's an elderly woman, was bathing, and clearly needs more constant supervision.

But when I walk into the room, that's not what I face.

The woman is young, mid-to late-twenties.

She's holding her arm against herself, her big brown eyes a bit dazed, and dressed in what I think are men's boxer shorts and an oversized, tie-dyed SpongeBob SquarePants tee shirt. Her hair is wet, pulled into a dark bun on top of her head. Mascara is streaking her cheeks.

She's a disaster.

"Thanks, Pam." I walk over to where the stunned woman sits on the edge of a table. "Hi, Gabrielle. My name is Doctor Brandt. You can call me Vic or Doctor Vic," I say. Patients usually find a first name basis more comfortable. Working in the emergency room, patients I see are generally already on another stress level, shock setting in. Every bit helps to calm them and gain their trust quickly.

"Hi," she says, her voice small and shallow. Looking at her, it's clear she's pretty, despite the stoner outfit and her mascara face.

"See you took a spill, huh?" She nods, a blush burning her cheeks. "While you were taking a shower?" Her eyes shift.

There is more to this story, that's for sure.

"Everything okay, Ms. Mancini?"

"Gabi."

"I'm sorry?"

"Gabi, you can call me Gabi." I nod.

"Okay. Is everything okay, Gabi?" She nods then shakes her head.

"Yes. Well, no. Yes. As okay as one can be right now, with what I assume is a broken wrist. Oh, my god." Her head tips back to look at the ceiling and shakes softly before she continues rambling. "Explaining this to my family is going to be a disaster. I'll never live it down. And Cassie's totally going to know. All the girls will. Stupid bridal shower. Stupid toothbrush." I can't do it. I can't fight the smile.

I've learned to take everyone's story and not react in this field. It's common decency—especially in the ER. You'd be shocked with the number of things I've had to help extract from asses.

You never laugh.

Compassion is the name of the game.

But right now, for whatever reason, it's failing me. So I smile as I ask, "Toothbrush?"

"I dropped it in the toilet today."

"And you fell trying to get it?"

"No." I smile again. God, she's kind of cute.

"What does a toothbrush in the toilet have to do with your wrist being broken?"

"It's broken?" I nod, moving the film so she can see. "Right there. You might need a pin or surgery. You'll definitely need a cast." Her eyes widen, mild panic taking over. I need to get her mind on a different track. "Toothbrush?"

"I dropped it this morning. In the toilet."

"Got that. What does that have to do with your wrist?"

"I should have known." I stand there watching her. To her credit, she's loaded with painkillers and talking reasonably, if not out of order. "It was a sign. I'm usually good at reading signs." And then it happens.

Whether or not I realize it, I fall in love with Gabrielle Mancini and her endless talking, her gorgeous mind, and hilarious personality.

"My boss literally reads red flags for a business, you know? That's what she does. She dates men to figure out what they're hiding, then she sets them up. A matchmaker, ya know? Though she's getting married, so, not sure how that's going to go. Anyway, she's also my best friend. Except for Paige, but she moved away out of the blue like a bitch. But I've learned a lot from her, about reading signs. And my mom is like, so superstitious." She rolls her eyes like she finds this exasperating. "*I should have known.* When you drop a toothbrush in the toilet in the morning before you go to a bridal shower, you don't do *anything* in the bathroom. It's a sign from the heavens above. It was probably a sign from my grandma! She totally loved me and would totally have done that in order to save me from this!" She jerks her wrist to show me, and I know that's it.

Her eyes go wide with pain that even the painkillers can't suppress and she yells, eyes rolling into her head.

That's the first time I hold her in my arms.

FOUR

-Gabi-

When I wake up, the room is spinning.

I'm not sure how strange that is, considering I just came out of surgery for my stupid, *stupid* wrist, but it's spinning all the same.

Three doctors are lined up in my line of sight, all three tall with brown skin and nearly black hair. I blink.

Nope. That's one doctor. One extremely hot doctor.

"Hello, Gabrielle. I'm Doctor Vic. We met earlier, and I performed the surgery on your wrist this afternoon. How are you feeling?"

Blink. Blink. Blink. My blinks go to the beat of the heart monitor, and it makes me giggle. "Gabrielle?"

"Does this look funny?" I ask, continuing to blink. It's not helping with the dizziness, but it's fun.

"What's that?"

"My blinking. Beep, beep, beep," I say to the beat as I blink.

"It does look funny, but you should stop. You could make yourself sick with the quick vision change." He's nice. A nice doctor, thinking about keeping me from getting sick. Though he's a doctor, so...

"You are super hot." He is. My sister Gia would call him "Daddy" material. And then my brother-in-law would roll his eyes at her in a way that makes my belly gushy and jealous because they are so freaking cute together. The doctor's white, perfectly straight teeth gleam from behind full lips.

A part of me thinks I should be embarrassed by having said that out loud. That it's inappropriate.

Wait. Is what I just said inappropriate? It's a fact, but still... my filter rarely works as it is. There's a good chance when I mixed in life-altering embarrassment and anesthesia, I broke it indefinitely.

"Thank you, Ms. Mancini." Well, that was nice. He has a nice smile. All white, and— "How are you feeling?"

"Dizzy." I look at the wall behind him. That hospital white color is supposed to be sterile and clean, but it's swirling with the cords and wires and posters on the walls, making for a stomach-churning look.

"That's to be expected. Here, let me help you sit up a bit." He moves, a warm arm touching bare skin where the back of my hospital gown is open, and I shiver as he moves me to sit. The shiver reminds me of my failed attempt to orgasm, which landed me with a broken wrist, surgery, and no orgasm.

"How's that?" he asks as he tips the bed up using a remote control looking thing.

"Good," I mumble. But I'm stuck on the feeling of his arm on my skin and the shiver it provoked.

My senses are coming back to me. Not totally, but enough that I can tell I'm thirsty as my tongue sticks to the roof of my mouth. I do it a few times, the sounds making me giggle again.

"Here, let me get you a water," the hot doctor says, leaning to pour some from the small plastic pitcher into a cup. Then he holds a straw to my lips like I'm a small child. Okay, now, *this* is embarrassing. "Slow sips," he says as I start to gulp. My eyes lock to his, a dark chocolate brown under thick lashes, and another shiver runs through me.

Good thing there's only one of him now.

That would be way too much of a good thing.

"Thank you," I say as I move my head back. He sets the drink on the small table beside me and sits on the corner of the bed where my feet aren't.

"So surgery went well. You have a cast, and there is a pin in your wrist to hold it together while things heal, but that's all. It's going to hurt for a few days, and you won't be able to get your wrist wet. There are stitches underneath the cast, which can come off in about six weeks." He continues to give me care instructions, and I really hope I leave here with a packet of papers because there is no way I'll remember anything he's saying. My mind is still spinning from the anesthesia and the pain medication and from the fact that this man is so freaking hot. How does he do his job? Do people actually listen to him?

"...you fall, Gabrielle?" the doctor says, and it's a question I'm supposed to answer. I know because he's staring at me expectantly. Shit. I wasn't listening.

"I'm sorry, wha—?" I'm getting tired. It would be rude for my eyes to close, though, so I keep them open, forcing the lids to stay as high as they can, blinking a few times until I can focus on him.

"I asked how you fell."

Something tells me I shouldn't answer this, but I can't remember why.

Why shouldn't I tell him how I fell? *Why, why?* My mind runs through all the excuses, but I can't find a single one. It's just... blank. I should have someone in the room, a chaperone, to make sure I don't say something stupid.

"In the shower." *Safe answer, Gabi. Good job.*

"Yes, I saw that in your chart. But how?" Everything is fuzzy, blurring the edges with sleep, so I can't even think about the fact that I should ask why he wants to know. Instead, my mind goes back to the shower, the handheld attachment, the building of pleasure; I was so close...

"I was so close!" I say, throwing my hands up. The IV line tugs in my arm, but it stays put. "Ow."

"Gotta stay still. Don't want that tugging out. If it does, Nurse Pam will come after me," he says with a smile. He has a *good* smile. Like a *really* good one. All straight white teeth surrounded by perfect brown skin. Cassie would call it a panty-dropping smile.

Red flag.

"So close to what?"

"I bet you could do it," I say, not answering his question. I bet he could, too. That face is gorgeous. He's tall and dark and handsome, which knocks him out early, that being the very first item on the red flag list, but I mean, maybe a red flag is what I need to finally make it happen. My eyes flit to his fingers, which are long and thick. I look at my own—tiny, dainty, even. "Maybe that's my problem," I say, looking from my hand to his face. "You know?" He's smiling still, confusion on his face. How is he confused?

It's *obvious*.

"Sorry, Gabrielle. You lost me."

"My friends call me Gabi. We can be friends."

"Okay, Gabi." There's a laugh in his voice, but I can't see the smile anymore.

"I really think we'd make good friends. The fun kind." My eyes have drifted, closing a bit as the picture of the kind of *friends* this doctor could make flashes behind them. It makes me shiver. Or maybe that's this freezing hospital room.

"What were you close to?"

"*An orgasm!*" I shout, my eyes opening again. He blinks at me, head moving back a bit in surprise. "I was so close! So close! Tara was right, you know. The shower method? Foolproof. Unless you're me, and you try it, and you break your fucking *wrist*." He's looking at me, eyes wide. "I know. I know, trust me, it's crazy to me too. Did you know some people use the showerhead to make themselves *orgasm?*"

I whisper it like it's a secret, which apparently it was to no one but me. His eyes are wide. Maybe it's a secret to him too. "You use the water. Not... the showerhead. That sounds... uncomfortable." Another laugh. It's rich and fills my veins with warmth. Or maybe that's the painkillers. Who knows? I look at his pants, the light green scrubs.

Hot.

"I don't think it works on guys. Though, what do I know? I think you're supposed to be sitting down. For the shower thing to work? I tried standing, and I was *so close*. But now, I'll never do it. The only time I ever got close, I *broke my damn wrist*."

"The only time..."

"I'm a freak, I know. 28, and I've never had an orgasm. I'm broken. I'm sure of it. Did you know that some people just genuinely *can't orgasm?* I think I'm one of them. The synapses don't work. I do it, and I get close, but then my brain goes BOOP, and it's a losing game. And I'm a *virgin*." Those eyes get wider, the smile growing too. "Believe me, I never thought I'd be here either." I blink, and it takes more effort to open them back up. "It was totally unintentional, you know. The virgin thing. But now I'm kind of committed to the cause."

"The cause?"

"The lucky guy has to pass my test. It's my only rule." I yawn, and suddenly there are three of Doctor Vic again. Shit. I blink and we're back to one.

"Your rule?" Jeez, he asks as many questions as I do.

"All of my rules come from Cassie, except for one, because I made that rule before I even knew Cassie." Blink.

The back of my eyelids are nice. Black and comfortable. But I open my eyes again to finish our conversation. "The only rule I have is if I'm giving it up to some random guy, he better know how to make me come, you know? Because I waited too long for it to suck."

Doctor Vic's smile is the last thing I see before the black of my eyelids takes over, and I fall into a deep, solid sleep.

FIVE

Six Weeks Later
-Vic-

Vivi and I were not close growing up the way some of my friends were with their siblings. Six and a half years separate us, so when we were school-aged, we never lined up. I graduated before she was even in high school. I wasn't far from entering into residency when she started college.

It also didn't help that where I was dying for unpredictability, to break free of the expected life our parents laid out for us, Vivi leaned into it. She picked a reasonable major "for a woman," intending only to attend long enough to find a man. She didn't date until she was 16 as per our parents' rules, and even then, it was only boys preselected for her. Boys whose parents our parents knew, and boys who fit the expectations of who my sister should at some point marry and procreate with.

Even now, my sister accepts the blind dates. Agrees with the advice my mother throws her way and attends the galas happily. She's accepted the predictability of what is expected of her.

Somewhere over the years, despite our differences, we've grown close. It's not that I didn't always love my sister growing up—I just didn't connect with her. She was so much younger, so different from me. She wasn't my people.

But now, after she weaseled her way into my life, she's one of my favorite people. I almost regret not spending more time with her when we were younger. But with time comes wisdom, I suppose.

Part of me wishes I had a closer relationship with her from the start or more siblings. More chaos. More fun. I wish my childhood was filled with more love in its explicit form, not buried beneath good intentions and high expectations.

But other times, like right now, I'm reminded of how different my sister and I are.

"So last week Mom took me to get my dress for the gala. Lots of eligible men will be there." Her smile is feline, like she's preparing to pounce

"I don't know how Mom talks you into that stuff."

"What stuff?"

"The parties. The galas. The meet and greets to find you a suitable husband."

"It helps that I want a suitable husband." I roll my eyes.

"So you can marry in exactly 27 months, wait 15 months, get pregnant and start your perfect family with your perfect 2.5 kids who will also become doctors and lawyers and politicians?"

"Please. If one of my kids became a politician, Mom would go into an early grave." I laugh.

"Yeah, god forbid someone tries to advocate for others. Though maybe one of those politicians who help the fancy people. Mom would like that. Gotta climb that social ladder, sis." Our mom isn't a bad person. She just has seen the negative of the word, growing up in poverty and pulling herself up the ranks to marry a man much wealthier than her. A man with money and prestige, but no time for her. She wants the best the world can offer us. In her mind, her entire life was lived to give that to us.

Even if it's the opposite of what we want.

"She's got another one lined up for you," Vivi says with a smile. It's the kind of smile little sisters have when they know you're about to experience some great irritation or disappointment, and it brings them a sick joy.

Vivi has perfected this look.

"Another what?" I ask, but I know the answer. It's the dynamic we follow. She teases me for something, and I act dumb so that she can have her fun.

"Perfect match." I groan.

"I told her I wasn't interested in a blind date."

"She told me you ran off to do some doctor emergency last time she asked." Shit. She's right. "Sounds like you didn't actually have time to say no explicitly. But knowing you, you would have given in anyway, so who cares?" She's not wrong. Telling my mom no is hard, at best. At worst, it ends in tears and manipulative exclamations of "I'm sorry I'm a bad mom," until the guilt takes me over and I just go on the damn date.

The date always sucks.

Basically, they're all versions of my sister, which is sick in its own way. Young, early to mid-twenties. Pretty things, but heads in the clouds. Usually focused on what comes next—the easy life. Marriage, kids, settling down.

I'm not opposed to any of that by any means. I want boys I can rough house with and girls I can spoil rotten. I want the wife I go to bed with each night and wake up for a new adventure every day.

But I *want the adventure*. That's the part that's nonnegotiable.

I don't want life to be boring and predictable.

My entire childhood was predictable. I woke at the same time every day, my dad already off to the hospital. My mom dropped us off for school and hours of extended learning and AP classes. The same lunches were packed each day with health and longevity in mind. Salads while my friends got peanut butter and jellies and hot school lunch. Then we were picked up and carted off to extracurriculars that would look impressive on applications.

Karate. Soccer. Latin Club. Ballet for Vivi.

Home, homework, extra homework my mom had teachers assign. Bed early, never staying up late for movies or TV shows.

I hated it.

I had friends who would tell me about their parents having movie nights packed with junk food and a fort. Friends who could choose which sport to play—or none. Friends who woke up at noon on Saturdays, and friends who got to be the masters of their own lives.

I wanted that. I wanted control.

And as I grew up, I realized it wasn't even that. It wasn't the control I wanted. I wanted excitement. I wanted to never know what was coming next. I wanted to be surprised, to roam free and enjoy the world instead of letting small pieces that fit into my life plan unfold as expected.

"It's Ramona," Vivi says, snapping me out of my daydream. *Ramona.* Why does that name sound familiar? "The girl down the street." Oh no. Not Ramona.

Ramona was born to be a princess but, unfortunately, was born in the suburbs of New Jersey. She's the kind who got homecoming queen not because she earned it, but because her mother demanded it. Head-to-toe designer. I've never seen her without a full face of makeup and heels. Once I saw her at a restaurant, complaining her ice water wasn't cold enough.

She's a nightmare.

If I could pick one person who would be my *worst* match, it would be Ramona Johansen.

"Shit." My sister laughs, a devious little sister laugh.

"She's adamant about this one, too, bro."

"What do you mean?"

"Mrs. Johansen was over again on Sunday for tea. I overheard them talking. Planning the wedding already."

"No fucking way."

"Seems Mother Dearest is getting tired of you being single. A winter wedding. Whites and blues."

"That sounds hideous."

"It sounds like it's from the pages of a bridal magazine." *Predictable.*

If I could choose a wedding, I'd elope.

A tropical island.

Bare feet.

My mother would go green at the thought.

"I haven't heard from her since that call, though. It was weeks ago."

"Well, I think she considers your silence a confirmation." I sigh. Of course she does.

"Fuck."

"You better figure out a plan. Even Dad's on her side. Saying you need to settle down."

Now, there's nothing reasonably that my parents could do to force me to date this girl. I'm a man. I pay my own bills. I live in my own apartment. But despite how obnoxious my parents are, my mother specifically, I love them. I understand they mean well, that they just want what they deem to be best for me.

It's just that our ideas of "best" collide.

"You need to figure out something to get her off your ass," Vivi says, sipping her water.

"I've been working on that for years."

"No, you've been agreeing to the bare minimum to keep her happy. You need a solution, not a fix."

"Oh, wise one, what should I do?"

"Date someone."

"I'm not going to date one of Mom's picks."

"No shit. They are so not your type."

"What's my type?" I ask with a smile.

"Fucking crazy." I nearly choke on my water.

"I'm sorry?"

"Every girl you date—though I wouldn't even call it that—is out of their damn mind."

"No fucking way." She blinks at me. "Emily —"

"Had that dog. Remember? She dressed it up in clothes and put it in a stroller?" Shit, she's right. The woman was sweet, but a little... well...

"Becca —"

"Asked everyone what their birth time was within the first three minutes of meeting them and then would decide if she could be within reach of their aura at that moment." Also true. In fact, she decided Vivi wasn't on the right wavelength when they met and insisted we never meet with her again. That relationship ended quickly.

"Sara—"

"She was two-faced."

"What?" If anything, I thought Sara would be the best fit of all of my exes.

"She was sunshine and rainbows when you were in the room. Cold as ice once you left."

"Why didn't you say anything?"

"I knew it wouldn't last."

"What?"

"Vic, you date women for two months, max. If you can even call it that. They're glorified fuck buddies." She cringes. "Though we're not talking about that."

"I don't sleep around, Viv."

"I know. But you do. You just do it in a way your conscience feels better about."

Shit. I always forget how observant Vivian is. "I just—"

"Don't want to settle down. Got it. But you've got a killer mental block, so you need to do it the good guy way. It helps that you land girls who also have no intention of settling."

God, when did she become so astute? "What are you doing, writing a dissertation on me?"

"I notice things. So what's your plan?"

"Plan?"

"For Mom. What are you going to do to get her off your back?"

"I'm not sure." She rolls her eyes and sighs.

"Men. Useless."

"I've been dodging her for years. I'm running out of options."

"You need something to distract her."

"Something to distract her?"

"Yeah. Give her hope. Give her hope that you'll be finding someone who will be a good fit. Help you settle down." I think about that. It's not a... terrible idea.

"Doesn't Ben have that friend?" I crinkle my brows together, confused.

"His friend is marrying the matchmaker, right?" How the hell does she know this?

"How do you know this?"

"I'm a nosy little sister. And Ocean View is a small town, especially in the off-season. Luke Dawson was an eligible bachelor, now off the market. Ben is next, I'm sure. Hattie told me Luke's bachelor party is coming soon. She had to block off his schedule."

Hattie is Vivi's best friend, though don't ask me how *that* works. Hattie is all tattoos and dyed hair and piercings. The polar opposite of my prim and proper, sugar and spice sister.

She's also the receptionist and an artist at Ben's tattoo shop.

Hattie and Vivi went to high school together, and even though Hattie went to art school and Vivi went to a traditional four-year state school, they stayed in touch.

"Anyway, you should do that. She like, dates people and then matches them up. I'm not totally sure how it works, but it sounds more reasonable than having Mom set you up. Plus, just telling Mom that you're taking control of your romantic future and thinking about working towards settling down will probably get her off your back. At least for a bit."

It's... not a terrible idea.

"That's not a terrible idea."

"I know. I'm full of not terrible ideas," she says with a roll of her eyes like she finds my doubting her annoying.

Valid though.

"I'll look into it."

"Better work quick. Mom's working quicker." I groan out loud, about to say something—convince her to talk our mother out of her plan, which will never work, of course—but the waitress puts down our lunches before I can: a burger and fries for me, a salad with the dressing on the side for Vivi.

"What the fuck is that?" She averts her eyes for the first time since we got here, actively trying to hide something.

"A salad."

"Why?"

"Because it's lunchtime."

"You know what I mean." She doesn't reply. "Why a salad, Viv?"

"Salads are delicious. Full of vitamins and nutrients and... stuff." She unrolls her utensils from the paper napkin, grabbing a fork and dipping the tines barely into the dressing before stabbing a piece of plain lettuce.

It's lettuce, a small variety of bland vegetables, and grilled chicken.

No cheese.

No bacon bits.

No croutons or anything else that would make a salad palatable.

"It's rabbit food."

"I don't think rabbits eat chicken." Jesus, she's annoying.

"You know what I mean." She rolls her eyes.

"If you must know, I have a gala next week and the dress is very fitted." It doesn't sit well with me.

"Viv—"

"It's just a salad, Vic. Nothing crazy."

I might deal with the pressure for perfection in my own way.

Vivian might shine effortlessly in front of others, but even though we weren't close as kids, I know.

She had her own pressure.

Still does, it seems.

"Viv, I don't like this."

"It's just a salad, Vic."

"You're eating? Meals?" Her eyes stay on the salad. *Shit.*

"Do I need to talk to Mom?"

"Vic, stop." Her head snaps up, her tough little sister mask on. "We're not doing this." From experience, I know pushing won't work.

"I worry, Viv." Her face meets mine, and I see it now; beneath her bubbly, proper mask is the other one.

"I'm good," she says. And I leave it at that, eating my burger, but keep my eyes locked to her as she silently finishes her lunch.

SIX

-Gabi-

THE CAST IS OFF, and I feel free without it. My skin is wrinkled and pale from where the sun couldn't reach it, and there's a small pink scar on the side of my wrist, but I'll take it if that means I can shower and drive normally again. I scrubbed my skin in the shower carefully for nearly an hour after it was off because six weeks of that cast meant six weeks of not washing my arm and six weeks of no regular showers. It felt *amazing*. The whole time I stayed mindful of where my feet were as they stood on the new grippy mat I bought. It's the kind of thing intended for the elderly or small children, but no way in hell am I going to fall in the shower and break my arm a second time.

The first was embarrassing enough.

When I got it removed, after a round of X-rays to confirm that it was well-healed, I was partly relieved to see it wasn't Doctor Vic removing my cast.

I hate to admit it, though; I was also partly disappointed.

I'm really fucked in the head.

Who in their right mind wants to see the man who she told she was a virgin and who helped to heal her wrist after she broke it in a failed attempt at masturbation?

Nevertheless, from what I remember of him in my painkiller addled mind, he was deviously handsome and had a charming laugh. When he came into the room both times, I felt strangely safe. Like some part of me knew he would take care of me, and not because it's his job, but because he's a good guy.

Instead, when I went in this morning, it was a tired-looking intern wielding a terrifying-looking saw—the opposite of safe and panic free.

And now, sitting in my bed in my pajamas, the book I was reading face down on my bed, I can't help but think of him as I stare at my wrist, slightly thinner now and definitely the wrong color.

My book, as with all the books I read these days, is hot. I've loved to read since the day I realized that if I taught myself to read early, I could break into my big sister Gia's room and read the diaries she kept in a shoebox under her bed. She never could figure out how her kindergarten sister knew all her secrets, using them as bargaining chips. My brothers were in second grade and I just studied their reading homework until I could figure it out, and boom. Blackmail for a solid three years until she went away to college.

The true win, though, was that I could turn off my brain by reading.

My mind has been wandering for as long as I remember. I can't get through a television show or a meal or a single conversation without it going somewhere else unrelated and unnecessary. And if I don't go with the thought, it just sits there, heavy and distracting, until I acknowledge it.

It's exhausting.

I can't turn it off.

When I started reading, I found I could transport myself somewhere else, somewhere my mind couldn't touch. It was magic.

But after reading all the basics—*Harry Potter*, *The Giver*, Judy Bloom, *Maniac Magee*—I felt it was time to be a grown-up. I needed to read "impressive" books. What would someone think of a girl who only ever got lost in the imaginary? In the fantasy and the happily ever afters? So I spent a good chunk of my life trying to read the classics. I wasted so much time reading what I thought would make me look smart, look cool. They didn't turn my brain off, but I thought maybe they would make my family take me seriously. I've always been the silly Mancini kid, the one everyone rolls their eyes at when I have a random thought or ask a dumb question. Some part of me thought maybe that would help. But all I wanted to do was live in a fictional world and let my mind run away from me.

There are only two times when my brain quiets down. Two times when the questions stop, the ideas pause, and my mind is blissfully silent.

One is when the music is loud and all-consuming.

The second is when I'm reading.

Once I ran through *The Great Gatsby* and *Romeo and Juliet* and *Catch 22* in high school, taking weeks if not months to focus long enough to finish a single one, I moved to self-help. To books that were supposed to help me be happier or live freer. Books that were supposed to teach me to save my money, prioritize my time, or figure out what I wanted to be when I grew up.

But I missed stories.

One day I was visiting my parents, and tucked in a corner was my old copy of *Forever* by Judy Bloom—my first romance. The first story that gave me full-on butterflies. Fifteen years after reading it for the first time, when I stole it from my sister's room, it transported me back to when I loved to read.

That same day, I ran to a bookstore and bought a dozen books.

None of them were classics.

None of them were beneficial to my brain or written as "self-help."

But each of them was good for my soul.

Each of them let me get lost and turn off my brain. Live in happily ever afters and watch the drama unfold and then wrap up neatly, unlike the real world.

That day I stopped caring about what other people thought.

That day, I realized I needed to live to make *myself* happy.

I stopped caring about what people thought about my being a virgin. I stopped caring about what people thought about my decisions, the way I dressed, and the way I decorated my apartment.

I stopped caring that someone could judge me for getting lost in my mind, lost in questions and thoughts.

My entire life, I've never been able to focus. My mind always wanders, always gets distracted, my thoughts interrupting the real world. My whole life I've had notes from teachers saying things like, "Gabi is a pleasure to have in class, but her head is often in the clouds," commentary on my ability to concentrate. My brothers rolling their eyes when I have yet another off-topic question. Friends getting subtly annoyed when they have to remind me of what we are talking about.

In middle school, they diagnosed me with ADHD, but it was manageable. I saw counselors and teachers who helped me work through it with strategies to focus, so there was never any need for extensive intervention, but it was always there.

My dad loves it—loves my brain. "My little *polpetta*, head always in the clouds like an angel," he says whenever he catches me off in another world. If we're at family dinner and someone asks me something I didn't catch, he'll wink at me and casually repeat the question.

He always answers my questions.

"Never let anyone, not even those jackass brothers of yours, make you feel like *tu cabeze* isn't a beautiful thing, my Gabrielle."

And while I have people who endure and family who love it and tactics to work around the constant chatter in my brain, the few times I can get it to shut off completely are utter bliss.

And one of them is reading.

That being said, it doesn't mean that when I'm reading, my mind isn't disconnected from my body. My body still reacts to the words—and right now, my body is responding to the scene I just read. My mind drifts to the feeling in the shower, how fucking *good* it felt, how close I got.

Maybe... Maybe...

I haven't tried again since the shower incident.

But maybe that broke some kind of wall. Perhaps I should just...

My hand slips down my body, grazing warm skin as my mind recaps the scene I read.

He pushed her onto the bed, fully naked, until she landed on all fours.

My fingertips dip below the waistline of the boxer briefs I wear to sleep in, grazing rough curls.

My breathing escalates.

I force myself to stay in my head.

"Fuck, baby, you're dripping," he said, running a finger up her inner thigh until he met her wet. "Is this for me?"

My hand moves, meeting where I'm wet. I breathe heavily as I move a finger to my slit, feeling the wet that gathered as I read and dragging it up, up, up, until I'm circling my clit. I let out a low, breathy moan.

It feels good.

Stay in the moment, Gab.

She moaned, nodding into the blankets.

"Do you want me to fuck you here?" he asked, a thick finger going into her. She nodded. "I need you to tell me with words, baby."

"Yes, I want you to fuck me," she said.

I moan again, my swollen clit begging for more pressure. Finally, I obey, pressing my fingers down and bucking my hips.

My mind stays on the scene.

He starts to slip in. "Jesus, so fucking tight. I can't wait until I'm buried deep in this pussy."

And then it happens.

My mind drifts.

Just like every single time I've ever worked to make myself come, every time I've been with a man who tried his hand at the task, my mind moves.

I wonder what it's like to have a man talk like that while he's fucking you.

I wonder what the hot doctor sounds like when he's turned on, about to fuck a woman.

Where the fuck did that come from?

The thought jolts me from the moment.

I spend a few seconds to confirm, circling my clit, testing, but nothing.

Goddammit.

Maybe I truly am broken.

SEVEN

-Gabi-

THE DAY after my latest failed attempt, I'm at the house on the outskirts of Ocean View Cassie and Luke bought together, getting ready for Cassie's bachelorette party, when she asks the question that, knowing her, she's been keeping in for *months*.

"Hey, Gabs?" Her voice is questioning and soft as her eyes focus on the mirror over the two double sinks she's leaning into. A brush is to her lashes, but she's not doing anything. It's a prop, at best.

"Yeah, Cass."

"I have a question."

"Are we swapping roles today? You get to be question girl and I get to be the wise, mentally stable one?" She rolls her eyes, swiping the brush on her lashes.

"Shut up, you dummy." Moving the brush back into the tube, her eyes stay locked to me in the mirror. "Why haven't you ever asked me to match you?" I always wondered why she'd never asked me this. Cassandra is nosy to an extreme, constantly poking and prodding everyone in her life. From her fiancé to me to her clients, she asks every question she thinks can help her better understand whoever is in front of her. But she's never asked this one question. "I mean, you *love* love. More than anyone I've ever met. You read those books all day long." She tips her head to where my e-reader sits on the chair, my having just put it down. I was reading while she got ready, totally engrossed in the story of an heiress falling for a lumberjack when she relocates to a small town.

She's not wrong. I love old bodice rippers and modern rom-coms —classics where falling is the focus and deeply dirty stories that are pretty much just sex. I love stories that make me laugh, and stories that make me cry, and stories that make me hotter than sin, but the only common denominator is the need for them to fall deeply, madly in love. Love that will last.

I love it.

It's also probably what made me so picky that I'm a single virgin at 28. No one lives up to the fictional men who live rent-free in my mind.

I sigh.

"It feels… weird."

"Asking me?" She turns to face me, crossing her arms over her chest and leaning onto the counter. "Why would that be weird?"

"No, not that. I mean, well, kind of. It seems weird to ask your boss to set you up on a date." She rolls her eyes.

"We're not like that, Gab."

"I know. But still. And it's not even that. Not really." I run a finger over the bottom edge of the sparkly black mini skirt she picked out for me. It goes up to right under my belly button and pairs with a cropped sparkly tank top. Not my typical style, but it's Cassie's day, and she's wearing the same in white, so…

"Then what is it?"

"I'm… well, you know." I roll my eyes to the side, avoiding hers as her brows furrow.

"You're what?"

"*You know*," I say, tipping my eyes to my lap.

"A virgin?" The blush burns my cheeks as I nod.

"So? Guys freaking love that. Shit, if Luke could go back to delete every guy I ever did it with and be the only one, he'd give his left leg." It's funny but also probably true. He's unbelievably protective of my best friend in the most beautiful way.

A true romance book hero come to life.

"It's not that... it's..." How do I explain? How do I explain it when I barely understand it myself? "It's going to be... awkward." Her brows scrunch together in confusion. "Sex. The first time. And honestly, the times after that. I don't know what I'm doing. It's going to be... no good." She's still confused. "Is it weird that I don't want whoever I end up with to remember me like that? I'm going to have to..." God, this is embarrassing. "Learn everything. Like from start to finish. I'm going to suck at it."

"It's like that for everyone, Gabi."

"Not everyone is 28 when it happens. When you're young and stupid, and you're both learning, it's normal. But it's going to be so uncomfortable in so many ways... I just... I feel like I'm stuck with this burden that I didn't plan on having or even want." I sigh, grabbing a curl and inspecting the ends. "I also don't want to just... get rid of it, you know? I've waited this long. I want it to be... good. I made that stupid pact with myself, and now I... I need to see it out."

"You know that's kind of weird, right? To wait to find the love of your life until *after* you lose your virginity?" She's smiling, poking fun, but not in a mean way. "Most people hold on to their virginity until they fall in love."

"That's because men are obsessed with purity and have brainwashed women to believe their virginity is some sacred moment in time that we must cherish and hand over to some guy who can't even find your clit." Cassie snorts out a laugh, but I don't. I feel a rant coming on. "Isn't the whole concept so strange? That we save this... thing for some man who is supposed to be our entire world. But most girls give it away to the first love they meet in high school who will break up with them three days later. You know that better than I do," I say. One of the reasons Cassie started this business is because a college friend experienced just that, and it crushed her. "And don't even get me started on how fucked up the double standard is, either. Because that shit is bananas. Do you know that when I was in school, my dad literally told my brothers to 'sow their seed while they can'?" Cassie gags.

I love my dad to the ends of the earth. I'm the baby girl in the family and treated as such by everyone around me, babied and nurtured and protected at all costs. But he is an absolute *caveman*. Most days, I let it go because I've realized neither of us will ever change our mindset, but other times... well, it ends in my storming out and my mom having to pave the way for us to hash it out and apologize. Her efforts usually include bribing me to come over for homemade manicotti.

My mom can cure nearly any grudge with food.

"But a girl decides she's not going to wait to give it to some theoretical 'love of her life' and instead to the first person who can make her come, and I'm the weird one."

"I didn't mean it like that—"

"I know," I say because I do. "I get defensive. My sister is constantly giving me shit for it. But like... I've heard all the horror stories. How it hurt, and they weren't ready, and he was a jerk, or she didn't come. I don't want that."

"So you don't want flower petals and candles for your first time; you want a screaming orgasm?" Cassie asks with a smile as she digs in her bag for lipstick. She pops the top off, widening her mouth and lining her lips with the pretty pink color while looking in the mirror again.

"Exactly," I say

"Makes sense to me. Hell, I wish I'd done that instead of giving it up in the backseat of Joey Petina's car when I was 16."

"Oh, so you've always had a thing for cars?" I ask with a laugh, remembering the drunken night Cass and I planned a wild excursion for her and Luke. Her eyes go even wider, her red painted lips dropping wide as she slowly turns towards me.

"I cannot believe you just said that."

"I cannot believe you'd expect any different," I say.

EIGHT

-Gabi-

Hours later, I feel *good*.

This joyous feeling in part is thanks to the two Long Island iced teas I chugged so far and part to the music blaring in the club we ended up in. It's loud, pumping through my system with an intensity that drowns out my other, usually incessant, thoughts until all there is in this moment is me and a random Ke$ha song.

Life is good.

Life is even better when I feel a warm body behind me, heat moving through the thin fabric of my skirt to my skin. It's not a demand, not an intrusion. It's more inquisitive than anything. Respectful. Cassie is dancing across from me, and my eyes go to hers in a "should I run or is he hot?" look. Her eyes widen with excitement, and a thumb goes up, giving me the high sign.

He's hot. I try to look back behind me with a smile, but the lights in the club are near blinding. Instead, I let the song continue to pulse in me, large hands settling on my hips and pulling me further into a body that's way taller than mine, a rough cheek that needs a shave scraping against my temple.

He moves well too. *Green flag*, my brain tells me. Technically, it's a red flag to Cassie—any man who knows how to move well could easily tip into sleazy club hopper territory, but to me? It's a necessity.

I grew up having kitchen dance parties with my mom and sister, always listening to Italian pop music, gyrating our hips to the beat, too young to know that it could mean more than just feeling the music and loving how it worked through us.

And since then, I've *loved* to dance. Not professionally, no, I love to go out, listen to music too loud, move and ignore the world.

Sometimes, when my mind won't stop and I can't find anyone to go out with me, I'll get dressed up and head downtown alone. I'm not looking to get drinks or to meet anyone. I just... I just want to space out and get that clarity. That numbness in my brain where the sounds, thoughts, and questions dim just for long enough for me to breathe.

The only time I've been able to find the quiet other than when I'm reading is when the music is loud and my body is moving. It's my own personal heaven.

But right now, with these warm hands on my hips, the noise stops even more than usual, quieting down to utter silence, my complete focus on those hands, on my movements, on my breathing.

And for a split second, I think I would do absolutely anything in the entire world to keep this feeling.

NINE

-Vic-

The music is blaring, and for a split second, I'm reminded of the kid who came in one night nearly deaf from a ruptured eardrum after standing right next to a speaker during a concert.

The perks of being an ER doctor. Everything in life has the potential for destruction. I just see the negative results more often.

I need to turn my brain off.

I didn't plan to come out tonight.

In fact, after a long ass shift that got longer when a car crash landed three patients in my ER an hour before I was off, I planned just to go home, eat, drink a beer, and go the fuck to bed. But my buddy Ben called right as I was changing out of my scrubs to tell me he was going out with some friends for a bachelor party and their last stop would be Sol.

The voice in my head reminded me that a night alone with a beer would be a great time to dwell on the kid who came in tonight with a broken arm that clearly came not from falling off a slide like his mother sporting a poorly hidden black eye told me.

So I agreed to meet him here.

Maybe this was exactly what I needed: a few drinks, a pleasant buzz, and a woman to bring back to my apartment and get lost in.

Yes, that sounds like exactly what the doctor ordered tonight.

I'd know.

And when the tiny, curvy woman dancing alone caught my eye, her friends coming on and off the dance floor to giggle with her before leaving again, I knew she was the one.

Short even in heels, she's wearing a tight black outfit designed to make a man wild, curves for days, a full head of wild, dark curls that she pulled on top of her head. Curls I'd love to tangle my hands in. I came up behind her, moving in time with her. Relief rushed through me when she didn't run, wasn't put off by my approach. But shit, I wanted more.

I wanted to grip her hips, pull her back, press her to me. But my mother would castrate me if I didn't treat a woman with full respect. So I waited until she looked behind her in the dark light of the club. I couldn't see much more than a wide, white smile before she stepped back, lining herself up with me and moving her hips in my lap. My hands went to those hips, once again tentative, careful not to cross any boundary before hands—tiny and soft—covered mine, pressing down to her hips to hold her there.

And then we danced, moving with the beat as one, stress and concerns and worry melting away with each thump of the bass. It reminded me of those boardwalk games where you add a quarter and it gets pushed to the edge by a blade, each press making coins drop. Except the quarters are every shitty moment of my job, every overwhelming feeling, and the push is the bass, knocking them all down with each beat.

As we continue, sweat building both from our movements and the confined area, her hands begin to move, shifting my hands from her full hips to her small waist, where her skin is bare and warm under my hands. She lets go, lifting into the air as her head moves back and forth to the beat of the song, her ass pressing back just a fraction into my crotch.

I need this woman.

She is a goddess, all sexuality and confidence and excitement.

My thumbs move, such a tiny movement it's almost unrecognizable, and they dip beneath the black sequined fabric of her top, grazing her ribs and where, in theory, there should be an underwire for a bra.

Nothing.

Fuck.

My breathing quickens, and for a split second, I wonder if I'm too old to take a woman into a bar bathroom and fuck her in a stall.

I've never done it myself, but it always looks like a blast in movies. It also usually exemplifies the need and intensity coursing through me right now. When she gyrates firmer this time, moving demandingly into me, it's clear she feels it too. God, it's like a magnet, some kind of all-consuming force between us. I need more. I need to see her.

We need a change in position. Hands still on her waist, I turn her in my arms, her own going directly to my neck as my hands go to her ass to pull her close.

I think about kissing her.

I think about moving her hips against me to make her feel as desperate as I feel.

I think about any number of other filthy things.

But all of that leaves my mind when I see her flinch, eyes wide and pupils dilated with liquor and lust.

All of my thoughts fly when she says those two words.

"It's you."

It's her.

The virgin who thinks she's broken.

"It's you," I reply, drawn into her wide eyes, shock and confusion written there. She tries to step back, to leave, but my hands tighten on her hips, keeping her in place.

She can't leave.

I won't let her.

I have not been able to get my mind off her for weeks: her goofy laugh while completely annihilated on painkillers, her words, her misconception that she's broken. The rambling. All of it.

She's stopped moving, though, so we're standing in the middle of a crowded dance floor, standing and staring at each other.

"Oh my god, I really said all of that shit, didn't I?" she asks, and to avoid looking like two crazy people, I move a hand to her hip, moving her to get us dancing again. She takes the hint.

"Said what?" I say. I need to shout it next to her ear, my breath moving, the scent of citrus and sweat coming off of her, and it smells like sex.

I close my eyes as I breathe it in, fighting any reaction. *Fuck, what is happening to me?*

"All of it!" She's panicking. I wonder if maybe she thought our conversations were a drug-filled delusion, all of them flying back now that we're in each other's presence again.

And for some fucking insane reason that I don't think I'll ever be able to fully understand even when I'm eighty and old and grey, I press my lips to her temple before saying in her ear, "Calm down, kitten."

By some miracle, she does just that. Her body goes limp and easy in mine, and she smiles at me when her head tips back before saying, "Let's dance."

Nothing has ever sounded like a better idea.

TEN

-Vic-

Hours later, I'm still perfectly and completely sober, holding a very not sober Gabi by the waist as she points the way to a table where her friends are sitting. Friends who have occasionally popped out onto the dance floor, I'm sure, in some effort to check that she was where she still wanted to be, to see if she needed a wingman to aid in her escape. And twice to bring her shots. She's out at a bachelorette party.

When we get there, it's no longer just her friends, as I've seen the few times I watched one of her posse walk back to their spot, but also a group of men. One is holding a woman as far gone as Gabi, pressing his lips to hers as she dips backward. She's in an all white outfit identical to Gabi's—the bride-to-be, obviously. And, hopefully, the groom to be.

As my eyes scan the group, I'm surprised to see a familiar face—Ben. He smiles his signature shit-eating grin, his specialty, half chill and smooth, half uptight and grumpy as fuck.

"Hey, man. You made it," he says, putting an arm out to shake my hand. Ben's tall, taller than me, and his arms are completely covered in tattoos. My mom would hate him and automatically assume he's a bad influence. I think a part of me forced him to become my friend after a pickup basketball game a few years back because of that fact alone.

I really am an asshole son.

In my defense, his equally tattoo-covered receptionist and tattoo artist has been Vivi's best friend since high school.

Mom... tolerates Hattie.

"Yeah, I've been here for... a bit." I look down at Gabi, who's smiling at me, the grin sloppy and sweet, all teeth and way more attractive than it has any right to be.

"You brought her back!" the bride-to-be yells. "Finally!" She tries to stumble over to us but is held back by her man, a smile on his face.

"Cassie—this is the *hot doctor*," Gabi says, clearly having a conversation her friend instantly understands

"No fucking way." Her eyes go wide, moving from me to her friend, and Gabi nods. "He *is* male model hot!" I'm not sure if I should run, with the way her fiancé is looking at me, or feel content that the woman I haven't been able to get out of my mind for nearly two months has also had me on hers.

"Right?!"

"The one you told you were a virgin!?" another woman shouts, about halfway between sober and Gabi, a man who might be Ben's twin standing next to her. No, not his twin. His younger brother. I remember meeting him once in passing at a party for the shop.

"You're a virgin, Gabi girl?" a man—Latino with dark hair and a five o'clock shadow—asks, a cocky grin on his face. "I can change that for ya," he says with a wink, and an uncontrolled rage runs through me, catching me off guard. It should be concerning how quickly it comes on, how fierce it is.

"Fuck off, Chris, or someone here will kick your ass," the groom says. Groom status is confirmed with the shirt that reads "groom" across his chest.

"Did you know she's a virgin?" the man—Chris—asks the groom.

"Yeah."

"Why didn't you tell me?"

"I didn't know I was obligated to share gossip about my woman's employee's sexual status with my childhood best friend."

"She's hot. Any hot single woman, I need to know about her."

"You're not allowed to fuck any of my friends, Christopher Jacobs," the bride says, angry eyes directed at him. He just smiles and winks. Then she turns to me, the look going from angry to friendly in the blink of an eye. It almost gives me whiplash, but no one nearby seems to find it strange, like this is just how she is.

"Hi! I'm Cassie! You're Hot Doctor."

"I uh... I guess so." I smile, and she returns it.

"Good smile."

"Thanks."

"Name?"

"Vic."

"Last name?"

"Brandt."

"I know you're a doctor. Where do you live?" Something tells me I shouldn't brush off this woman's questions. They sound like they're coming from a list, rehearsed well enough to be recited in her drunken state.

"Apartments on fifth."

"The waterfront? Fancy."

"Enough interviewing him, sweetheart," her fiancé says. *Interviewing?*

"I can't help it. It's my job." He smiles at his woman, kissing her hair before Ben speaks up.

"So, what's the story here?" He seems mildly confused, but also very much intrigued. His eyes have been volleying between everyone as this introduction went on. Thankfully where their table is, the music isn't as loud, so it hasn't been an obscene screaming match to be heard through this very awkward conversation. "You know Vic?" he asks his friend. I see now Ben's shirt says, "groomsman." This is the party I was invited to crash, more or less.

"I don't. Gabi does."

"I don't technically know him. He just healed this," Gabi says, wobbling just a bit and waving her arm with a clear demarcation line from where her cast was.

"Hey, let's get you in a seat before I have to fix that again, okay?" I say into her hair, pulling over a chair and placing her into it. Unfortunately, it's a stool, so I need to stand behind her to keep her on it.

"Unfortunately" is a very loose term here.

"Ooh, I like you. *Can* I interview you?" the woman—Cassie—asks. I'm confused.

"Uhh..." I start as Gabi's head looks back at me, and she nearly falls over as she does. She's not in a good state. "Can you get me a bottle of water?" I say quietly to the bartender walking past. They nod then head off.

"Cassie's a *matchmaker*. She interviews men to decide if they're hiding things and are a big red flag. Like *Chris*." She glares at him. I remember her mentioning this the first time I met her in the crazy tie-dyed shirt.

"Me? Red flag? No. Pink, maybe," Chris says with a smile. I know the smile. I've *made* the smile. It says he knows he's a player, knows how to get a woman to like him, and he's proud of it.

A man not ready to settle down, who likes life the way it is.

My mom would call him a kindred soul to my own.

Before I can say anything, the bartender brings me the water and I crack the seal, handing it to Gabi who swats it away. I dip down until my lips are to her ear.

"You need to drink this or you'll regret it." My nose is in her hair, and fuck, she smells good—citrusy and earthy and like salty sweat. It's from dancing, but my mind, the primal side of me, instantly attributes it to a different action. My breath tickles her neck as I speak to her, and she shivers, the reaction combined with her scent affecting me way more than it should.

All of this is a terrible, horrible idea.

She is way past drunk.

And she's a virgin.

Absolutely not.

"If I'm a good girl, will I get rewarded?" she asks me, her voice low and husky, and Jesus fuck, I feel my cock hardening despite the fact everything about this is so incredibly wrong and never going to happen.

Ever.

Hear that, Little Vic?

Never.

"She's gone," Cassie says, her eyes wide and on Gabi. It seems she must have heard Gabi's words too. Looking around, I'm relieved it seems no one else did, just her best friend, who clearly cares about her. Why that's a relief, I'm not sure, but I also know Gabi would be unbearably embarrassed if anyone else heard her say that.

"Okay, honey. I think it's time to get you into bed," I say, helping her to stand from the stool.

"Where are you going?" The groom—Luke—says, stepping in front of me like some kind of bossy big brother. Seems this crew is tight.

"She needs to sleep this off."

"We can take her home." Luke tips his head to Cassie.

"Man, this is not the night you want to be dealing with a drunk girl. She is one hundred percent going to get sick." Even though she's nearly as gone as Gabi, Cassie looks concerned. The concern is sobering her a bit.

"She doesn't drink. Not this much, at least. And she hasn't drunk even a glass of wine since she broke her wrist. I should have... shit. I should have thought of that and stopped her."

"Not your fault, sweetheart. She's having fun. We'll take her back to her place."

"She can't be alone tonight," I say, a strange sense of protectiveness and worry coming over me. "She drank way too much and is recovering from an injury. It's a recipe for disaster."

"We'll—"

"Look, nothing will happen; I'm going to take her to my place, keep an eye on her. I'm an ER doctor. I've seen this exact thing go bad way too many times to walk away."

"The fuck you are. We don't even know you," Luke says.

"Ben knows me." I tip my head to my friend. "He invited me here to meet you guys. Seriously, nothing is going to happen. Doctor, remember? Ben can vouch for me."

"He's a good guy, Luke. Nothing will happen if he says nothing will happen."

"I'm not cool with this."

"You don't have to be. I'm taking care of her, regardless."

"I want to go with the hot doctor," Gabi says, rubbing her face onto my shirt like a kitten.

"Luke, he seems—"

"Gabi is innocent." Luke looks at Cassie. "She doesn't know the things—" Gabi's body stiffens, her head lifting to look at her friend's man through squinted eyes.

"Are you fucking kidding me? I'm so tired of this. I'm not a baby. I'm tired of everyone treating me like I'm some precious thing that needs to be protected. I know what the world is like. I know about sex! Shit, I want to have sex! I just *can't* because I made a *stupid* pact with myself and no man can fucking *make me orgasm* and I sure as fuck am not giving my v-card to anyone who can't even do that. No way, no how." She takes a deep breath and I feel the intake on my chest. Looking around, I see nearly every face has wide eyes, shocked that this little powerhouse is losing it.

Seems they may have never seen this side of her.

Interesting.

"I'm so tired of feeling like I'm some innocent flower. I don't *want* to be innocent. I don't want my flower! I'm just... stuck here. I'm tired of everyone protecting me. I have five fucking brothers. A lifetime of being protected. I don't need more, thank you very much, Lucas Andrew Dawson. Jesus. If I want to get drunk and dance crazy and go home with some doctor I met because I broke my wrist trying to make myself come, then so be it. Maybe I'll let him fuck me! Who knows! He looks like he can make a woman come." She turns to me, and I know what she's going to say before she says it. "Can you?"

"Can I what?" I'm not sure why I want to hear her say it. But I do. Really badly.

"Can you make a woman come?" Ben laughs, and I shoot a look in his direction.

"I've had no complaints."

"Well, some women don't like to complain. They just... endure."

"I'm pretty sure the women I've been with haven't just... endured."

"How do you know?" I smile at her. I kind of like this. She doesn't just take my smile and go gooey-eyed. She's questioning me.

"I'm a doctor."

"What does that have anything to do with anything?"

"A woman's body feels different when she orgasms, Gabrielle. It's easy to know if she's faking it if you know what you're looking for." Her eyes go wide.

"He's not wrong," Chris says.

"Of course, I'm not."

"Maybe I *should* let you fuck me. You know bodies and stuff. I bet you could make me come. Do you think you could make me come?" she asks, and her eyes are dreamy, like she's envisioning it already.

I don't know if I could, but I'd love to try.

"You're not fucking the doctor tonight, Gabi. You're coming home with us. We'll keep an eye on you," Luke says.

"No, I'm not."

"Yes, you are." He clearly has the older brother thing on lock.

"She's not, honey," Cassie says, her hand on Luke's arm.

"What?" His head swivels to his fiancé, confusion and surprise on his face.

"She's not coming home with us. She's a grown woman. Ben vouches for this guy." She looks at me. "Sorry, what's your name? I'm pretty sure it's not Hot Doctor."

"I mean, if you want to call me that—"

"Watch out, man. That's my fiancé," I smile.

"Yes, a good smile." She scrunches her nose. "Could go either way," Cassie says, tilting her head left to right like she's weighing the pros and cons.

"Vic. My name's Vic. Victor Brandt." I stare at Luke. "Look, man. You've got better things to do than take care of a drunk girl who I'm sure will get sick tonight." Reaching into my pocket, I grab my wallet. "Here. Take my bank card. And take a picture of my license. And my keys." I grab those as well, twisting off the apartment key, and then I'm holding them out to a stunned-looking Luke. "I'll drop her off in the morning. Then, when you see she's safe, you give me them back. I get it. You're a good friend. But I've got her. You enjoy your night."

"He's cool, Luke. Trust me," Ben says. Luke stares at me, still not grabbing the keys.

"God, stop being an ass, Luke." Cassie reaches out and grabs the keys. "Here, give me your number. I'll text you our address. Gabi knows it, but I want your number too." I do as she asks, watching Luke take the keys from his woman and pocket them. "I expect you to drop her off by eleven a.m. at the latest. A minute after, I'm calling in the cavalry."

"The cavalry?"

"She has five older brothers. You seem tough, but they could take you." I smile. I like that. A tiny, hellbent woman with an entire crew of people who would protect her, even though she clearly doesn't want their protection.

It's endearing,

Even more endearing are her next words.

"Yay! I'm going home with Hot Doctor! See you in the morning when I'm not a virgin!" Gabi yells, grabbing my hand and stumbling towards the exit.

This is going to be interesting.

ELEVEN

-Vic-

Once we're in the cab, Gabi starts talking again, eyes glazed, nursing the water bottle she still hasn't drunk from. She needs to.

"So, what position should we do first?"

"I'm sorry, what?" My mind shifts from water consumption to Gabi's words.

"Position. Like... sex?"

"Kitten, I'm not having sex with you tonight." She pouts—a full-out pout.

"Why not?"

"Where should I start?"

"The beginning." She's pouting like the child she is adamant people not treat her as, and it's adorable. Unreasonably adorable.

"Let's make a deal. You drink some water, and I'll give you an answer." She crunches her nose.

"I'm not thirsty."

"Sober you will thank drunk you if you drink that." Another scrunch, another pout. But she does what I ask.

"For one, you said you have a rule about who gets that v-card."

"The guy needs to make me come."

"I've never done that."

"I bet you could." *I bet I could too.*

"Maybe. Drink," I say, tipping my head to the water, watching her drink until it hits the 1/3 mark. Looking out the window, I see we have about five more minutes. "Even if I could, I'm not fucking you drunk."

"Why?"

"I want you to remember it."

"I don't forget anything. I'm an elephant. My brothers hate it because I have something on *all* of them. My oldest brother, Dom, snuck a girl into the house and she puked in my mom's roses when he was home from school. I was nine and caught him. He gave me five dollars not to tell our mom. But like, what is five dollars, ya know? So I took the money, but I still use it to get my way sometimes. That's not even the worst of it." I smile. That seems like something she'd do and I don't even know her that well. I like it too. It reminds me of Vivi and her constant pestering.

"Well, I want you to have all of your senses."

"My senses?"

"Yeah, baby. Your senses. All of them." The cab slows to a stop in front of my building, and I extricate us from the vehicle. She shivers with my words, and as I help her out of the cab, her eyes are wide.

"Oh. My *senses*," she says and then instantly starts giggling like crazy.

Cute.

I wave off the cab as I put an arm around Gabi's waist, helping her to the entrance of my apartment and tossing the empty water bottle into the recycling bin.

"You said you have theories about why you've never come?"

"Of course I do."

"Well?"

"Well, what?" *Elephant my ass.* She can barely stay in this conversation. Thankfully, her steps are less wobbly, be it from the water or time, I don't know. Despite that, I hold her, liking the feel of her little body pressed to mine.

"What are your theories?" I press the number 17 to get to the floor of my apartment before the doors close, caging Gabi and me in the small box.

"Oh." She looks up at the digital display, watching the numbers go up with each floor. "My brain is broken. It's not my body. It's my *brain*."

"I'm sorry?"

"It never stops." She pauses, but I don't fill the silence. This is an interesting development. "Does your brain stop?" she asks, looking at me. This is the slowest elevator on the planet, so I have time. I turn her to me, pressing her chest to mine, wrapping my arms around her waist.

"Yeah, my brain stops." *Especially when you're around, it seems.*

"Is it ever quiet in there?" she asks, reaching up and tapping my head.

"Yeah, kitten. My mind gets quiet. Yours doesn't?"

"Never." The word is a whisper. A quiet, embarrassed term.

"You can't focus?" She scrunches her nose, neither a confirmation nor a denial. "On coming. You can't focus? Because your brain isn't quiet?"

"I get close. I get really close—it feels nice. And I think I'm almost there and then my brain... moves to something else. Like... what's for dinner. Or if I remembered to shave or if I should be doing something... different. And I lose it."

This is the most coherent I've seen this woman, which isn't saying much. I wonder what she'll be like in the morning, once the liquor has worked its way out.

"Have you ever told anyone that?"

"My parents. Teachers." She waits. "I have ADHD."

"Got that, kitten," I say with a smile. "Doctor, remember?" She smiles back. "I meant to partners. Have you ever had this conversation with them?" She shakes her head.

"No way. That's embarrassing. I'm only doing this because I'm drunk and my filter is gone. In the morning, I'll hate myself." She tries to turn her head away from me.

"Hey, hey. Stop. No." My hand goes to her cheek, turning her face to me. God, her skin is soft. "Never be embarrassed about something that makes you *you*." A blush forms on her cheeks and it's gorgeous. "I just asked because that's good information to know. There are... things we could do. To get you over that."

Now, why did I say that? *We could do...*

"We?" she asks, somehow despite her state catching my slip, her face hopeful. I don't answer, her eyes still locked to mine, the elevator making its slow climb. "Will you kiss me?" Her words are a whisper, and she looks at me with those big brown eyes, gorgeous eyes, eyes that, despite her words and her fire, hold innocence and trust and admiration. I hate what I have to do next.

"No, kitten. I won't be kissing you. Not tonight." Her face falls.

"Why not?"

"Because when I kiss you, I need you to remember it." Those eyes go gooey and soft.

"When you kiss me?"

"Oh yeah. When," I say, my breath grazing her lips with my words.

And at that moment, I want nothing more than to kiss her. To say fuck it and kiss her even if she's beyond gone, which goes against my moral compass.

But the elevator dings and the doors open, having reached my floor.

Saved by the bell.

"Come on, you. Drink this," I say, handing Gabi a glass of water as she sits against the wall next to the toilet, eyes closed and head back. I wonder if she might have fallen asleep, but one pretty brown one opens up to glare at me.

I wasn't wrong when I said she'd get sick.

I spent the last 15 minutes holding Gabi's hair, rubbing her back, and swapping out cold washcloths as she brought up everything in her stomach. It wasn't much, mostly liquor and then bile as her body fought to get out any remaining toxin. Thankfully, I'm pretty sure she avoided alcohol poisoning.

"And these," I say, handing her a handful of saltine crackers. She looks at me, face still green, hair in a scrunchie Vivi left here.

"No, thank you." Her voice is low and hoarse.

"Didn't give you a choice." I shake my hand.

"You're bossy."

"I'm a doctor."

"Does that mean you have to be so bossy?" she asks with an annoyed look. The drunk seems to be wearing off more, especially with the liquor out of her stomach, but a crankiness is creeping in.

How fucked in the head am I that I find it cute?

So fucked.

"When it comes to health? Yeah. It's literally my job." She grabs the square crackers from my hand and munches, sipping the water. "Slow." Another glare from her and another smile from me as I settle on the floor across from her.

"What did you eat today?" She cringes. I think it's at the thought of food, but when she avoids my eyes, I know it's something different. "Gabrielle."

"God, you sound like my brothers. Or my dad."

"What did you eat?"

"Mozzarella sticks."

"What else?" Silence. "Are you telling me all you had for dinner before going out and drinking was mozzarella sticks?"

"There was marinara sauce."

"Yeah, that's really gonna absorb the liquor. Jesus, Gabi. Did you have breakfast?" Her fingers tug at the hem of my shirt she's wearing. It looks good on her.

Too good.

"No." Her voice is low and quiet.

"Why not?"

"I forgot."

"You forgot? To eat breakfast?" She pauses, and when she says her next words, I can tell she doesn't want to admit them.

"And lunch."

"Jesus. How do you forget to eat?"

"I get... distracted—a lot. I can't... my mind. It wanders. Remember?" I do. And I know that's normal for people with ADHD, but still.

"You need to eat, Gabi."

"Yeah, got it. Next time I plan to go out, I'll make sure I have three square meals." She rolls her eyes like I'm annoying, but there's also a small smile on her lips. "I didn't expect to drink so much. Or for it to affect me too much. I don't drink a lot, but I like a glass of wine. I haven't had one since my accident, though." Makes sense.

"I mean other days, though. You need to eat daily."

"Yes, doctor," she says with another roll of her eyes. How is that not giving her a headache?

"It could help with concentration. Hunger can worsen ADHD symptoms. Especially if you skip breakfast."

"I hate breakfast."

"It's the most important meal of the day."

"That's bullshit."

"It's not. It helps you get a boost of glucose. Increases your alertness and energy first thing in the morning." Her eyes drift shut as she chews the last cracker, drunken exhaustion taking over.

"I haven't had breakfast since I lived under my mom's roof," she mumbles, and again, I smile. I seem to do that a lot around this woman.

I think about arguing, telling her she needs to eat breakfast, that she needs someone to keep her on track, a man to remind her to grab a protein bar or make her eggs and toast, but I stop myself before I go too far.

Whose mind is wandering now, Brandt?

Her eyes slink shut, the chewing no longer forcing her awake.

"I'm tired," she mumbles, and before she gets a chance to lean over and crack her head on the toilet, I'm scooping her up into my arms.

Tiny. She's absolutely tiny.

"Then let's get you to bed, kitten." And with that, she nuzzles into my chest and falls asleep before I can tuck her in.

TWELVE

-Gabi-

When I wake up, the bed smells like cologne and dryer sheets, the kind my brother Dom uses on Sam's clothes.

This is not my brother Dom's bed, though.

I carefully open one eye to take in my surroundings and shut it quickly, the sun near blinding me.

Nope. Bad idea. Terrible idea, even. And this is definitely not Dom's bed. The sheets are crisp, the comforter an immaculate white.

And it's huge.

I test this theory by stretching out my arms and legs, trying to find the edge. I can't. This isn't necessarily strange, since I'm short, but this bed is much bigger than what I'm used to. I roll once to the left and can finally touch the corner.

I lie there for another minute, adjusting to being in the land of the living and taking in the world around me. Moving my arms again, I feel nothing, no warm spot, definitely no additional body. I think the other side of the bed is still made.

Good news.

My hands run down my body.

I'm not in the black miniskirt and cami from last night,

Bad news.

No bra, but a soft oversized tee shirt. No pants, but my own panties are on. I'm pretty sure they're mine at least. I put the blanket over my head and crack an eye carefully to check.

Yup, those are mine.

Good news.

My feet are achy, which makes sense since those heels I shoved them into last night are the furthest thing from comfortable. Nevertheless, my mind continues, noting every inch of my body.

I don't feel sore between my legs.

I'm pretty sure if I lost my virginity, I'd be at least a bit sore, right?

I really hope I didn't and then forgot. I don't normally forget things. I have a killer memory except for things like doctor's appointments or why I went into any given room at any given moment. I'm like an elephant, I—

Then it comes back. I remember telling someone that last night.

Telling someone that I found Dom sneaking in a drunk girlfriend when I was nine and using it against him.

Vic.

Hot Doctor.

It all comes back to me in a rush that has me burning from head to toe with embarrassment.

Not eating all day and then drinking way too much, considering I haven't had even a glass of wine since my "accident."

Dancing.

Vic being there.

Dancing with him.

The way he made me feel...

Him taking me back to Cassie.

Luke fighting with Vic about taking me home.

Cassie *giving in*. Cassie *never* gives in.

My tantrum about everyone thinking I'm so innocent, needing to protect me.

The cab ride home. Telling Vic about my ADHD and how it affects me.

The elevator.

Vic refusing to kiss me.

"Because when I kiss you, I need you to remember it."

Oh, my god. The barfing. I barfed. And he held my hair back and forced me to drink water and eat saltines and gave me shit about not eating.

My eyes open finally. I don't want to see those memories anymore. I fight a wave of nausea, but it goes away quickly as I sit up. My head is pounding, my mouth disgustingly dry. Oh god, this is terrible.

But despite all of that, I can't resist looking around, taking in his room. The bed frame is black. So are the dresser and the chair in the corner. The walls are white. Plain. Minimalist? Or just boring. I think about my funky apartment. I think about the plain black pants and cream shirt he wore yesterday.

Boring.

I think about the tea-length skirt with the dinosaurs all over it I wore to Cassie's yesterday afternoon.

A life without color isn't a life at all.

The dresser in the corner is big, the top empty.

My mind wanders to one of Cassie's many red flags.

A man without photos in his home means he's hiding something.

What could he be hiding?

My mind wanders to those true crime podcasts Cassie is always begging me to stop listening to because then I start obsessing over them and assuming everyone I meet has the potential to be a serial killer.

Bare room.

No photos.

No personal belongings.

Nothing on the walls, plain black and white.

Oh my god, he could totally be a charming serial killer—a Ted Bundy or a John Paul Knowles.

Without my mind's approval, my body shifts so my feet are dangling over the edge of the surprisingly high-up bed. When I stand, the shirt drifts down until it's almost to my knees and I giggle a bit, twirling like a little girl in her mom's dress.

Focus, Gabi! Potential serial killer alert!

I look around. There's a plain black nightstand where my phone blinks with messages.

Okay, good sign—if he was going to kill me, I doubt he'd give me my phone.

Tiptoeing to the dresser, I open the top drawer.

Underwear. I dig around, hoping to find... something, but it seems it genuinely is just an underwear drawer.

Is that a good sign?

Doesn't everyone keep a secret or two in their underwear drawer?

The next small drawer to the right of it holds women's clothes.

Red flag: he has women's clothes.

Maybe he's into drag?

Except they're all size small. Hmm.

I slide the drawer shut, about to continue my investigation, but there's noise at the door. My eyes swing there and as the sounds get closer, I panic, jumping back into the bed and covering myself in blankets, but not before I grab my phone, slipping it right under me. Just in case.

THIRTEEN

-Vic-

I'VE BEEN STANDING outside my bedroom like a freaking stalker for what feels like an eternity. My entire body aches after moving closer to the door every few minutes, hunched over to listen, and sleeping on the couch last night. But when a rustling comes through the door indicating she's finally up, I walk to the kitchen, grabbing the water bottle, crackers, and aspirin.

I'm sure she's going to need it.

I knock at the door.

"Gabi?"

"Yeah?" Her voice is quiet, nervous.

"Can I come in?"

"I, uh... yeah?" I try not to smile at her hesitance, her confusion, as I carefully turn the knob, trying not to drop everything, and push it open.

She's lying in my bed, tan skin and dark hair tumbling over white, blanket-covered shoulders, the white bedding and room only showing her off more, framing her in a way I've never gotten to see her before.

She's tired and definitely hungover, but she's still gorgeous.

Yeah, I'm going to kiss her. And then some, if I can get to her agree to the fucked-up plan I hatched up on the couch, staring at the ceiling and attempting to get comfortable, long after she passed out in my bed.

"Hi." I get the feeling that she's rarely this reserved, this nervous. Is that a good sign?

"Hey, how are you feeling?" I ask, handing her the water that she takes eagerly, the blanket falling to her waist, before snapping the top off and bringing it to her full lips. She takes a deep drink as I set the plate of crackers and aspirin on the bedside table before backing away. Hoping to give her space, I sit in the chair in the corner.

She's vulnerable right now. She might want to be strong and independent and be treated like she's not innocent, but she's still a woman in an unfamiliar place after an unfortunately drunk night. I have no idea how much she remembers, what she remembers, or how she feels about it.

"Vic, right?" she asks, her cheeks going pink.

"You can call me Hot Doctor if you want."

"Oh my god," she murmurs, putting her hands to her face before peeking through two fingers. "That really happened, didn't it? I called you Hot Doctor to your face."

"Technically, your friend Cassie did it first."

"She has a big mouth."

"You're good. It was a compliment. Happy to know you remembered me after all of that. How's your wrist, by the way?" She looks at me, confused. "Seems to have healed well." She turns the discolored wrist to look where a small pink scar is. It will fade, but she'll always have that reminder.

If nothing at all, it will be a hilarious story.

"I got the cast taken off early this week."

"I know. I checked your file."

"You checked my file?" I shrug, avoiding the answer and tipping my head toward her.

"Take those. I'm sure you have a headache." She looks at the plate.

"What are they?"

"Aspirin. And crackers."

"How do I know you're not drugging me?" The question comes and I don't think she thought about it much before saying the words aloud, since her eyes go wide with shock.

"You want the bottle? I also have one that's unopened. But I'm a doctor. If I drugged you, you could get my license taken away."

"If you didn't kill me first," she says under her breath, and I laugh out loud. It feels good. Vivi would love her.

"I have much better plans for you, kitten."

"What?" Her eyes are wide, and if I'm not mistaken, a memory resurfaces, a memory of our conversation from last night.

"Let's get those pills and crackers in you before you start asking your questions." Staring at me for a small moment, she puts the pills into her mouth, washing them down with water. She quickly eats, chasing each cracker with more water until the water bottle is empty and there's nothing on the plate. Then she sets it aside and crosses her arms on her chest.

"Okay, go." I smile. She's fuckin' cute. When she's not drunk or high on painkillers, it seems she's not just cute, but also funny. "Hello?" And possibly a little impatient.

"You're the baby?" She squints. "Last night you said you have five older brothers."

"I have an older sister and five brothers. All older than me. Gia by 12 years. Each of us is two years apart."

"Your parents were busy."

"They're in love."

"Kids don't equal love."

"In my family? It does." I think about that. In my family, kids are an obligation to continue the family line, to please your parents, strengthen your family, and introduce even more highly achieving children into the fold.

"No wonder you're so bossy," I say instead.

"What?"

"The baby of the family. You ever not get your way?" She looks to the side. There's my answer. Never. I laugh.

"So what better plans do you have, Doctor Brandt?"

"You have a problem." Might as well say it straight out.

"I'm sorry?"

"You told an entire club last night that not only are you a virgin, but you've never had an orgasm. And not by choice on either count." She blushes. "Tell me about your rule."

"My rule?"

"Your rule. A man needs to make you come before you have sex with him?"

"It's common sense." She's ruffled by my question and what I assume she interprets to be an accusation, a taunt.

"I agree." Her face screws up with disbelief, nose crinkling and eyebrows coming together.

"You do?"

"Well, yeah. Virginity isn't precious, not in real life. It's not even really a medical condition, just a status. Maybe in a society obsessed with purity culture it's precious and guarded, but in real life? It's nothing. But you've been taught it's special your whole life. At the bare minimum, you should be made to feel good when you give it away." She glares at me.

"Do you have sisters?"

"One, yes."

"If your sister were in my place, what would you say?" This is a test. I'm not sure if it's a test because she wants to see my reaction or wants to know if I just want to get into her pants, but...

"First, I'd say I don't want to know in any way, shape, or form about her having sex. Ever. Then I'd tell her to be safe. Then I'd tell her it's her choice. Her body." It seems the answer was the right one.

"I didn't want to be a 28-year-old virgin. I wasn't holding out for marriage or..." She pauses, moving her head from left to right. "Well, not really. My family made it a thing my whole life, but when I got older... it's kind of fucked, you know? The whole virginity thing." I nod. I agree. "But like... Everyone says it sucks—their first time. So I want it to be special. I don't want it to suck. I want an orgasm."

"But..."

"You know the rest."

"Tell me now that you're sober." She sighs and rolls her eyes.

"I can't come. I'm broken."

"You're not broken. And I can help you." After our conversation last night, I'm pretty sure I can. I'm pretty sure I know where she's failing and the workaround.

"What?"

"You don't know your body."

"Excuse me, but I—" I cut her off. This is going to be it with her, isn't it? Constantly arguing about non-issues.

Why does that sound strangely appealing?

"You don't know your body in the context of pleasure. And you're so hyper focused on coming that you distract yourself from your actual end goal." Acceptance washes over her face.

"But... how can you help me?" she asks, pulling the sheet up to her chest again. She's tiny, the tee shirt I helped her into last night down to her knees, but she's clearly still nervous about the lack of clothing. Before I even answer, I walk to my dresser, grabbing a pair of sweatpants from the top right drawer where I keep some extras in case my sister stays over and tossing them to her. The relief in her eyes tells me it was the right call as she grabs them, but then the nerves are back when she opens them.

"They're my little sister's. She stays here sometimes." Skeptical. That's fine. "I can help you, Gabrielle," I start as she puts the pants under the thick downy blanket and pulls them up. "Because I'm a doctor."

"I don't think I need medical intervention, Vic."

I laugh, and for the first time in a while, I feel it all over. She's cute. Really cute. "Yeah, got that. But I took a lot of anatomy classes."

Her eyes widen. "I guarantee your issue is part mental block, part not knowing your body enough. Sex education classes don't teach girls about their body, much less where the clitoris or the G-spot are." A blush forms on her light brown skin. "No one tells them where the sensitive spots are, when to go fast, when to go slow." My voice goes low, even to my own ears. *Shit, don't get too excited, Vic.* "I could show you. I'm more than qualified."

"Because you mess around a lot?" she asks, face unimpressed but her blush still present, and I nearly choke on air with a laugh.

"I'm not a virgin." More of a blush, but this one is more shame-driven. "I didn't mean it like that, kitten." Wide eyes. Fuck, her face is so expressive. To be fair, I'm not sure why I called her that, other than she reminds me of a kitten. She's tiny and scared, easily spooked, and though I'm sure she'd argue the fact, fragile. She also seems like she's got claws. Kitten. I like it. It fits.

"Because I'm a doctor. I know women's bodies." Her eyes go wide and disbelieving. I can't blame her. It's a good line. One I've heard colleagues use, the results always churning my stomach with how disgusting it sounds. A line that felt as sleazy coming out of my mouth as I always thought it would. "Seriously. I took entire classes on it." I try to recover. "I could... help you. With your problem."

"So you're telling me you could help me learn to orgasm? And take my v-card in the process?"

"Only if you want." I pause, staring at her. "Look, last night you were upset about it. It... We live in a strange contradiction of a world. Being a virgin is sexy and cool until it's not anymore. You're right—most people who find out you're a virgin at 28 will think you're either intentionally saving yourself or you'll be a clinger-on after. It's a cliche for a reason." She blushes and opens her mouth to argue. Shit, I can't get a single aspect of this conversation to come out right. "Not that I think you would. I'm just agreeing with you." She seems to take that in, take in my words. "I'm just saying, if you're looking to figure out what it takes to make you come, I might be able to help if you want me to. "

"And... what do you get out of it?" She's smart. Her untraditional mind and innocent face betray it, but she's sharp. Even hungover in the bed of a near stranger, she doesn't let her guard down.

I don't answer right away. I've fucked this up enough and walk a thin balance beam.

Generally speaking, I'd love to be this woman's first. Something draws me to her, and even though I only saw her for thirty minutes nearly two months ago, I haven't been able to get her off my mind. It only took an hour of dancing with her in a club before I was crafting a mental plan for how to get her and make her mine.

"My mom."

"Your mom?" She raises one thick, dark eyebrow.

"My mom is on me to start dating. To settle down." She now rolls her eyes. "She's a pain in my ass, never stops bugging me. If I don't at least look like I'm searching for someone, she'll start setting me up on blind dates. Again."

"Blind dates aren't that bad, you know." Yes, the matchmaker that curates blind dates. *That's my in.* It's also the perfect cure. The fact that these stars are lining up, the fact that Vivi was just talking to me about her business, has to be a sign, right? A sign that this is the path I should take?

Hopefully, it's not just my dick talking because I'm going for it.

"They are when they are with the perpetually unwed daughters of my mom's mahjong friends." Her head tips from side to side like she's agreeing in her mind but doesn't want to say it aloud. "Look, I'd help you for free, no strings. You're gorgeous and I love..." I pause, smiling at her. It's the smile I use on the nurses when I need a favor from them. "A challenge. It wouldn't be a burden for me, kitten. But if you want to even out the scales, get me through your blind date schtick. You need to date me, right? That's how Ben said it works. You date me a few times, get to know me, make sure I'm not a douche, and set me up on blind dates. Right?"

"I mean, yeah, in theory, but—"

"Look. My mom is getting itchy. I need the blind dates to end.

My sister told me she was planning my non-existent wedding with her friend the other day. I'm desperate." Gabi shivers, eyes wide. It seems she gets the direness of my situation. "If I tell her I'm working with a matchmaker, she'll back off. It's the perfect fix."

"Except that's not my job." My plan comes to a screeching halt.

"What?" No, this needs to work. It's actually perfect.

"I'm Cassie's assistant. I don't do the dating. I just... organize things." I see the statement for what I'm sure it is—a diss to herself. "I'm supposed to start training soon so Cassie can have more free time. The business is growing fast, with lots of happy couples and word-of-mouth referrals. But she's only one person and about to be a newlywed so—"

"So you're getting a promotion."

"Kind of?" She stares into the room, eyes locked somewhere on the wall, but she's not here. She's nervous about that new job addition and what it will entail.

"You're anxious about it. The promotion."

"I'm not... nervous. I just... I'm weird."

"No, you're not." I feel inexplicably defensive over this and the fact that she feels that way.

"You barely know me."

"Know you enough. You're not weird. You're sweet. You're... Gabi." Why do I feel a sudden urge to knock out anyone who has ever made her feel like she's weird or different instead of beautiful and intriguing?

"Spend a whole day with me and you'll think differently." A self-deprecating laugh accompanies it as she stares at her hands, playing with a loose thread on the comforter.

"Gladly." She blinks. Shakes her head. Shifts in the bed. It makes her uncomfortable, the focus being on her. She grazes over it by continuing the conversation.

"Whatever. Anyway, I'm nervous I won't be... good at it. It's not my thing. People, that is. Cassie's great at it. I don't... I don't know. People's love lives are on the line, you know?" I see the shift in her—

she's about to go on a tangent. I sit back and smile. I hope this is normal for her because it's fucking cute. "Okay, so the women coming to Cassie—they've tried all the things. The swiping and the blind dates and the setups from friends. They pay Cassie because they're tired of it and losing faith. They're tired of getting fucked over, tired of being disappointed." She looks at me, waiting to acknowledge that I understand where she's going. "So they come to Cassie because they're on the verge of giving up. And Cassie helps them. It's what we do. Find love. Make it work. Find that forever kind of love they can rely on and not have to worry that someone has some hidden shitty part of their personality. We help people find forever, the kind of forever they can rest knowing isn't a facade." She stops, contemplating. "I mean, for a while there, Cassie just thought she was helping women avoid major red flags but that everything would eventually end because she's a big old pessimist and her family is the freaking worst. I don't know how such a good person came from those assholes, you know?" She stops talking, waiting for my confirmation.

I nod in agreement, though the only time I've met Cassie was in passing last night while she was drunk and I was wrangling Gabi.

"Anyway, people who come to us are... They're fragile. Cassie is amazing at her job, at finding red flags."

"Red flags?"

"Oh, yeah. That's Cassie's specialty. She finds red flags. All of those little things men do that hint at their true self? Cassie finds them and decodes them and decides if they pass or fail. The guys who pass with just little ones—like, pink flags, because everyone technically has a few red flags—they get added to Cassie's ex files."

"So a file of exes she's dated." I'm getting it, I think.

"Yes! Exactly! So she's good at seeing red flags. I'm not bad, but mostly because I take excellent notes."

"Notes?"

"Oh yeah, I have a list of like... one hundred red flags Cassie has pointed out since I started working for her. It's nuts. Some things she tells me sound totally fine on the surface, but once you dig in, you're like... wow. Yeah. Totally a crazy red flag." I'm intrigued. I don't think there's a man alive who wouldn't love to read that list, to get an insight into little things they're doing to raise the alarm.

"Like what?"

"Girls' clothing in his house." She smirks at me, raising that eyebrow, taunting.

"I told you, they're my sister Vivian's. You can call her to confirm." I reach in my pocket, ready to grab my phone, but she rolls her eyes and waves her hand.

"I'm not worried about your flags. We're not dating."

"What if you *were* worried about my flags?"

"What?"

"Look, I need to give my mom hope that I'm looking for a wife on my own time. I work a ton. I don't feel like going on a million dates when I'm not working. But if I told my mom I'm working with a matchmaker, she'd back off. I'd buy myself at least six months of peace." The more I think about this, the more I think it's genius.

"So you want me to..."

"Date me. Vet me. Whatever you'd be doing for Cassie. I could be your test subject. Nothing is on the line with me."

"And in exchange..."

"I'll help you come." Her eyes widen. "As I said, I'd do it free of charge, but I think you're the kind of person who needs things to be reciprocal." She nods. I knew it.

"And when this is... done?"

"When this is done, we'll see. Maybe if it's a good fit, I'll have Cassie set me up. Either way, it will buy me some time without my mom breathing down my neck." I love this idea the more I tell Gabi about it. It's genius, really.

"I don't know, Vic. This all feels very... icky." My back straightens.

"Icky?"

"Yeah. Icky. Creepy crawly."

"What part is icky?" I can't believe I'm saying icky this much

"The exchange part? Like... it's a purchase or something."

"Friends with benefits."

"What?"

"I like you. You're sweet. You're a blast when you're drunk and that filter you have a tight hold on falls. We're friends. I'm helping you with your... issue, and you're helping me with mine." She pauses, nose scrunched like she's still not sure. God, she's cute. *God, I want this to work.* "If it's too much, if at any point you feel like it's feeling wrong, we stop. Stay friends. Your best friend is marrying my best friend's friend. Chances are we'll run into each other in the future."

"Well, what happens if you're a total dick?" I laugh.

"What?"

"If you're a total dick. Like you said, I'm probably going to see you occasionally. It will be weird if you're a dick and fail all the red flags."

"For one, if I'm a dick, I think Luke would hunt me down and wreak his revenge." She mulls on this thought. "And two, Ben would too. He's a good guy. If he gets wind I'm a shithead to sweet women, he'll probably be cornering me in an alley and giving me his thoughts too."

"Great. Just what I need."

"What?"

"I have five older brothers. I need more like I need my dad to know I'm negotiating my virginity away."

"Yeah, well. You've got it." Another roll of big brown eyes before her hand tries to run through her curls but gets stuck halfway through. It takes everything not to smile at her frustrated glare as she looks up at her hand like it betrayed her somehow.

"So, what do you say?"

"About what?"

"About our deal? I help you come, prove you're not broken, and you help me avoid blind dates for a bit." She stares at me for a long moment, taking me in. Reading me.

Despite her concerns that she won't be good at vetting the men her boss has her dating, I can already see she's good at it—a good judge of character and intentions.

For a split second, I panic she'll say no.

Legitimate panic washes through me.

What the fuck.

But then, before I can open my mouth and say something stupid, say something to convince her to agree, she smiles.

It's big. And beautiful. It lights up her entire face, full cheeks pushing into her eyes, black mascara smudges beneath them.

Then she sticks out her hand.

"We've got a deal."

Fuck, she's cute.

Fuck, this is going to be fun.

Instead of saying anything, I move.

Walking over to her, I reach out my hand, grabbing hers where I pull, tugging her up and to me until her feet are on the ground, the sweat pants magically fitting. The shirt covers nearly every inch, though, going to her elbows and down past her ass.

Something about the look sets off something primal in me, seeing her in my tee, how big it is on her.

Shit, I sound like a cliche.

"You wouldn't kiss me last night."

"Nope," I say, our lips near touching now. Our breaths mingle between us with tension so thick, I think I could dip my tongue out and taste it.

"Why?"

"I wanted you to remember it."

"Remember it?"

"Yeah, kitten, the first time I kissed you, I didn't want there to be even a single chance you doubted what was happening between us."

She stares, long and hard.

"Even then?" Her words are whispers but confusing.

"What?"

"Even then. Last night. You wanted to kiss me?" This girl is cute. I smile and chuckle, my breath playing on her lips.

"Yeah, Gabi. Fuck. I think I wanted to kiss you when you were babbling about toothbrushes and signs." Her breath stops, but mine doesn't. "I don't just want to kiss you because I'm gonna be the lucky fuck to prove you're not broken." She tries to butt in, probably to tell me not to get my hopes up or some other fucked-up shit. "I want to kiss you because every time something comes out of your mouth, it makes me smile. Because your hair is crazy, and you're gorgeous, and clearly a good person with so many people fighting to keep you safe from assholes like me."

"Are you an asshole?"

"Never to you, kitten." I move a hand to push one of those crazy curls back behind her ear. "Gonna kiss you now, okay?" Panic crosses her face. That's unexpected.

"You can't kiss me now."

"Why the fuck not?" I feel my brows furrow with confusion because I am going to kiss this woman in front of me, wrapped in my arms, wearing my tee. Right now, if she'll let me.

"I haven't brushed my teeth." Her voice is quiet. I just smile at her.

"I don't give a fuck about that." And then I move the fraction of an inch forward to press my lips to hers, gently, barely a graze, a simple press.

A test.

Then her tongue dips out to taste her lips, to taste the imprint mine left. As it does, her tongue grazes my lip.

That does it.

I part my lips, tapping my tongue to hers, her mouth opening to me as I move to deepen the kiss, to turn it into something so much more. More than anything I've ever experienced. She's not hesitant as I'd expect, not innocent or shy. Instead, her leg hitches up to wrap around mine, grinding on to me as I nip her lip, my hands pulling up the shirt until I can touch the bare skin of her lower back.

So fucking soft.

A mewl comes from her as my other hand moves up into her hair, tangling there.

And then she breaks the kiss.

"I bet my hair is a mess right now." I stop all movement, confused. "What?"

"My hair. It's probably ratty and knotted. I bought this new shampoo, but it's making my hair super tangly, so I need to get a new one, but every time I'm at the store, I forget." My hand moves against her scalp, caught in her crazy mess of curls. It is a mess, but in a pretty way. A way I like a fuckuva lot.

But why the fuck is she talking about shampoo while she's dry humping me? "Is that what's on your mind right now?" She blushes.

"I mean, not really. I mean, yes? But not... on purpose. If that makes sense. I mean, of course, it doesn't. It just... popped in. If I don't... If I don't say it out loud, my mind goes off with it." She tries to hide in my chest, but I stop her with my hand in her hair, tightening just a bit to keep her still. Instead, she just looks down between us. She's embarrassed.

There's no need. It's becoming evident I find everything about this woman unbearably adorable. I am so fucked.

"Is that what happens when you're trying to come?" The blush spreads to the tips of her ears and she nods, but my hand once again keeps her from hiding.

"I don't mean it to. But I can't help it. I told you. I'm broken."

"You're not broken, kitten. You've just never found a man willing to work for it. Telling you right now, that man is me."

And my job is lined up for me.

FOURTEEN

-Vic-

For once, I'm grateful for my nosy, intrusive mother since I have a bag of bagels from the bagel shop I love individually wrapped and frozen in my freezer, thanks to her. She thinks if she doesn't stock my fridge, freezer, and pantry, I'll starve to death.

Just another reason she believes I "need" a nice little wife to keep me in line, make sure I get home in one piece each night, feed me, and, of course, give my mom lots of grandbabies.

But at this moment, I'm grateful as Gabi sits across from me, chewing on one with butter and a cup of coffee.

Despite my perpetually empty fridge, I always seem to have butter—it doesn't go bad the way cream cheese does. The only thing I can almost always be counted on to have that isn't expired is cream for my coffee. But as she chews, her face gets contemplative, distant. She's thinking. Her mind is wandering.

I've been in a mostly sober Gabi's presence for nearly two hours and I've seen this face at least ten times. Sometimes it accompanies a distracted look for a few minutes, clearly exploring some random idea in her mind. When those are done, she usually does a slight nod to herself, like she's satisfied by the answer she came to on her own.

Sometimes, she asks me a question. About me, about my apartment, about medicine. None of them on the topic at hand, clearly just something her mind stumbled upon and she needed to ask.

I love her mind already, finding the way it works fascinating.

This face is new, though.

This reaction has her eyes drifting to me, full of hesitance.

Why?

"So..." She pauses, moving around seeds from the bagel that fell to her paper plate. She shifts in her seat, uncomfortable. Interesting. But she doesn't finish the thought, eyes moving from me to her finger to me and back again.

"So...?" Her eyes stop on me before she sighs, building up... the confidence? For what, I'm not sure.

"So, like... you want to fix me?"

"You're not broken." She rolls her eyes.

"Whatever."

"You're not, Gabi. You're just... different."

"Great, even better."

"It is." I'm not lying. I've had my fair share of women, women who fall over me, know what they want, see an expensive apartment, hear "doctor" and ask for the moon.

Gabi is... not that.

"Whatever. So you want to—"

"Help you." Another eye roll, those chocolate brown eyes rolling back in clear irritation. I can't hide the smile it brings. In fact, I think I've smiled in her presence more than I have in the past two years combined.

It's not that I'm not happy or don't show it on an average day—I am, and I do.

But because she just... makes me smile. A lot.

"You want to help me?" I nod, circling a hand to prompt her to continue. "You want to help me with my... problem."

"With your seeming inability to orgasm."

"And my virginity."

"Let's get past this hurdle first, okay?" She stares at me, blinking. I expand. "First, I'm going to make you come. Then I'm going to make you comfortable with coming. And then I'm going to make you come on my cock, Gabi. Those are the steps. Got it?" She blinks again, but it's accompanied by wide eyes, parted lips, and increased breathing this time. Shallow, increased breathing.

Shit, this woman is responsive.

How the fuck has no man been able to make her come?

I stare at her and smile until she collects herself out of the dazed state.

"Okay, so how does that... work?" she asks, shaking her head.

"What do you mean?"

"Are you gonna like... finger me after we eat?" I can't help it—I choke on the coffee I had just taken a sip of. "Oh my god, are you okay?" Her eyes are wide as I cough to clear my airways. "Shit, are you choking? God, this would be a fun one to explain. 'I killed a doctor because I asked him when he'd be fingering me and he choked on coffee, and I couldn't remember those first aid classes they forced me to take in high school because the dummy was creepy and they made us use a dental dam, so I never learned, not really, and boom—he died.'" I continue to laugh as I cough. "Shit, shut up, Gabi! Go..." She stands up, chair scraping, and starts hitting my back—much harder than you'd expect from a five-foot-two Italian princess.

"I'm good, I'm good. Just took me off guard." I say, grabbing her wrist. I scoot my chair back to make room and tug until she's sitting in my lap before I move her hand around my neck. I'm slightly surprised when the other hand follows.

This feels good.

This feels right.

This feels fucking dangerous.

"I'm not going to finger you today." Her face drops.

"Oh. Are you just gonna like... rub it then? Is that where I've been going wrong? I guess that makes sense because that one time in the shower, it was just, like, water pressure and no... you know..." She looks at me and whispers the next part like she's embarrassed others will hear in my empty apartment. "Penetration."

I have to fight a laugh.

"No, kitten. I'm not going to rub you, either. As tempting as it is, I'm not doing anything with you but feeding you and taking you to your friend's house."

"But..."

"You need time. A day, two, at least. You need to decide if you want to do this. Last night you were drunk. This morning you're hungover. Even though you don't see it as such, this is an important decision. As much as I would love to make you come right here in my lap, I won't." Her body shifts.

"I mean, I'm sure. Trust me. I think I'd... really like that." I smile and shake my head. Her body shifts again and fuck if my own isn't responding. Her eyes widen, and the look is so... delicious. Every time she does it, it's like she's shocked I'm attracted to her, shocked she holds such power. "Is there anything I can do to change your mind?" Her voice has dropped now, going sultry, her body relaxing and wiggling again, this time with intent. I hesitate, not wanting to admit that yes, she could very easily convince me if she just kept that up...

"No, Gabi."

"Why not?"

"I just told you. Look, I want this, but I want to do it right. You're going home tonight, and you're going to think about it. You will text me no earlier than tomorrow morning to confirm our arrangement. This arrangement will be you interviewing me for your boss to get my mother off my case and me helping you to orgasm, teaching you about your body. This is important, though, Gabi. I don't want you to just... do it. Do you understand me? I won't be a regret you look back on."

She stares at me, the heat melting into something still warm, but in a different way. Warm and sweet like honey. It melts through me, the feeling pleasant.

I could see that feeling becoming additive.

"So you're going to text me when you've thought it over. Not a second earlier. I want you to really think, Gabi. And once you do, you text me. Then we'll set up our first date."

"A date?"

"Consider this lesson one, kitten. If a man is going to make you come, you expect at the very least a meal from him. You'll come here. I'll make you dinner, and then I'll make you come." She flushes.

"Are you always this bossy?" she asks, some mix of pride and stubbornness coming out as she tightens her grip on my neck.

I can't resist it any longer.

I lean in.

My lips brush hers with each word.

"You think on it and decide this will work for you? You'll find out." And then I press my lips to her, kissing her in a way I wish I never had to stop, her moving on me as it gets heated in a way that makes me wish I didn't just give some gallant gentleman speech.

When I drop her off at Cassie and Luke's, walking her in and letting Luke give me the once over like some overprotective big brother, I kiss her once more as I leave, whispering, "Text me *tomorrow*," in her ear.

But as I think I can come to expect, she doesn't listen.

My phone buzzes at 8 p.m. An unknown number.

It doesn't matter.

The words clue me in.

> I don't follow rules written by men. I accept your proposal. When are you free next?

This is going to be a wild ride.

FIFTEEN

-Gabi-

"How was it?" Cassie asks as soon as I walk into the office on Monday carrying two coffees as is tradition—whoever comes in second gets the coffee. "I couldn't grill you while Luke was around because he's a pain but now it's just us. Tell me everything."

It's usually me getting the coffee.

When I first started at the Ex Files, I was early every day. I hate being late; the panic sends me into a tailspin. But also, mornings are my kryptonite. So now that I'm settled here and we're in a rhythm, Cassie is already going through messages more often than not when I walk in. Of course, it helps that Cassie gets up at the crack of dawn with Luke, who works early mornings down at Jeff's Garage.

"How was what?" I ask as I pop the coffee onto her desk and walk to my own as if nothing happened. There's no avoiding this barrage of questions, but I like to pretend.

"Don't you 'how was what' me, missy. I'll call Gia, tell her you went home with some random man on Saturday." A roll of my eyes.

"Gia wouldn't care. She'd just ask when you can babysit next."

"Then I'd call your brothers. Dom, maybe?" She names my most protective brother, the oldest because she knows that's who would come down on me the hardest.

I have five brothers. Dom, Nico, Enzo, and the twins, Gio and Dario. All are overbearing, all are older, all hotheaded, Italian Americans that think I'm still 12 instead of 28.

"I'd quit," I say, looking at her deadpan.

"No, you wouldn't."

"Yes, I would." Although, to be honest, I probably wouldn't, but also, if she drags my brothers into it, I might have to when I run and leave the country.

"Are you going to stop being stupid and tell me what happened? I might not call your brothers, but I'd definitely engage the phone tree. Call Luke who would call Ben who would call... What was his name again?"

She knows his name. She gave him the fifth degree when he dropped me off, even if he was only in her home for a solid five minutes before he had to go off to the hospital.

"Vic."

"Ah, yes, Hot Doctor Vic."

"Don't call him that."

"Ooooh, possessive! Love this. So! What happened? I know you didn't lose it because you don't have that... glow about you. You're also not waddling. I feel like he's tall and you're so tiny... You'd definitely be waddling."

"Waddling?" I cringe. Cassie laughs but doesn't answer my inquiry.

"So?" I sigh, logging into my computer and scrolling through emails as if I can end this conversation before it starts. I sip my coffee, trying to decide what to tell her. But that entire plan gets derailed when the email in my inbox blares at me, and I spit coffee on the screen.

"What the fuck?" Cassie says, walking over to my desk. I stand in a panic.

"Oh my god, oh my god!"

"What is going on?"

"My email. My email!"

"What's in your email!?" She starts walking around to see the screen and I start pacing in a panic. "Is it a dick pic!? Did a potential client send a dick pic?! Oh my god. Ew!" I can't even focus long enough to laugh or gawk at that prospect.

"I can't believe—my work email! And he... oh god. Oh god!"

"Gabi what the—" And then she stops at my desk, her eyes scanning the screen. And then she sits her ass in my chair, leaning forward to read like she's three times her age and forgot her reading glasses.

"You're gonna fuck the hot doctor?!" she says with a screech, leaning back in the chair so quickly it nearly tips backward. I stop moving and glare at her, but she's already looking back at the screen. "And match him?!" My head looks to the ceiling. It has those weird panels that they move over in scary movies or thrillers for the bad guys to escape through. I wonder if I could do that, avoid this conversation. "Gabi!"

"I'm not fucking him." Yet.

"He's gonna try!"

"He's going to try to make me come. And then if he can, he's going to fuck me."

"Same difference."

"It won't work."

"I saw that man, Gabi. If anyone can make you come, it's going to be him." And isn't that part of the problem? Because what happens then? If he tries, if he fails—what then? My mind doesn't get the time to stop there and panic. Cassie's already talking. "So what, he's going to give it a college try?"

"I have no idea what's happening! You're the one reading the email!" I only got in a few lines before my mental meltdown occurred.

"Ahem," she says, leaning back to read aloud. In another universe,

I'd blush. I'd push her out of the chair, delete the email, and run down the stairs screaming. I'd never come back because I'd move to Mexico and learn how to make friendship bracelets and sell them at the smoothie shack I'd end up working at.

But then I realize I hate smoothies, and my hair hates humidity, and I might have failed geography, but I'm pretty sure Mexico is humid.

So instead, I sigh and sit on the edge of my desk while she reads the email aloud.

"Dear Gabi,

I hope it's okay I'm sending through this email—it's the only one I could find and this didn't seem like a thing to send via text. As per our conversation last weekend, I'd like to set up a time to enact part one of our deal. I feel dinner would be a good start—that way you can ask some of your questions for the matching aspect and calm down a bit. I need your mind clear for what I'm going to do to you." Heat flashes through me but it's not entirely embarrassment—a different kind of heat coils in my belly. Cassie uses a hand to fan herself as she looks over at me. "Jesus, girl! Hot and he wants your mind clear?!" The blush takes over my face, burning deep into my bones.

"Please send over your schedule and I can compare it against mine at the hospital. Also, please run this by Cassie—I don't want you to get in trouble with her." Her eyes shift to me again. "Oh, it's been run by me. And I *so* approve!" Her eyes scan the rest of the message, mostly dates and times, before he signs off with a strangely formal, "Sincerely, Doctor Brandt."

"So, you're matching him?" The noise is half question, half accusation, and I feel the urge to cover my face and hide from this inquisition. I don't because that would add fuel to Cassie's fire and send her on a rampage. It's best to sit back and let it pass.

"I need to talk to you about that."

"Yes."

"What?"

"Yes!"

"Cassie, you—"

"Don't care. Vet him! It's perfect. Way more comfortable than the normal two dates, so you'll feel more confident when I throw you to the wolves for real. I told you—I need someone to help take on some of the vetting. I can't spend every night dating other men and never my own husband." The word makes her eyes go dreamy and I smile. I love this for her.

"I didn't mean to... offer. Without consulting you."

"Babe, I trust you. Trust your opinion." I sigh before telling her the other half of what I assume she's figured out.

"We have a deal."

"Got that. What is it, exactly?" I feel the blush burning. It felt crazy when Vic and I were having the conversation, just the two of us. It felt crazier once I was back at my place, going over his proposition again and again in my mind. Even crazier when I hyped myself up on the drive here to ask Cassie.

But now? Standing in front of her and having to say the words out loud?

I try to remind myself that Cassie met her fiancé when she mistook him for Roadside Assistance and yelled at him for taking too long then agreed to date him temporarily while she vetted him so he could be her date to her father's wedding. It was as messy as it sounds, but it turned out well...

My romance-addicted mind quietly hopes that maybe mine will turn out just as well.

Nope. No. No. Can't go there.

I spill before I can sit too long on that. "The scales need to be balanced." She nods, knowing me, understanding me. She's not much different in her need for things to be even. "So he's going to... help me. Well, see if he can at least."

"Is he going to fuck you?"

"He's going to... teach me. About my body. He's a doctor, after all."

And then, because we can and the situation I've gotten myself into truly is laughable, we both giggle at the idea.

"And then if he, uh... succeeds, we'll... uh... you know."

"Okay, and in return?" Cassie has her boss lady face on, and I'm half shocked that she doesn't have a notepad in front of her, writing one of her pros and cons lists.

"So, his mom keeps trying to set him up with the single daughters of her friends." Cassie cringes. This is a theme we've heard a lot in clients: many women—and now men—come to Cassie because they think taking their dating future into her own hands is better than dealing with nosy parents. "Exactly. I don't know if he just doesn't like the options or if he's not ready for it, but he wants some breathing room." Another nod. "So he's going to tell his mom he's working with a matchmaker and buy himself some time without her bugging him. If he passes the vetting, he said he'd be open to being matched."

Cassie's head moves from left to right, and although there's no paper in front of her, I know she's got the pros and cons list drafted in her mind. But then, her face gets serious, all joking and excitement done.

"Are you sure about this?"

"What?" She was gung-ho a minute ago. Now she has that look Gia has when she thinks I'm about to make a stupid decision that could hurt me.

"This. You and Vic. Are you sure? Gabs, he's got red flag written all over him. Jesus, that man could be a model for red flags on sight. Tall, dark, handsome, cocky—"

"Panty-dropping smile, I know."

"Exactly. You could..." She looks around, not wanting to say what's coming next. Like everyone else, Cassie thinks I'm innocent in more ways than just that no one has ever been between my legs.

"I could get hurt." She nods. "I won't." Pity crosses her face. "Seriously, Cassie. It's just... potentially sex. That's it."

"It's never just sex." The words are a whisper, a whisper full of knowledge and experience. My back straightens.

"Millions of people on earth disagree."

"It's never just sex for women like us, Gabi." There's a knowing look in her eyes, the look Gia gave me when I told her I thought Mom might be Santa. Not quite pity, but the look a woman gives another when she knows she's in for disappointment.

"It will be for me." She keeps staring. "I'm tired of this…. burden. That's all it feels like anymore. It's not special or memorable. It's a burden." She tries to speak. "I know what you're saying. And I appreciate it. But I'm going to do this. I'd like… your support. And advice. You're right—it's a good training exercise. If you're against the matching aspect, that's fine. We'll figure something else out. It's your business."

"No, Gabi. I actually think it will be good for you to vet someone over a longer period of time. A learning experience. I just worry about you." I open my mouth to protest, but she speaks over me. "But you're right. It's not my place to tell you to be careful or watch out. You're smart and capable."

She smiles, and I smile back before we hug, the tight kind friends give each other when a big moment happens.

Because as much as I'm downplaying this, just like Cassie, a part of me knows something big is happening.

SIXTEEN

-Vic-

EVERYONE HAS a friend who will pick at you to put you in your place and attempt—keyword being attempt—to help you think rationally about the world.

My friend is Ben Coleman.

He's the tattoo artist extraordinaire, family black sheep, and an unapologetic straight talker, and over the years since he's moved to Ocean View, he's become my best friend.

I hate to say it out loud because it makes both of us look terrible, but when the tall, dark, and objectively handsome brown doctor and the broody, tattooed motorcycle-riding guy go out together, we get our pick.

Whether we cash in on that pick is another story. That's why when my phone beeps with a text from Gabi, I know I'm in for it. There is no way that Ben will let me breeze right past what happened last Saturday and roll right into her joining us for drinks without giving me some shit.

As I walked to the bar a few blocks from my apartment, warm

summer weather and sea salt scented air clearing my mind, I had sent her a text.

> Headed to Sol and Sal to meet up with Ben. Want to meet us for a drink?

I don't know what made me send it. No idea other than for the past three days, our schedules didn't mix to meet up, and I've been able to think of nothing but kissing her.

Gabi has taken over my mind: talking to her, the strange but endearing way her mind jumps from topic to topic, the way she is unabashedly herself. She isn't ashamed of who she is or how she is. Except when it comes to her sexual history, of which she is very much embarrassed.

I have to admit, if only to myself, part of me has wondered if the deal we struck isn't just too far on the wrong side of manipulative. She wants her virginity gone. I want time with her, however I can get it. I'm inexplicably drawn to this woman.

This seems like the perfect solution to all of our problems.

That being said, when I see my phone flashing with a new message right after I order, it takes everything in me not to smile.

It's hard though, reading her reply of, "Sure—Cassie's tagging along. See you soon!" followed by an intense string of crazy emojis, which made no sense in the context. So Gabi.

"Gabi's coming," I say, fighting a smile I can't seem to shake as I stuff my phone back in my pocket. "With Cassie." The smile takes over my face, even though I'm sure this will be a third-degree style of interrogation by Gabi and her boss. An interrogation that my friend will be privy to and make fun of me for, for an eternity. Picking up my beer, I avoid Ben's eyes.

He's quiet.

I know what this is.

I might not have known Ben since we were kids—we met about six years ago now, but we're close in the way men who are single but not looking are—my sister calls it a bromance. While I hate the term,

I can't deny he knows me pretty well. And I know that if I look up at him...

I do, and my suspicions are confirmed. A thick black eyebrow is cocked at me, a half-smile on his face.

Shit. It takes everything in me not to look away. It's like an older brother staring you down, waiting for you to crack. Not that I have an older brother, and not that Ben is much older than I am. But still.

"Gabi, huh?"

"Mmhmm." Don't commit to an answer. Don't commit, Brandt.

"The virgin?"

"Jesus, man. You don't have any other way to describe her?" Why does it drive me insane that he knows that about her, that he's using it as a descriptor? A layer of red frustration coats my nerves, a stubborn layer I can't brush off.

"Dude, she announced to an entire group of people, one of whom was her boss—"

"I don't think that counts. They're also best friends, from what I understand." Ben gives me a look, telling me he knows I know what he meant.

"She told a group of men that she was a virgin, but not by choice. And then when Luke gave in and let you take her home, she announced she was going to, oh, what was it again?" I cringe. Those words are burned in my brain forever. It would be a good burn if it were just me hearing them. But knowing Ben remembers... "Oh yes, 'fuck the hot doctor.'" His deep laugh has female heads turning our way, and my fingers itch to hit him.

"Man, shut up. And don't bring that up when she gets here, okay? She might not have been that night, but she's shy. She's sweet, drank way too much, and didn't eat near enough." His smile tells me he's not buying it.

I can't blame him.

"So did you?"

"Did I what?"

"Fuck the cute virgin?" I'm genuinely offended.

"Fuck off, man. I wouldn't—" Ben laughs again, a hand on his chest right over the logo of the tattoo shop he owns.

"Jesus, man, calm down."

"I wouldn't fuck a woman I don't know when she was that drunk and unable to tell me she wanted it."

"I know, I know. But fuck if you could have seen your face." He comes down from his laughing jaunt, a smile still on his face. "So what did happen? Clearly, it wasn't just a place for her to crash and never see you again if she's coming to meet us for drinks." I roll my eyes. I want to have this conversation about as much as I want to go on that blind date my mom is dying to set up.

"She got sick as soon as we got home. Threw up and then I got her to bed."

"Where'd she sleep?"

"My bed." He smiles.

"And where did you sleep?"

"The couch, you dumbass. She was hammered. I figured there was a good chance she wouldn't even know where she was when she woke up. No way I was courting that kind of panic."

"That's a gentlemanly sacrifice—your couch is crazy uncomfortable." I roll my eyes and flip him off, and that laugh comes rumbling through. I have to wonder if he teased his brother Tanner this much when they were growing up. If so, I pity the guy. "So what happened when she woke up?"

"We... talked."

"Did she remember the night before?" I shrug.

"Somewhat."

"What does that mean?"

"I told you, she was embarrassed." He accepts that answer, and for a moment, I'm relieved. It's a mistake. It seems he just has a bigger, more pressing question to ask.

"When she saw your apartment, did she think you were a serial killer?"

"What?" I say with a laugh.

"A serial killer. Your apartment is like, textbook murderer." I blink at him.

"You'd know that how?"

"Hattie watches a lot of true crime. I'm forced to take part." Hattie is the receptionist and artist at Coleman Ink and one of Ben's best friends.

"You're insane."

"Your apartment looks like a fuckin' crash pad. Like you're a creepy killer who bought a fancy-ass apartment on the ocean to lure women into but doesn't decorate it because then you'll just have more things to move when you relocate or evidence you'll leave behind."

"You've really put a lot of thought into this, haven't you?"

"Hat and I have talked about it. Theorized."

"My apartment doesn't look like a serial killer's lair."

"Place has no fuckin' life in it."

"Fuck off, man."

"Ask her. She'll tell you." I roll my eyes, but a part of me wonders if he's right. My sister says the same thing, but she's also my little sister and lives to give me shit about everything and anything.

"So, why are you meeting up with her?"

How much do I tell him? I take a sip of my beer.

"Oh, fuck, there's a story there. What's going on?"

"Nothing." He stares.

Truth be told, I'm dying to talk about the deal I made with Gabi with someone rational. I still don't know what possessed me to make it. Sure, I want to try and make her come, and fuck if the idea of being the first man to do it doesn't make me all kinds of crazy. But it was... more than that. There's some kind of crazy chemistry there that we both feel. I know it.

I told her my end of the deal was to get my mother off my back. In any other case, it wouldn't be far from the truth. But the reality is, that's an excuse. When I suggested it and created the tit for tat I somehow knew she needed, it made sense. My mom's bugging me. A matchmaker would help ease that.

But really, I could have done that years ago. I didn't have Gabi in my corner to hire a matchmaker, but I wasn't interested in looking. I've never even been tempted. So why now? When I sat with my own thoughts after dropping her off, I realized that the matchmaking was just my way in.

To get to know her.

Learn more about her.

Figure out if this attraction and chemistry could be more.

Pick that crazy brain apart.

And, of course, to get the chance to hear her moan my name.

Does this plan make me a huge fucking dick, though? This deception I'm concocting?

"Would it be fucked up if I told Gabi I wanted her to help me with matchmaking to get my mom off my back, and in exchange, I'd help her with her problem?" I blurt the words out with no nuance, throwing them out into the universe.

Ben chokes on his beer.

"You good?" I ask as he coughs, face red, wiping at his mouth.

"Did you just say you're going to a matchmaker? Luke's matchmaker?"

"I'm going to Gabi, technically."

"Same difference." Actually, it's a huge difference, and I want to correct him, but he keeps talking. "And you're doing it to get your mom to stop setting you up on blind dates?" I nod my head because that's the jist, even if it's not the full motivation. "And in exchange, you're..."

"Going to help her figure out how to reach an orgasm." Professional. That's a good idea. If I treat this like a patient and it will seem less—

"That's crazy."

"What's crazy?"

"A date for an orgasm?"

"Okay, when you put it like that..."

"When you put it *any* way, it's insane." I look around the bar at a loss. He's not wrong. What am I doing? I run a hand through my hair, resting my head in my hands on the table.

"Holy shit," Ben says, his voice a shocked whisper.

"What?" I say, head snapping back up. I expect to see Ben looking around; maybe Cassie and Gabi are here already. Maybe they brought Luke. Maybe Luke has a baseball bat, having learned of my plan and ready to go all big brother on me. Maybe I should be looking for a rear exit.

Instead, Ben's looking at me.

"You like her."

"What?"

"Holy shit, hot shot doctor likes a girl. A girl who wears dinosaur skirts and heavy metal tees and calls it an outfit." I've never seen said outfit, but it fits my mental idea of Gabi. "Holy fuck." His eyes are wide like he's seen a miracle, like he's shocked beyond belief.

"I don't—"

"You do. I saw it when Luke fell for Cass. When Tanner fell for Jordan. You've got that look when you talk about her. All dazed and fuckin' stupid."

"I don't like her. I've met her three times. All three, she was impaired in some way, shape, or form."

"Doesn't matter. You like her." It's gone from shock to what feels like a grade school tease.

But still, his words have me thinking...

Do I like Gabi? Is it more than just some crazy chemistry I need to feel out? I mean, I think she's sweet. And sexy. And hilarious, and the way her brain works absolutely entices me. But like-like her?

Shit, I can't even remember the last time I like-liked a girl.

Shit, now I sound like a preteen boy.

"I don't think—" Ben cuts me off.

"Shh, they're here. I'll make fun of you about this shit later." Ben stands, a big shit-eating smile on his face but not directed at me— directed at tiny and tinier, two completely opposite peas in a pod.

Cassie is dressed in a tight but professional black dress and heels, hair pinned up in a nearly prissy way my mother would love, her glare pointed at me.

The look is half excited and half ready to rip me a new one.

Definitely going to have an interrogation.

Gabi is wearing what my mother would call a tea skirt, poofy and ending at her knees, but instead of a demure pattern or solid color, it has giant daisies with cat heads in the center. Her tee shirt has the KISS logo, Gene Simmons's crazy makeup and crazier tongue on display.

It's a complete contradiction of an outfit, half groupie, half preschool teacher. Her wild curls create a dark halo, bright red lipstick is painted on her lips, and when I look down—Vans. Checkered Vans.

It's essentially what my sister Vivi would have killed to wear when she was 12 and in her rebellious phase.

Or a toddler who dressed herself to her mother's chagrin.

But on Gabi, it just makes sense.

"Hello, Benjamin."

"Hello, Cassandra." I don't know if I've ever heard anyone call Ben Benjamin. Gabi rolls her eyes at my confusion.

"They do this. It's weird." And then something crazy and unexpected happens.

She hugs me hello.

Her tiny body comes over to mine, head barely hitting my chest, arms wrapping around my waist, and then she looks up at me with a slight smile, a quiet flash of second-guessing, but the smile stays strong.

Sweet.

Cute.

Sexy.

My arm dips down, wrapping her waist and gripping her tight.

"Hey there, kitten," I say, just barely loud enough to be heard over the bar's music. Her smile becomes less tentative and more confident.

"Hey."

"One for the pros," I hear, and my eyes move to Cassie with an eyebrow raised. She's taking us in.

"What?" I ask, confused.

"She's making a list. Pros and cons." Gabi looks from me to Cassie. "I told you to be subtle."

"Why?" Cassie says, still with the mix of glare and humor.

"Because you'll scare him off. He's not the dating type."

"Con," Cassie says, and I move my eyes to Ben, whose eyes are flitting back and forth between the three of us, fighting a laugh.

"Kitten?" he mouths, and I roll my eyes. "You like her," he mouths before throwing an arm around Cassie's shoulder.

"Pros and cons?" I ask into Gab's hair as Ben asks Cassie where her fiancé is.

"She does that. This is kind of an interview. Preliminary." There's a smile, a teasing smile, and I'm relieved for some fucked-up reason.

"Got it. I'll be on my best behavior."

"That's usually a con. She can sniff out being fake," she says and laughs. "Be yourself. That will be enough."

And although I spend the entire night out with Ben, Cassie, Gabi, and later Luke, who gives me the same mix of glare and humorous looks all night, half threatening me and half inviting me over for beers and a game next week, those words run through me. Over and over again.

Words I've never heard.

Be yourself. That will be enough.

SEVENTEEN

-Gabi-

"Hey," I say as I stand in the doorway of his apartment. Vic gestures me in, a hand on the small of my back as he closes the door behind us.

My hands are still shaking. It seems the twenty minutes I spent reminding myself that everything will be fine in the parking garage only took a slight edge off.

I sat there, unnecessarily early because being late makes me nauseous.

I'm never late. That's my thing. I'm pretty sure it's because I spent much of my elementary school days waiting for my big brother Dom, and then Nico when Dom went off to school, to pick me up.

He was always late.

His being late meant that a teacher had to wait with me, burdening her. Knowing my having to stay late made someone else miserable made it so I never wanted to make anyone wait again.

Instead, I get everywhere way too early and then fret about how early is too early in my car. Thankfully, Vic doesn't live in a house where he could see me panicking about it. The only person who witnessed my mini-meltdown was the security guard, and I mean, he seemed pretty bored anyway. He deserved a little entertainment.

"How was your day?" he asks, pressing his lips into the back of my hair as he walks me to a stool at the breakfast bar.

I melt, anxiety leaving my body,

Magic.

"It was good. Uneventful."

"So, what do you do? Day to day. I know Cassie's a matchmaker." Okay. This is easy. I can talk about work. I love my job.

"I'm her assistant. So I do a lot of busy work, like inputting notes and doing preliminary matching and vetting. Background checks, making sure men aren't, like, married." Vic laughs, a surprised noise as he walks to the stove.

Shit, why is that surprising?

Is he married? Was that not a laugh but a choke, like he's worried I caught on? Oh god. My mind is creating scenarios where this is his crash pad and he has some sweet wife and a perfect 2.5 kids in Oklahoma waiting for him to come home for a long weekend.

"Oh my god, are you married?" His head snaps to me, part confusion, part humor on his face.

"What?"

"You found that funny. Why would you find that funny? Are you married? Is that some kind of funny haha coincidence thing? Like, you laughed because I caught you?" Oh, my god. "Because that disqualifies you. Period."

"Kitten, calm down. It's funny married men are going to a matchmaker, that's all." His white teeth gleam against brown skin, temporarily stunning me. That makes sense. I guess it *is* kind of funny, in a sick and twisted way. Shit, why am I like this? I'm absolutely insane.

"Sorry. I mean. Yeah. That's funny. I mean, not for the wife. But I can see how that would be... funny. It's funny." I'm rambling like an idiot. What is wrong with me? "But only some of them come directly to Cassie. Some we find on dating apps. We have a few set up to capture leads. So I'll go through them and swipe to find potential clients for Cassie."

"And then she dates them?" I nod.

"Yup. Cassie dates all potential matches to vet them for red flags."

"So, she's the only one who dates them?"

"For now. Eventually, I'll be dating random men too," I say with a laugh, the idea still making me anxious. He stills, but I keep going. "As per our agreement, you're my first assignment. Vetting you while we, uh... you know."

"Have you told Cassie?"

"Well, yeah. I had to. It's her business I'm vetting you for. I thought you knew—pros and cons list at the bar and whatnot. Plus, you kind of told me to run it by her."

"No, I mean about our deal." My eyes move from side to side. Oh. That.

"She, uh, saw your email." I pick at my nails, remembering Cassie's shriek-fest. I half expect him to show some kind of remorse or apology, but he doesn't. Instead, he laughs.

"How'd she take that?" My mind drifts back to the conversation we had the Monday after her bachelorette.

"She thought it was... very professional." He laughs, sending a rush of ease and calm through me. "She appreciates professional."

"Oh, I am. The utmost professionalism when it comes to making deals." He smiles then turns away, headed for the oven. "And first dates."

"Is this our, uh, first date?"

"What else would it be?" I hesitate. "The time you broke your wrist?" I blush. He smiles. "Or when you drunkenly ran into me, called me hot doctor, and then puked in my bathroom?"

"Oh god, I had forgotten about that. Thanks for reminding me." I bury my face in my hands and groan before looking back at him. "I was thinking more the other night? Drinks with Ben?"

"We weren't alone then." His back is to the kitchen counter, leaning on it with his feet crossed like he has all the time in the world to fuck with me.

"We weren't alone in the hospital, either. Or at the bar." He tips his head in challenge.

"Fair. But we were alone when we were here after the bar."

"No, we weren't. My intoxication was very much present."

"Touché." I smile, taking my win as he turns his back to me, moving across the kitchen and opening the oven, pulling plates down. I watch him meticulously as if I'll be given a test.

A test I'd fail since my mind is in another universe. A universe where this is normal and I always come here on nights he's not on call after work. Another universe where instead of boring white plates, he has multicolored milk glass ones, antiques I found while shopping with Cassie or his sister. Photos on the walls and a funky throw on his couch. Life.

This apartment needs life.

I'm so far gone into my delusion that I'm shocked when a plate is placed in front of me.

"Where did this come from?" I ask, staring at it in confusion. It looks like... real food.

"What?" On the plate are chicken, a roasted potato, and green beans. I look from it to him and back again.

"Where did this come from?"

"I just... I just made it?"

"You cooked this?" He nods with a smile, grabbing silverware. "When?" His smile grows.

"While you were sitting here sipping your wine and explaining your day to me."

"Where the hell was I?" How did I not see Vic cooking? It seems like a crime, not seeing that. I would really like to see Vic cooking.

"In that gorgeous head of yours." A blush burns my cheeks and I look down at my plate. Plain white. Boring. Lifeless. But he doesn't let me avoid the conversation. Instead, his fingers touch my chin, tipping it up so I'm stuck looking at him. "No. Don't do that."

"What?"

"Look down. Get embarrassed. I like that, how you get lost in your mind. Like seeing things work in your eyes, seeing you talk and get excited about things."

"You like it now," I say, moving so I can busy myself with a fork and knife. People like this part of me when they first meet me. The quirky part, the part that makes them laugh and smile.

Until they don't. Until they realize it's not some cute act I put on, it's just me. My mind never stops. I ask a million and seven questions, nearly all of them with no real purpose. I space out, my mind ignoring reality and moving at its own speed.

"Yeah, I like it a fuckuva lot right now," he says, his hand moving to my chin again, grabbing it this time so I can't move. "Stop, Gabi. Stop now. One thing to know about me is I will never lie to you. I like your brain. Like how it runs off and the places it takes you. If I find out you're hiding that from me, hiding that part that's so you it drives me wild, I'll get mad."

"And then what? You won't have sex with me today?"

"Not having sex with you tonight, regardless." He turns from me after dropping that bombshell to grab his own plate.

"What?" He sets his own plate down across from me and sits.

"I told you, Gabi. There are steps to my master plan. Step one is to make you come. Step two is to help you explore, to learn. Neither of those is me fucking you." And then, fuck my life, I feel it. I pout. It's a byproduct of being the baby girl in a family where my dad thinks his girls are princesses and my brothers were trained to believe the same. So instinctively, I pout, and he laughs.

"Don't worry, babe. I'll fuck you sooner or later. There's no rush though. Now eat. You'll need it." And then the man fucking winks at me before he digs in.

My pussy quivers in response.

I am so fucked.

And not in the way I thought I'd be.

EIGHTEEN

-Gabi-

When my hands are busy drying dishes as he cleans, Vic starts the conversation again.

Dinner was shockingly good—and apparently made by him. I need to run this info by Cassie—is that a good thing or a red flag, a man who knows how to cook? I don't remember her ever mentioning it one way or another.

"We need to set some ground rules," Vic says, and my hands freeze.

"Ground rules?" He hands me a white plate, ceramic and plain, just like the rest of his apartment. Like his bedroom that's white and black with not much else. No art, no photos, no goofy magnets from his travels on the fridge. Not a notepad to jot things down or a vase for flowers. Even his chargers are in a fancy, minimalist charging station.

It's kind of a shock, but it seems he's boring as fuck.

"Ground rules. I want to make sure we're on the same page."

"That sounds foreboding."

"Everything in life should be laid out in front of you. Planned. That makes sure no one gets hurt."

"Forget foreboding. That sounds super boring." He laughs, handing me a fork.

"Making sure no one gets hurt because expectations weren't set is boring?"

"Well, yeah."

"How's that?"

"If you plan your entire life, you never get a surprise."

"I work in an ER. My life is one big surprise."

"That's a controlled surprise. And it doesn't affect you other than what work you're doing day to day."

"What's wrong with that? Who wants a life of surprises?"

"You're like Cassie." I decide with a roll of my eyes. Cassie is boring too.

"How so?"

"Before she met Luke, she had these crazy rules and no social life. Like, she didn't date or go out with friends at all. She just worked."

"Nothing wrong with that." Why does this not surprise me?

"She was a matchmaker who didn't believe in love."

"Is that wrong?"

"Well, yeah. She was selling love, for lack of a better description. She sells the dream to her clients. A dream that, before Luke, she didn't believe was feasible." Long seconds pass as he watches me before he speaks.

"Do you?"

"Do I what?"

"Do you believe in love?" I sigh and blush all at the same time. There's no way around it, and I promised myself I wouldn't be fake if I did this.

"My sister met her husband when they were in middle school. She knew she would marry him, came home, and told my dad. I was five, and I remember how red my dad's face got. But she's married to him and they have two boys together. Totally in love." I grab a spoon, wiping it with a white dish towel. "My parents met and hated each other. Couldn't stand to look at each other." I laugh. "My dad was my mom's best friend's boyfriend in high school, and she thought he was an ass. He thought she was an uptight princess." He laughs, and I shrug. "She is. And he is. But...

"Years later, they met again and fell in love. The math says Gia was the reason for a shotgun wedding, but my mom insists Gia was a premie, that they were just so in love they couldn't wait. Had a city hall wedding and a big party after. There is not a single picture of my wine-loving mother holding a glass, though." Vic laughs.

"So you believe in love." I mull on that. I lose a lot of potential men with this next one.

"I read romance."

"Okay?"

"A lot of it."

"My sister likes that. Nothing to be ashamed of." I smile. He's sweet.

"Oh, I'm not. But... you read that, read those stories, read about human emotion and love and trials and tribulations that a couple goes through to wind up together... you can't not. Believe in love, that is. It's out there. I've seen it at work. With my parents. With Gia and Ant. With Cassie and Luke and all of the Ex Files clients." He's quiet, and I think... I think I fucked up.

"I'm not saying I need that or want that. I just..." Vic stays quiet, stopping the faucet as I dry the last plate. My mind runs off, panicking that I did it wrong, I spoke wrong, I... "Okay, so, losing my virginity. It's... it's embarrassing. Having it is embarrassing. And like... when I find him... When I find the man I want to be with for the rest of my life, I don't want him to remember our first time as awkward or painful. I don't want to be... inexperienced. I want to know what I'm doing, you know?" Oh my god, my body is on fire. This might be the most embarrassing moment of my life. Worse than telling a hot doctor my hair was soaking wet because I was masturbating when I fell in the shower.

Granted, that doctor was also Vic.

Kill me now.

"This is so embarrassing. I should just leave. Shit, this was a terrible idea. So bad. Oh, my god. I'm just going to.." I turn in a circle, looking for an out, looking for my keys. On the second spin, I spot them on a black side table. "I'm gonna go. Thank you for dinner. This was... such a bad idea. I must be insane." I turn to him, halfway between my bag and where I was standing. The plate I was drying is still in my hand. Why am I like this? "Why would you—Hot Doctor with a capital H—want to... what? Train me? For some future husband?" I smack my head. "I'm a moron. I'm a freak! Please. Forget this ever happened. I need..." I turn again, going to my purse. I can't watch Vic anymore, his face blank, leaning against the breakfast bar, arms crossed on his chest. His chest that looks good in a thin gray tee shirt. His chest that I will never get the chance to look at without said tee shirt.

Dammit.

That's a shame.

But as my hand reaches out for my bag, mere inches away, he finally makes a noise.

"Stop." I do. It's like his voice is the key to my body, and every muscle freezes up. A part of my brain argues, telling me to *move, move, move*, grab my bag and run from this embarrassing as fuck situation.

But my body doesn't listen.

It's not mine anymore.

"Turn around." I do. Shit, my body turns around. But I keep my eyes to the floor, refusing to look at him. He's wearing loafers. Loafers. Who wears loafers? There's a small tab on them, on the tongue, and I wonder for a split second if there's room in them to put a penny or if it's for show.

Not the time, Gabi.

Actually, it might be a great time. Perfect time to zone out and let my mind leave my body. Are loafers a red flag? Does that red flag differentiate if they're legitimate penny loafers or if they're fake?

"Look at me."

What the fuck? His words cut through my self-induced haze.

Well, that's new.

My head moves to look up at him.

He's smiling.

"Not a single part of you is something to be embarrassed about."

"Falling in a shower while I attempt to masturbate and breaking my wrist?" The words fall from my mouth.

"Okay, maybe that." I can't help it—I smile. "But the rest? No. Being a virgin? Who cares? Being inexperienced? Kitten, that's every man's dream. Teaching a woman? Helping her be confident in bed? Ensuring what she learns is what *you* like? Fuck, Gabi. Nothing hotter." My entire body flushes with his words and the way his voice goes low and gravely.

"Oh."

"Yeah, oh. So, I will never make you do anything. Ever. You can feel safe with me. If you want to leave, I'll walk you downstairs and you can leave. If you're serious—if you want to do this—I would be honored. But know that none of what we do should be because you're embarrassed. None of what we do should be because of some fictional man you may meet in the future. Any man would be honored to have you in his bed, Gabi. Experienced or not. This would be for you. All for you."

"How so?"

"Can you put the plate down?" he says, moving his eyes to my hand still holding the white plate. Shit. I take one step and lean forward just enough to stay far from him but still reach the island's edge as I slip it onto the marble. He rolls his eyes at me before continuing. "You need to know yourself. Know your body. Get the confidence to know you're not broken, Gabrielle." His words are near angry. "In fact, I never want to hear those words come from your mouth, okay? Ever again." I nod, not telling him that those words didn't come from my own mind but from an ex who was angry he couldn't "fix" me and thus get my v-card.

I think that would end terribly at this moment.

"You want to decide now, we're good. You want time, want to sit on it, we can watch a movie, or we can talk, or you can go home. I had a good time with you tonight. I enjoy your company, Gabi." His words now sound... foreign. Like he's not used to saying them. Like they taste unfamiliar in his mouth. "But no matter what, I need to know you're sure."

I don't even wait.

His words... They mean everything to me. To hear them, to be validated. To feel... normal.

It's a rare moment in my life where I feel normal.

So I nod.

"I'm sure, Vic. I want... I want to do this." I take a deep breath before I add, "With you." His eyes darken with those two words, and something tells me they were the right words. *Game on,* they seem to say to him.

He walks from the kitchen, past me, sinking into the couch, eyes locked on me.

"Come here," he says, his voice low and gravelly, the sound instantly pulsing at my center. His voice is the sexiest part about him, I think. The way it's low and soft and strangely comforting all at once. I do as he asks, walking until I stand between his legs where he sits on the deep couch, his eyes looking into mine as his hands go to the outsides of my bare thighs, right above my knees, just barely under my skirt. "You good?"

Am I good? I'm a mix of anxiety and excitement and fear and resolve. "Maybe?" His lips twitch.

"If at any moment things feel weird, you tell me, and I'll stop." Warmth runs down my spine. His hands move up and down my legs, caressing the backs of my thighs. Not sexual, but in a reassuring way.

"Okay." My voice sounds breathy even to my own ears, and when his thumbs join the party, stroking the insides of my thighs, I quiver all over.

"What do you have on under here?" he asks. His voice is lower than I've ever heard it. Through my hooded eyes, I see his are locked to his hands, watching them disappear under the fabric, watching his wrists lift it ever so slightly. Every pass up, he gets closer and closer to where my pulsing is dying for him. The look in his eyes tells me everything I need to know.

I'm going to orgasm tonight if it's the last thing he ever does.

"What?"

"Under this skirt, kitten. What do you have on?" Another shiver. I look down at the flouncy, bright purple skater skirt I paired with a flowery blouse, watching his thumb disappear and reappear, each swipe like a match on sandpaper. Igniting.

"Uhm. Underwear?" I pause, unsure of what he's looking for. "Blue. Boy short?" I probably should have worn something sexier, knowing why I was coming here.

"Next time, wear nothing," he says as his thumb goes up, up, up and grazes the line of my panties.

"Oh," I breathe, the sound nearly silent, but he catches it. His eyes move up to mine, my mind not missing the fact that, unlike every time his hand has grazed up, it's staying there, running back and forth on the line of my panties. I can see at this moment how having none would be a perk. Noted.

Then one hand moves out from under my skirt to the top of my hips, pulling me down. I squeal in surprise, landing on Vic's chest before the arm is around my waist, moving our bodies until we're both lying on the couch. He's on his side, his back to the back of the couch, while I'm splayed next to him, the deep couch giving me more than enough room.

But that hand. That hand is still grazing that line, back and forth, back and forth.

I feel my lips part, his eyes locked on them.

I'm turned on.

This isn't... new.

But it's new to feel it this easily with a man.

And then his head tips forward, his lips touching mine, tasting, his tongue dipping into my open mouth to distract me as that thumb stops grazing and dips under the line of my underwear.

A low moan falls from me, swallowed by his mouth as that thumb runs up and down my slit, not going in, just dragging the moisture I can already feel.

"God, you're wet, Gabi," he says against my lips, and the words, the tone, his hand... it all has me lifting my hips for more.

He chuckles.

"Slow, kitten," he says, but I shake my head.

"I don't want slow," I say in a whisper. I've waited 28 years. I want this so badly, I feel like I'm going to combust if I don't get it. Become a pile of ash and indignity on this crazy expensive couch.

"Slow. We're not in a rush," he says, moving his hand from my panties, and I mewl a sound of disappointment. Another chuckle. "Hips up, kitten," he says, his fingers creeping up and hooking into the waist of my underwear. Oh, my god. I do as he asks and gently he uses his hand to scoot them down slowly. Torturously slow. When they're past where he can reach, I bend at the knee, helping him until I'm free. He lifts them, looking at the light-blue boy short panties I wore under my skirt.

"I changed my mind," he says, and my stomach drops. Oh my god, were they *that* unsexy? So bad he needs to end this before it even starts?

"What?"

"I changed my mind. Next time you come wearing these. I need to see you bent over this couch in nothing but these." My belly flutters, my center clenching as he flicks the underwear to the floor. His hand lightly trails fingers back up my thigh, flicking the skirt up and exposing me, the warm air of the house hitting bare skin. "Beautiful."

Knowing his eyes are there, I instantly start rethinking every life choice I've ever made, if I should have shaved better or gotten waxed, or—

"Don't you dare," Vic says, moving my legs, which were trying to cross, to hide myself. "Don't you dare try to hide this from me. Right now, this pussy is mine." His words have me clenching, a small mewl working from my throat. "Ahh, seems my girl likes words," he says, and I'd be embarrassed, probably blush, or maybe even try to sit up, except his hand is further parting my legs, giving him room, and his hand is running up my thigh, using his thumb to part me. "She likes to read; she likes my words. Perfect." That thumb moves up my slit, exposing me to his watchful eye.

"Jesus, look at you. Already so wet." The thumb starts from my entrance, dipping in the slightest bit before running up to my clit, lightly circling me there. My hips buck. "Feel good?" he asks, his voice a sultry caress, an additional layer to the erotic tease that is Vic. I moan as his thumb presses lightly where I'm dying for more. "Answer me." His face goes into my neck as he whispers the words before nipping my ear, pulling it into his mouth.

"Yes," I whisper, lifting my hips.

"Good girl," he says, pressing on my clit with more force this time. *Oh my god, that is so hot.* Should that be hot? Why is that so hot? "This is all we're doing tonight. I'm gonna make you come." He breathes heavily, a sigh. "You're going to come for me tonight, okay, kitten?" I nod, biting my lip, my back arching as he continues to circle my clit, spiraling in towards my clit then back out.

"For a woman who's never had a man make her come, you're responsive as fuck." His fingers go down, dipping barely into my entrance again, two fingers gathering wet, and fuck, I want that too.

"Please," I say, the words a beg.

"What, baby. What do you need?" Try as I might to fight it, the blush burns from my cheeks down to my neck. "Nothing to be embarrassed about. I have never seen anything sexier than you writhing on my couch, wanting more. What do you need, Gabrielle?" Another moan, another buck of my hips. *Why is my full name so sexy?*

"I need… your fingers."

"You have them," he says, returning to my clit. It feels swollen, oversensitive. I've never felt this, never felt this… much.

"Inside," I whisper, still embarrassed but quickly losing that. I need him. I need more.

"Not tonight," he says, and my eyes snap open, looking at him. His eyes move from where he's staring at his hand hungrily to my eyes, and he's smiling. "Not tonight, Gabi. Tonight is about making you realize you're not broken," he says, and the words I spoke in a drunken fit of tears break down a bit of the wall. A wall I didn't know was there; a dam that holds me back.

My pleasure rises as the wall falls.

"Tonight, I'm going to make you come on my fingers, hear you moan my name, and revel in the fact that I'm the first one not just to make that happen, but to witness you coming. Then, tomorrow, I'm going to jack off to the knowledge that I made you come when even you couldn't." I moan deep, the sound not even my own. The wall crumbles, the feeling closing in on me, building in my lower back, moving up my inner thighs. It's so much more than I felt in the shower, more than I've ever felt. Each word that comes from Vic's lips breaks the wall and fills that bubble inside me a bit more.

He's panting in my ear, just as turned on as I am as his hand moves feverishly, the wet sound of him rubbing my clit in this perfect motion hitting my ears, like an erotic crashing of waves, pounding at that wall until it's just a small heap of pebbles, the barrier almost gone.

"I'm… I think I'm close," I say, and I expect Vic's hand to move, to do something different, but he doesn't, he just keeps going, the same rhythm, the same pace, the same pressure as it builds and builds, as I reach for it…

But I can't. I can't get there.

And as his hand continues, as the feeling builds to an excruciating level, as he continues to pant in my ear, as I continue to moan, I wonder if maybe I really am broken.

Because if I can't focus with Doctor Victor Brandt touching me, when will I?

"What, baby? Get out of your head," he says.

"I can't... I'm so... but I can't..."

"You're so wet for me, Gabi. I know you can do this," he says, and another stone falls from the wall, my body responding in kind. "Fuck, you like when I talk to you?" Another pebble, another clench, another rush of wet. "Fuck, Gabi. I can't wait to hear you when you come. I want you to say my name, okay? When you come for me, you say the name of the man who made it happen." I moan deep, a new, more profound feeling taking over. A blooming of warmth fills my lower back, my breathing becoming erratic.

"Fuck, I... I..."

"Fuck yeah, baby, you're going to come for me. You're going to come so fucking hard right now, and all it took was my fingers. Imagine what it's going to feel like when I'm fucking you. I have so much to teach you, and I'm going to have so much fun doing it," he says, and it's that—the idea of more, the idea of learning, and, admittedly, of Vic fucking me that does it.

I explode, his name on my lips, my back arching, hips moving to get more, to get anything I can from him as I scream. Vic lays his entire hand on my soaking pussy, rubbing hard to draw out the last of my orgasm, the orgasm I never thought I could have. My body trembles with aftershocks as my mind comes back into focus slowly, his hand slowing its movements.

And when my eyes open, when I look at Vic, who is looking at me with a mix of adoration and awe and lust, it happens.

I cry.

NINETEEN

-Vic-

I'm making Gabi breakfast the morning after making her come on my living room couch.

The morning after she cried in my arms because she finally realized she was not broken.

The morning after I realized that wasn't something she created in her head—someone told her she was broken. Some asshole didn't put in the work, got frustrated, and told her she was broken and she believed him. She confessed this late into the night, long after I thought she had fallen asleep in my arms, and it took everything in me not to demand a name so I could hunt him down.

Show him what broken felt like.

I shake my head, trying to remove that feeling, that reaction.

That is not me. I don't know *who* that is.

"You ever wonder why there's no West Brunswick?" Gabi asks, staring off at the black side table that holds a globe that was my great grandfather's. It's the only decoration in the room, so I know that's what she's looking at.

Shit, I never realized how… empty it is in here.

"What?"

"There's East Brunswick and North Brunswick and South Brunswick and New Brunswick."

"Okay?"

"But no West Brunswick." I stand there for a moment, flipping bacon from my grocery run, before I look over at her as she picks up her phone and starts scrolling absentmindedly. "You ever wonder why?"

The answer to her question is no. I have never once wondered about that. But now that she brings it up… "No, but you're right. Also, Plainfield. There's a North Plainfield and a South Plainfield and also just Plainfield. Why didn't they just break Plainfield up and call it north and south?"

"Like the Carolinas." Her words are hesitant.

"Or the Dakotas," I say, grabbing toast from the toaster. Her face moves away from what I now realize is nervously scrolling to meet my eye.

"Are you messing with me?" she asks. My eyebrows furrow at the question. I don't understand it.

"What?"

"Are you messing with me?" Now her voice is near angry, the words coming out harsh.

"In what way?"

"By talking to me about this."

"You lost me, kitten." Her eyes are skeptical, suspicious, and guarded as they narrow on me. She pauses, continuing to stare at me before she decides to answer, to explain seemingly begrudgingly.

"I'm annoying." I burst out laughing at her words.

"What?"

"I'm annoying. It's fine; I've come to accept it and the fact that I'll always be this way." I continue to stare at her. "Weird things pop in my mind all the time. I can't stop it. Sometimes it's stupid, like… what kind of fruit would be the best to live in, and sometimes it's even stupider, like why isn't there a West Brunswick. I've spent my entire life knowing that when I say these things out loud, people think I'm a little crazy. I learned the lesson early. I keep them to myself. But sometimes, when I'm nervous, they pop out. Usually, I get the looks, and I change the subject quickly. But you were entertaining them, so I need to know: are you being serious or are you messing with me?"

Something about that look makes me hurt for her. Something about her thinking she's annoying makes me want to go after everyone who ever made her feel that way. So, instead of answering her question, I ask one of my own.

"Who said you're annoying?"

"Everyone." The word comes easy, like she thinks it's obvious.

"Who?" I ask again, and even I can hear the demand in my tone. I want names. And addresses.

"Kids at school. My brothers. I... They mean well, I'm just... annoying."

"You're not annoying."

"Yes, I am. It's fine—I'm the baby of seven kids. I was born to be annoying. I've also accepted this fact."

"You're not annoying, and if I hear you say that again, I'm taking you over my knee." Her eyes go wide with shock and surprise, and I know she's a virgin and we have a lot of other "firsts" to go over, but fuck, I like that idea a lot. I keep on talking. "You're normal. You have a brain that's always wondering and always working. I think that's beautiful." She stares at me for long moments, trying to decide if she can believe my words. "And for the record, the answer is a coconut." More silent, confused, staring.

"Coconut?" Her word is a whisper.

"A coconut. A coconut is the best fruit to live in."

"Is a coconut a fruit?"

"It's a drupe. Which is technically a classification of fruit." There's a long moment where she stares at me in shock before she speaks.

"How do you know that?"

"You're not the only one who wonders things, Gabrielle." With my words, she relaxes, her body going limp in her seat on the couch, and she sets her phone aside.

"Why not a watermelon?" The anxiousness from before melts. She's looking at me with a small smile on her face. But something in that look tells me she can't believe I'm playing along with this, and she's wondering when I'm gonna turn it into some mean joke.

I'm not though. Not even a little.

And the fact that her brilliant, creative mind has been a sore spot for her in the past, the fact that it hasn't always been seen as brilliant and interesting and exciting, makes me want to go hunt down her siblings and beat some sense into them.

"A coconut is hard. It'll dry out to make a better permanent structure once you scrape out the edible part. A watermelon would rot." She blinks at me. "And a coconut would smell good." More blinking. She keeps staring at me. "What?" Silence. And then she speaks.

"You don't think I'm crazy."

"Why would I?"

"Because I say dumb shit like what's the best fruit to live in. Because weird thoughts come into my mind and I can't get them out until I say them out loud." Her eyes move from me to the TV that's still off, but I can see her face is a shroud of shock and confusion, even in her profile. I almost say something, almost talk, but a voice in my mind tells me not to. That voice begs me to be quiet, to be patient.

My patience pays off.

"I have six brothers and sisters. There was always someone talking in my house. But I was the one that when I said something, everyone would go, 'oh, here goes Gabi,' because everyone knew I was about to go on a tangent." The next time I look from the pan to her, her eyes are on me again. "There have only ever been two people who went along with the chaos in my mind. My dad and now, you."

And even though she doesn't elaborate more, even though I still I kind of want to go kick the asses of her brothers who made her feel like some kind of nuisance, I know deep down that means something to her.

And I love that I gave that to her.

TWENTY

-Gabi-

On Monday, I walk into the office with a giant smile on my face, carrying two drinks—one for me and one for Cassie.

I can't wipe the smile off.

It's been stuck there since Vic walked me down to my car after breakfast, him needing to go into the hospital at noon. I drove home grinning, catching my goofy face in the rearview mirror. I cleaned my house, prepped for the week, and called my sister to confirm her bringing her tyrants over on Saturday, all with that same smile.

And now I'm walking into work with it, my insides still a mess of sunshine and rainbows and fairy tales and amazing orgasms.

When Cassie catches my face, her phone to her ear, her face falls.

"Gotta go, babe. No, I'm good. Gabs walked in," she says, swiping her phone and keeping her eyes on me as I walk to her, handing over the drink. "*Oh, my* fucking god." I smile as I step back, headed to my desk. "Oh, my *fucking* god!" she repeats as I pull my chair out. "Oh, my fucking *god!*" Her voice is rising with each word, each change in enunciation.

"Quiet, Cassie. The neighbors will call the cops on us again," I say, reminding her of when we squealed so loud the neighbors in our office building thought something had happened and sent over the police.

"And I'll tell the cops that my best friend just had her first orgasm in 28 years!" The smile stretches until it hurts my cheeks, but a blush comes to my face to join it.

"Cassie, can we not let the poor accountants next door know I had my first orgasm this weekend? It might give the guy a heart attack."

"Or a boner," she says, and I gag, thinking of the little old man next door who is always just this side of inappropriate.

"Ew, Cass. You're fucked up," I say, sitting at my desk. Despite that, my smile stays in place. Is it bad for teeth to be exposed to this much air? Or sun? Do teeth need sunscreen? I guess not since they're usually behind lips, but if they're not, should I protect them? Like sunglasses for faces?

"Get your ass up. We're getting breakfast," Cassie says with a demand, already putting her bag on her shoulder.

"We have work."

"Like I could work under these conditions. I own the business. I make the hours." I roll my eyes but agree nonetheless.

"My place or yours?" I ask, because there's no way in hell I'm having this conversation at Pete's Diner.

An hour later, we have pastries from the coffee shop down the road (they gave me a weird look since I was there just ten minutes earlier, getting coffee) and are sitting on the killer emerald velvet couch in my apartment.

My place is quirky and perfectly me in every way. As soon as I got a place of my own, I took the chance to make it... mine. In all honesty, it matches the chaos in my mind. A dangly crystal chandelier hangs in my living room right over the couch that I found on Facebook Marketplace and forced my brother Dom to help me lug up the stairs.

That ended in Dom calling Nico, and they lugged it up while I gave them directions. It was all very *Friends* "PIVOT!" but I promised Dom I'd take Sammy for two days to do girly stuff, so it was worth it for him.

There's a black and white bullseye rug under my antique coffee table I painted a light, dusty purple on a whim, and on top is a stack of coffee table books, from the history of rap through photos to a giant *Where's Waldo*. My niece loves that one.

On the small table in my kitchen is a vase full of fresh wildflowers. The vase is a teal T-rex, a Christmas present from my nephews that I cherish more than nearly any other item in my home. My curtains are pink and white gingham, the appliances in my kitchen a bright yellow, and my walls are littered with everything from family photos to thrift store art to pictures my niece and nephews have drawn.

It's... Gabi's place.

That's the only way I can explain it.

As Cassie sits, unwrapping the cheese danish I picked, I grab plates—a light pink milk glass set—and put them on the coffee table.

"Okay, spill."

"Spill what?" I ask, suddenly shy. Over a year ago, Cassie and I sat on this very couch while she spilled to me about Luke—about their whirlwind romance, their stupid deal to date until he took her to her father's wedding, all of it. In a way, their relationship brought us together as friends.

It's strange being on the other end of it, though.

"Gabi. I know I'm your boss, but that hat is off. I'm officially best friend Cassie right now. Best friend Cassie wants to know about the first orgasm you ever received." My cheeks burn. "Okay, let's start small. How did the night go? You got there and..."

"He made me dinner. By himself."

"He made dinner?" I nod and I see the wheels turning. "Okay, that's... interesting."

"Interesting how?"

"A man who can cook either likes food, was tight with his mom, or uses it to woo women. It could really go either way without more info." And this is what I need from Cassie right now. I'm still learning all the red flags to look for, but there's still so much I don't know. *Not that it should matter to me, other than to vet him.*

I don't get a chance to ask anything else before she's talking again.

"Okay, so dinner and then..."

"And then we were cleaning up, and... well, I got all weird and I almost left."

"You almost left?"

"But he didn't let me." Her eyes widen.

"He didn't let you?" I shake my head. "Did he like..." Her face blanches. "Gabi, did something bad happen?"

"Oh, god, no. He just talked to me. He was... nice."

"So you didn't..."

"Oh, no, we did." Cassie screams, a shriek that I've never heard her make, and my body jolts back in shock.

"Gabi, are you still a—"

"He refused to have sex with me." Cassie looks crestfallen and I can't blame her. "For now."

"For now?"

"He has some master plan." She rolls her eyes, clearly done with the games.

"Okay, enough dropping hints. What the fuck happened?"

"He fingered me."

"He fingered you?" Her eyes are wide, but I tip my head from left to right—that's not entirely true.

"Well, not really."

"Gabi, what the fuck?"

"Okay, so he's got this plan, right? Day one, make me come. Then he wants to help me... learn things. Be comfortable. Then... we're gonna do it. So he touched me. But refused to... go in." I can feel my face burning even more as Cassie doesn't respond. I fill in the silence with mental vomit. "Is that weird? Like... maybe I did something wrong, and he didn't want to go too far because he wasn't interested anymore, but he wanted to like... prove himself? I haven't heard from him since yesterday and.." My gut falls. "Oh my god. I did something wrong. And now my first and probably only orgasm that was life-changing and amazing, and oh my fucking god, so good, is going to be forever remembered as the time I scared off Hot Doctor. What is wrong with me? I—"

Cassie cuts me off.

"Jeez, Gab, breath. You're fine. It makes sense. I'm just.. impressed."

"That he made me come?" God, did even Cassie think I was a lost cause?

"No, Gabi. That was a given. Did you see him?" I did. I nod. "I'm impressed that he's thinking that far ahead. He seems... committed."

"He's not." Cassie's face scrunches, not buying what I'm saying. "Not in that way. It's not his style, I don't think. This is just... a way to help me."

"What does he get out of it other than a hot girl coming for him?" I roll my eyes at her, winding my hair and shoving in one of the millions of sparkly pens I own to keep it in place, brushing my blunt bangs to either side of my face.

"We talked about this. His mom is always trying to set him up. I'm his out. I'm vetting him for matching, remember?" Is she so caught up in wedding prep that she forgot?

"I'm not stupid, Gabi." She rolls her eyes and throws a napkin my way. I watch it flutter to the ground. "I just mean... he could have gotten with a matchmaker at any point to avoid his mom. Why now? How come when you stumble into his ER, he decides he needs to get set up?" My thoughts have ruminated on this once or twice before. Each time, I instantly shift mental topics. "And he's not actually looking to get matched, right? Just have an excuse for his mom, and then maybe, possibly, have us match him?" She has her digging face on, the one she wears when she's putting together pieces of someone's personality to get the whole picture. I don't like it.

"I mean... yes? But no? I don't know."

"This sounds... confusing, Gabi." It does. It is.

"I know." Cassie doesn't say anything, picking at the buttery pastry in front of her before she finally looks at me.

"Look. You know I love you, right?" I nod. "And I don't want you to get hurt." I nod again. "I've... I've seen it all." Of course she has. Between her ass of a father and all the men she's dated over the years, she's seen every form of crappy guy. "You're sweet. And you *love* love. The idea of it." Her eyes travel to my bookshelf filled with smutty books and happily ever afters. "The real world? It doesn't look like those."

"I know that, Cassie." The words sound defensive even to my ears.

"Not trying to offend you. You see the best in everyone. I see the worst. It's why we work. But that is how you get hurt."

"If I recall, Miss Cassie, that's also how you almost fucked everything up with Luke." I stare at her, standing my ground and reminding her that she let Luke go because she saw the worst. Saw the potential for bad and ran from it.

"You're right. I just... I worry about you. Virginity is dumb, I agree. Definitely a creepy, misogynistic social construct. And yeah, if you want to get rid of it with some random guy who can make it good for you, do it, by all means. But... whether we want it to or not, the first time means something to most women. It's fucked up and totally bullshit, but... it does. I don't want you to get hurt. Or to fall for a man who has player written all over him." I pause. This is what I've been afraid to hear.

"Does he?" Cassie sighs, like a big sister about to break bad news.

"Walking red flag, Gab." I know this. He ticks off a lot of the "red flag" boxes on the list of red flags I've collected over the years working for Cassie. But still...

"He said a coconut is the best place to live." Cassie's brow furrow in confusion.

Of course it does.

Normal people require context, Gabi. Duh.

"You know how I say random shit all the time?" She nods without hesitation. Not surprising. Everyone who knows me knows what I'm talking about. "I was talking about how West Brunswick isn't a place and that's weird, and then I mentioned what would be the best fruit to live in. Normally, if I say something like that, people make a face."

"What face?"

"That face," I say with a wave of my hand at her, smiling. She blushes, rearranging her features. "He told me a coconut would be best."

"Not a cantaloupe?" She might not always get it, but she tries. And this is why she's one of my best friends.

"He said a fruit like a watermelon would rot. A coconut would get hard." She nods.

"I mean, that makes sense." She's the logical one of us. "But what does that..."

"He doesn't think I'm weird and annoying."

"You're not."

"I mean, I am. But I'm fine with it."

"Gabi, I—"

"No, stop, that's not what I'm saying. I'm saying... he went with it."

"And that... that means something to you." Understanding blooms on her face. I nod.

"It means something to me," I say, and she sighs, one of resignation. Here comes logical Cassie.

"Babe, that's why you need to be careful. I see it now, Gabi. You could get hurt. I don't think... You could get wrapped up in this and then..."

"I'm not going to fall for him."

"You could though, without even knowing you are." She says this not because she's warning me, but because it happened to her. Cassie and Luke were supposed to be temporary, and then she was supposed to match him up. That was until... it wasn't.

"You can match me up after." I let go of my secret weapon, one I've been holding on to for months.

"What?"

"When Vic and I are... done. You can match me up. Find me my soulmate." Her eyes light up.

"Really?"

"Really." She looks at me, contemplating my plan. Then, big sister mode activates before my eyes, and her back straightens.

"I need you to write a list of the pros and cons of this guy. That way... when we need to—" I know what she's saying.

"If we need to."

"Fine. *If* we need to, you can reference it. Remember that this is... temporary. A hurdle to make you understand yourself better so you're confident when you meet the Luke of your life."

"The Luke of my life?" I ask with a smile. It's an easy way to move the conversation forward, and we both know it. She gets it, gets why I need to do this.

"I think that's what I might start calling perfect matches. Lukes." I roll my eyes, but I take the diversion for what it is. I find a paper and tugging the pen from my hair, and together, we write a pros and cons list of Victor Brandt and giggle the whole way through.

We never make it to the office that day.

TWENTY-ONE

-Gabi-

My phone beeps with a text on Saturday morning.

> You want to meet up tonight? I'm off at three.

We've texted back and forth all week, trying to make plans, but nothing has worked.

I sigh, staring at the two dark-haired boys sitting on my velvet couch, eating sugary cereal their mother would never allow into her home, much less their little bodies.

It's the only reason I keep it on hand.

> Can't, watching my nephews. Tomorrow?

He texts back nearly instantly. Hmm. That's technically a green flag. I add it to the "pros" side of the list.

> Deal. Time?

> I'm free all day,

He sends me back a time and a string of random emojis that take me a long time to interpret, but once I do, I blush like all hell.

It seems our next "meeting" will feature a new "lesson."

I can't dwell on that too long, though, because Gino is slurping the last of the sugary milk from his bowl and tossing it into my sink. Fun aunt time is starting.

"Okay, boys, what are we doing today?" I ask my nephews as they move from the table and stand in my very un-kid-friendly apartment, waiting for the fun now that their bellies are full. Gia is taking a much-needed day off from mom duties, which means cool AF Aunt Gabi (Okay, I've given myself this title. Sue me.) is in the house.

Well, they're in my house.

But you get what I mean.

Gia dropped them off with a backpack of kid crap and a wave before she rushed back out the door with barely a glance behind her.

And now I have a five- and seven-year-old staring at me expectantly.

I watch them often, usually spending the night at my sister's on Friday nights to babysit and do cool aunt stuff, but they rarely come here.

And every time they do, and I see that it's basically a kid death trap here, I'm reminded why.

Great.

"Park!" Gino, the five-year-old, yells.

"Beach!" Nicky, the seven-year-old, screams.

I can do this. Cool aunt mode activated.

"How about the beach with the park on the sand?" I counter, crossing my toes because it can turn into a WWE Smackdown in the blink of an eye when these two argue.

Don't show weakness, Gabi.

They look at each other, clearly weighing the pros and cons, some silent brother talk I've seen my own brothers do transmitting in the space between them.

"Deal," they say at the same time.

"But we want pizza," says Gino.

"And ice cream," says Nicky, clearly thinking they got one over on me.

I roll my eyes and smile as I grab my bag, thinking that I had planned to do just that the entire time.

Score one for cool Aunt Gabi.

Two hours later and bellies full of boardwalk pizza slices the size of Nicky and an ice cream cone the size of Gino's head, I'm sitting on a bench taking in the warm sun as they giggle and chase each other around.

This is what I remember as a kid, the reason I moved the half-hour south to the shore. Weekends where we'd all pile into two cars (two adults and seven kids meant we never had enough seats in one) and head down to the shore to run crazy on the sand, chasing seagulls and finding seashells. The boys would bring a football and toss it around and eventually, as they got older, they'd drift off and go find girls to flirt with.

"Aunt Gabi! Look at me!" Gino says, standing on one of the structures and reaching for the monkey bars. "Are you watching?" I tip my sunglasses down to my nose and give him a thumbs up.

"Go for it!" I shout, watching him reach and grab, reach and grab, reach and—

And then it happens.

The slip.

His fingers don't quite make it to the next bar, slipping, but not before his other hand already started to let go. The moment of panic on his face will be burned into my brain forever.

He hits the sand.

And then he's crying.

I run over, panicking. Kids get hurt all the time. I've seen the boys go up to their mother with a bleeding elbow or a split lip and she basically shoos them off to continue playing.

But this is different. It's confirmed when every adult head in the area swivels our way, panicking to see if it's their kid making that noise.

"OWW!" he screams in my ear as I scoop up his tiny but surprisingly heavy body. His father is tall, and my brothers are tall. Gia and I are tiny, thanks to our mother. But Nicky is nearly as tall as me, and Gino isn't that much smaller.

But like someone lifting a bus off of an injured family member, I get adrenaline-induced super strength, lifting my nephew as I tip my head to my other nephew in a "please follow me as we GTFO of here because this is bad" gesture.

I don't have to though—Nicky knows. His face is pale, his body tight as he runs over to us. I sit down on a bench with Gino in my lap.

"It hurts, Aunt Gabi! Sooo bad!" he says.

"Where, buddy?"

"My arm!" And then I see it, his forearm bulging and swollen already, and I *know*. He broke something. There's no way in hell that's normal. *Shit*.

Why the fuck am I supposed to do?

I am not trained for this kind of chaos.

I am the cool aunt.

I'm an assistant.

I don't even have the brain capacity to do much more than organize someone else's schedule.

I reach for my phone in my pocket as I stand with Gino, one arm hooked on my neck with an almost suffocating force, and he's wrapping his legs tight around my hips. I don't even really have to hold him. His arm is cradled between us and I'm cautious as I walk not to jostle him too much.

Phone in my hand, I open up a search but pause.

What am I doing?

What am I going to do? Google "Five-year-old broken arm. What do I do?"

Plus, Google is always a terrible idea for anything even closely related to medical stuff. My mind goes off with diagnoses. If I google something, I'll worry about gangrene or amputation for at least a month.

How long does it take for gangrene to set in? Longer than an hour, right?

Shit. Is Gino going to be one-armed forever because his dumb-ass aunt told him to try the monkey bars?

No, Gabi. Kids fall off things and break bones all the time.

Hell, each of my brothers has broken at least one limb.

I check the time. Gia is still in her massage. She's going to be stressing enough once she finds out. So I call Ant, her husband.

No answer.

Shit, shit, shit.

Mom? I should call Mom. I start to dial her as we walk the four blocks (Why didn't I splurge for a closer lot?) to my car but then I decide against it. The last thing I need is to give my mother another reason I'm flighty and a disaster.

So I call the only other person I can think of. It rings only once before there's an answer.

"Hey, kitten, give me a minute and I'll get somewhere quieter," Vic answers, his tone playful, beeping in the background.

"Vic, thank god." He must note the panic in my voice because he instantly switches gears.

"What, what is it?"

"It's Gino... Oh, fuck. Come on, Nicky, come here," I say, carrying a crying Gino to my car, Nicky scrambling to keep up.

"Gabi, what's going on?"

"The monkey bars!" I shout, voice full of panic. "The goddamn monkey bars!"

"What?"

"It hurts, Aunt Gabi!" Gino shouts, his tears soaking my tee shirt through to my skin. I bleep the lock and Nicky runs over, opening the door. His face is pale, and I remember I need to keep Gino calm—if I fuck this up, Nicky will be traumatized by this experience as much as I am most definitely going to be.

"Gabi, what is going on?" Vic says, and the noises around him go quiet like he's gone into a private room. I put Gino into his car seat and see the arm he's holding is already bruising and swollen. *Fuck, fuck, fuck*. His tears continue to stream, and I try to put on my calm voice that, to be honest, I rarely have to use. Because I'm a single woman with no kids of my own and work as an assistant for a matchmaker.

"Alright, guys. It's all going to be okay. I'm gonna talk to my doctor friend, and we'll get you all fixed up."

"Gabi, for fuck's sake, what is going on!" Vic says, the words loud in my ear as I shut the door on the boys.

I lean against the car, breathing deep and trying not to freak the fuck out.

"I think Gino just broke his arm," I say.

"What? Who's Gino?"

"He was on the monkey bars. I should have known he's too little for the monkey bars but he's always trying to catch up with Nicky and he's a stubborn little asshole, so if I tried to say no, he'd have wanted to do it more. And he was doing fine!"

"Who's Nicky?" I ignore him.

"But then his hand slipped. Shit, I knew once he fell. Isn't sand supposed to be soft? I guess it makes glass, but like, it's soft normally. But when it's wet, it's kind of hard and it's always wet under that top layer, so I guess it's hard. You know?"

"Gabi, stop talking about the texture of sand and tell me what is going on." He doesn't sound mad—he sounds calm. He's coaching me through this. "Are you okay? Who is Gino? Who's Nicky?" He's right. I need to focus. Focus, Gabi. Why is it always so hard to concentrate when you're told to focus? Because now my brain is jumping to that movie where the lightning hits the sand and makes glass and then he says, "So I can kiss you anytime I want," and years later makes an entire business and it's so damn— "Gabi!" *Shit.* Vic. Gino.

I walk around to the front of my car, stopping with my hand on the door handle.

"Gino is my nephew. I'm watching them. His brother is Nicky."

"Okay, kitten, good. Now, he fell off the monkey bars?" His tone, his calmness, his concise question... it grounds me. I can focus.

"Yes. At the park on 5th."

"On the beach?"

"Yeah."

"Come to the hospital."

"I need to—"

"Call your sister when you get here."

"I can't. I need to—"

"I'll meet you in the emergency room, Gabi. I'll be there. I'll help you. We've got this, okay, baby?" Crystal clear focus pours over me.

This is easy.

Obviously, I need to go to the hospital.

That's priority number one. Gia would want me to get him to a professional and then call her.

"You'll be there?" The thought of walking in with two kids, one injured, neither even my own, terrifies me.

"Walking down there now," he says, and I hear the ding of an elevator confirming that. "Now, Gabi. Get in your car, and drive them here."

"Can you..." I pause. I'm embarrassed. I should be able to do this alone.

"I'll stay on the phone, kitten. Get in the car, start it. Drive down here, yeah?" Relief washes through me, and before I can even wonder how he knew what I was going to say, I'm opening the door, tears and sniffles hitting my ears instantly as I start my car.

"I want Doctor Vic to sign it first!" Gino says, sitting happily in a hospital bed and eating his third chocolate pudding cup one-handed. Despite the dried, dirty tear tracks on his face, he's all smiles.

"Not me?" Gia asks, feigning hurt.

"Doctor Vic is way cooler." When he says that, Vic is suddenly standing in the doorway, Sharpie in hand.

"Did someone say they're looking for my signature?" he asks, a handsome smile on his lips. He winks at me as he walks toward my nephew. "Where?" Gino points to the top of his hand, clearly a spot of honor.

"Right here. I want to show everyone at school," he says, smiling up at Vic like Superman instead of a doctor.

Right now, he's also my own personal superhero.

True to his word, Vic sat on the phone with me through the entire three-minute drive, dealing with the drama via Bluetooth and even making the boys laugh with what I can only describe as dad jokes.

Vic was at my car door when we parked, knocking for me to unlock it before he ducked in and grabbed the sniffling Gino into his arms, carrying him into the ER. We bypassed the main desk and stopped in a room where Vic inspected his arm before pulling me outside, leaving Nicky making latex glove animals with a nurse while Gino laughed.

"It's probably a break, but we need an X-ray to be sure. You need to call Gia now." I'd nodded, not enough time to even ask how he'd remembered my sister's name.

I made the call to my not very surprised sister, who sent over my brother-in-law to meet us first since he could get here quicker than her.

The rest of the afternoon rushed by in a blur, from the X-ray, where Vic introduced the boys to the tech and made silly jokes the whole time, to getting Gino the actual cast, Vic instructing the orthopedic cast technician to let Gino pick out whatever color he wanted.

He disappeared for an hour or so to do actual work, probably some kind of important emergency, before he came back to check in just now.

"I guess we can't stay at Aunt Gabi's tonight," Nicky says, pouting.

"You were never staying there, Bud," Antonio, my brother-in-law, says. "You were gonna be home for dinner."

"We thought maybe we could have Aunt Gabi ask if we could have a sleepover." My eyes go wide. These two.

"I think your Aunt Gabi needs some alone time and a huge glass of wine after dealing with your drama, Nicolas." Mom-tone activated. "And where were you when your brother was on the monkey bars, sir?" Nicky looks away. "This is your fault, you know." He looks at his shoes.

"Wasn't it just last weekend when you were teasing him for not being able to make it across?" Ant asks, glaring at his oldest son. Shit, Nicky's in for it.

"Pop—"

"Don't you 'Pop' me, Nick. We'll talk about this when we get home." I make a nervous, cringy face with wide eyes at Gino, and he giggles. "And you—didn't I tell you you're too little for the monkey bars?"

"I almost made it!" he says.

"Until you broke your damn arm, Gino." He can't argue with that.

"I think we're just about good to leave, Gabs, are all of their things in your car?" I nod.

"Yeah, their boosters and backpack are in there. They had a big lunch, but that's all." I look at my watch. "And that was hours ago."

"No worries. We've got it from here. You comin' to dinner Sunday?" Gia asks, grabbing her bag and handing Ant her keys. "Can you go to Gabs's car and move the stuff over?" He nods, walking out before I answer my sister.

"Do I have a choice?"

"Not now that you broke her precious grandbaby's arm," Gia says with a smile.

"I didn't break his arm!"

"Yeah, thanks for breaking my arm, Aunt Gabi," Gino says, and I look at him, wide-eyed and mouth open.

"You little—"

"Yeah, Aunt Gabi. That wasn't very *responsible* of you," Nicky says. That's his new vocab word, and he sure loves to use it.

"You two are little shits."

"Aunt Gabi said a bad word!" Nicky shouts.

"You are little shits," Gia confirms. Then I feel a warm arm around my waist as a chuckle hits my ears.

"Is it always like this?" Vic asks. I lean into his body, his warmth. I know this isn't... that. But god, it feels nice, especially after this day,

"She's the baby of seven. Pretty much," Gia says, her eyes filled with questions and intrigue. Shit. "You coming on Sunday?" she asks again, but not to me this time. To Vic.

"Yeah, we'll be there." Gia's mouth spreads into a huge, taunting smile, and my entire body freezes as I look over my shoulder at him with wide eyes.

"Have you warned him?" my sister asks.

"No!"

"Warned me about what?"

"Nothing, you're not coming," I say to him through gritted teeth, eyes locked on my sister.

"Warned you about the family," Gia says, rolling right over me. "We're insane."

"My family's also insane. I like insane families."

It takes everything in me not to stomp on Vic's foot. But this is not what we are. We are not a "come over for Sunday dinner with the fam" kind of arrangement.

We are a "convince your mom you don't need a blind date and help me lose my v-card" kind of arrangement. And my family doesn't need to know about that.

I chose this man in part because no one knew him.

And now everyone is going to know him.

Shit.

"We'll see you on Sunday, Gia," Vic says before kissing my head and backing up. "Call me when he's discharged; I'll drive you home. You're still shaken up, and I'm just about off shift," he says to me, backing up. "Nice to meet you, Gia. Nicky, Gino. Behave. Be good for your mom."

"Bye, Doctor Vic!" they shout behind him as I stand there, face in shock.

"Uh, details. I need details," my sister says as soon as she assumes he is out of hearing distance, but I still hear Vic's laugh as he walks down the hall.

I'm so fucked.

TWENTY-TWO

-Vic-

Hours after the chaos at the hospital, Gabi and I are back at my place, having eaten takeout and watched some dumb show neither of us really paid attention to.

After Gabi's day of drama and stress, we're having a sleepover.

It took some convincing, but there was no way I was letting Gabi drive home after the boys left with Gia. Gabi's hands were still shaking slightly, her eyes still hollow and filled with shock and concern.

"You're coming home with me," I said, grabbing her hand and hefting my work bag over my shoulder.

"What?"

"You're coming home with me. I'm driving."

"Vic, there's no need," she started, trying to pull away.

"Don't care, it's happening."

"Vic, seriously." I could hear her argument brewing. For a tiny, sweet, virginal thing, she's fiery and stubborn. But meeting her sister, learning more about her family and seeing her interact with others, it became clear.

There's more to Gabrielle Mancini than meets the eye.

Instead of getting into it right there in the hospital hallway, I tugged her hand into an empty patient room, closing the door and pressing her back to it.

"You're going home with me or I'm going home with you. Either way, we're leaving this hospital together, and you're staying by my side all night so I can keep an eye on you."

"I'm fine—"

"You're pale and your hands are still shaking," I said, lifting them to press against the wall beside her head, fingers entwined with my own. Her breathing became labored, matching mine. "I'm driving you. Are we going to my place or yours?" I asked, breathing in her air. She blinked a few times, deciding the answer, probably trying to figure out if arguing would help.

It wouldn't.

I'd already decided, and regardless of how stubborn Gabi could be, I could be more stubborn.

"The boys destroyed my apartment," she'd said, eyes still wide.

"Does that mean we need to go there to make sure it's still standing, or you're spending the night at my place to avoid it?"

"I don't want you to see the mess," she said, and I just smiled, pressing my lips softly to hers. Perfectly right, just as it's been every time before that.

The truth is, the more I play with Gabi, the more I wonder if I'm playing at all.

That brought us here, hours later, lying in my bed after dinner.

Her little hand picks at threads in the comforter as she waits for me to settle next to her.

This is because when we were eating, she made her expectations clear.

"We're doing... stuff tonight, right?" I nearly choked on my bite.

"What?" I looked over, her face ablaze with a deep red blush.

"Tonight. We're... you know. I mean. We have a deal. Might as well..." Her voice trailed off. "Do... things." I smiled, the movement feeling lazy on my lips as I tried to ignore my body's near immediate reaction to the suggestion.

Since the other day on my couch, I haven't been able to think about anything but rubbing her until she came.

The sounds she made.

How she was fucking dripping.

How the thing that took her over the edge, the thing that ended her 28-year losing streak, was my voice. My cock throbbed just remembering it.

"What kind of things do you want to do?"

"Sex." The word came out quick and embarrassed.

"We're not having sex." Her face fell.

"But... You made me... you know."

"I made you what?" I wanted to hear the words.

"You made me... orgasm." She said it in a quiet voice that took everything in me not to laugh at.

"Yeah, and?"

"My rule was I wouldn't lose my virginity until a man made me come. I don't want a shitty first time." Her unbearably attractive confidence was back, the indignant voice in place, and all embarrassment gone as I leaned over and put my hand on her face.

"Honored, kitten. Honored, I'm the man to do that. But I'm not fucking you until we're good and ready. We're going slow." A part of me wondered why not. Why wouldn't I just fuck her and get this bargain over with?

The other part of me knows. I'm just not ready to admit it just yet.

"But I want... sex."

"Good. You'll get it. Just not tonight." Her nose had scrunched in frustration. "You'll get something tonight though. I promise I'll make you feel good, Gabi," I'd said, and her eyes flared with my words before returning to her food.

With that in mind, the look of interest still blazing there, I feel the need to quell this awkwardness. She's clearly uncomfortable.

"You know we don't have to do anything tonight, right?"

"Of course I do. But... I want to. I think it would be good... you know. To get my mind off it?" I do, having spent my entire life using outside distractions to ignore everything around me: family drama, family expectations, work stress. Gabi might be drowning in distractions, but I'm always reaching for them. The perfect fit.

Her next words knock me out of my confusing mental state. "But I want to do something... for you too. Tonight. If... that's okay." God, this woman. My cock twitches, awakening at the mere insinuation that he'll get something.

"You want to do something for me?"

"Well, I know you're not going to... you know... tonight."

"No, I will not be fucking you the night your nephew was released from the hospital with a broken arm." Her face shutters. "Shit, I didn't mean—"

"I know what you meant." Her hand traces the shapes from the stitching on my comforter as we sit beneath it, near fully dressed. I don't usually sleep in pajamas, but when she grabbed Vivi's sweats again and one of my tee shirts to pull on when she disappeared into the bathroom to change, I dug out an old pair my sister bought me a few years ago. It feels like a 90s sitcom, both of us in our sleep clothes as we dissect the day. We just need a laugh track.

We need to get this train back on the "distract Gabi for good" track.

I turn to my side to face her, my hand moving to her hip and turning her to face me until we're nearly nose to nose, breaths mingling between us.

"What do you want to do tonight?" She blushes, and fuck, it's so cute. Everything about this woman is a perfect mixture of sexy and sweet, the literal manifestation of a sex kitten. Her lip is pulled into her mouth, tiny white teeth denting the skin there.

"Gabi." Her eyes lift to mine. "What do you want to do tonight?" I wait, holding my breath to hear her response. I need her to guide this.

"I want to see you come," she says, and fuck if that, said in her breathy, nervous voice, isn't the sexiest thing I've ever heard. Jesus.

"I want to see you come too, Gabi. Been thinking about it since last week." Her little hand moves, going straight for my dick, and it takes everything in me not to laugh at her eagerness. Even more, not to just let her. I don't feel the urge to laugh because I'm making fun of her, but because I find so much fucking joy in her, in how excited she is for this. "No, no, no. That's not how we're playing this today."

"What?"

"We're doing this my way."

"Do I get to touch you this time?" I smile.

"I would be devastated if you didn't." A small smile graces her lips as she reaches for me again. "No, kitten. Slow."

"I don't want slow. I want distraction." Warmth runs through me from knowing and understanding. She scared herself today; guilt ate at her even though everything was totally fine. She needs this.

"I know, honey. You'll get it. But slow."

"Why?" The hand on her hip moves up, dipping under her shirt, my thumb swiping left and right, left and right as it creeps up her smooth skin, lifting her shirt as I go. I've been dreaming about what her body looks like under her girly skirts and funky tops for weeks, months, if I'm being honest.

"Well, for one, I fully plan on getting you naked today," I say, and the blush creeps up again. "And for two, I fully plan on eating your pussy today. If we go too fast, I won't be able to enjoy it." There's a sharp intake of breath that accompanies my words, but I swallow it as my lips brush hers, tongue dipping out to taste her lips. "Have you ever done that?" She looks at me, eyes wide, licking the lips I just tasted before she gently nods and then shakes her head no. I raise an eyebrow.

"Yes, once. But not for long. I didn't... like it."

Shit, no wonder she's never come.

No one's ever tried.

Between that and the barrier she built up around the idea, that's enough to ensure she had to wait 28 years before she fell apart in my arms.

"Another first," I whisper against her lips before I kiss her, less tentative this time, more all-consuming. My hand continues to creep up as she kisses me back, the tongue that was nervous last week, brave and seeking, tasting me.

The kissing ends when my thumb brushes the underside of her breast and she gasps.

No stopping now.

My hand goes up, up, thumb gently brushing the nipple and drawing another sharp gasp from her until its weight is in my hand. "God, perfect," I say, circling her erect nipple with my thumb. Her back arches, trying to get more. So I give it to her.

I dip my head down, circling the peaked flesh over the gray shirt and sucking hard, pulling it and the cotton into my mouth as she moans, the sound low and deep, reverberating through her chest and into my mouth before I nip once and release. Her hand is in my hair as I move back just enough to see my handiwork: a dark, wet circle on her shirt.

"That's a beautiful sight, Gabi," I say, smiling up at her, but her eyes are glazed over, her mouth open, lip pouting without intention. Then, like seems to be the norm with the woman, she shocks me when she pushes my head forward, moving me for a repeat movement on the other side.

God, this woman.

It's beautiful witnessing her slowly gaining confidence, the beginning of losing that embarrassment and fear of rejection or humiliation when we're together like this. I do as she asks, pulling fabric and skin into my mouth, pulling a deep moan from deep in her chest. The sound has me moaning, too, against her skin, and the vibrations move through her, her hand moving to keep my head in place.

That's fine.

I'd happily stay here for as long as she'll have me.

Well, maybe there's one change I'd make. My hand moves back down towards her hips but then back up. This time though, I'm determined to get this shirt off. Up, up, up, until my hands meet where my mouth is, still separated by fabric. My mouth moves back to the first nipple, sucking it and the fabric back into my mouth as my hand holds her tit, full, the perfect size. My thumb swipes the nipple that I abandoned, the skin wet and already sensitive after just moments in my mouth.

Her hips buck up, and a low moan drags from her.

"Oh, shit, Vic!" I laugh against her then continue my assault with my fingers, gently swiping, barely even there.

But she's sensitive. And I love it.

When my fingers meet, though, I move my mouth to watch her face, watch her action. I pinch and pull the tender flesh, watching as her eyes that were drooped with lust snap open, her mouth dropping open and her back arching, trying to get her breast further into my hand.

Yeah, she likes this.

With my mouth moved, I tug the shirt over her head, my hands both going back to hold her breasts now as I sit up, resting on my heels.

I take in what I've revealed.

Miles of tan flesh.

Curves for days.

At some point without me realizing, she kicked off the sweats, leaving her in just a tiny pair of underwear.

No bra, and pink, hard nipples.

A mess of dark curls on the pillows.

Fuck, this woman is what wet dreams are made of.

I lean forward with no warning and take her nipple into my mouth, pinching tight with the other hand, and she screams my name.

The sound is forever cataloged instantly, a life-changing moment that I'll use when I need to jack myself off until I'm 103. It's that amazing.

Her hands go into my hair, losing themselves there and tugging hard then pushing my face in further. I groan around her nipple.

"Jesus, Vic, this is too good."

My head pops up. "Oh, baby, I haven't even gotten started. Wait until you see what else my mouth can do.

The words have the desired effect. Her eyes roll. Her lips tilt. I love this side of her most—this one that doesn't melt at my lines. The one that wants me but isn't afraid to knock me down a notch.

"Well, Dr. Brandt, maybe you should show me. Convince me." The words are a challenge, one I'm more than willing to take up.

"Oh, it's on, Ms. Mancini," I say and she smiles, but that smile falters as I start to move, hooking my thumbs in the waistband of her underwear.

I kiss a path between her breasts, down her stomach, stopping at her navel where I dip my tongue in, her belly contracting with her intake of breath, then stopping at the panties. I kiss the soft skin right above them, eyes locked to hers, and I tug the underwear down her legs.

She's panting, a foot kicking as lace hits her toes.

Then the underwear is gone. I move down the last new inches.

And then I'm there.

Face to face with what I've been daydreaming about all week.

If I'm being honest, despite every oath I've ever taken, every ounce of propriety and professionalism, some sick part of me has been dreaming about this since she first came into my ER, a scrambled mess.

I run my nose along her center.

Soaked.

"Oh, god, Vic," she moans, the words low.

"So pretty, Gabi." Not wasting a moment of time, I flatten my tongue, running it over her, tasting.

Perfection.

I moan against her, and the sound reverberates up her, pulling a deep moan from her in exchange.

I laugh against her.

"Vic!" How is it that such a deeply sexual experience is also... fun? I've never felt this way with another woman, equal parts turned on and like I want to laugh and enjoy being with her. My head comes up to lock eyes with Gabi. Her head is on the bed, staring at the ceiling, but her eyes move to me.

"What the—"

"You need to prop yourself." She looks confused. I start to move, but her hand goes to my hair, keeping me in place.

Laughter. It's bubbling in my chest, in my veins. This woman.

"Where are you going?" She sounds panicked. Panicked with sexual desire she's not sure will be sated.

"Don't worry, baby. I'm going to take care of you. But I need you focused. You stare at the ceiling, you can drift." I move to help her put pillows behind her back to prop her just enough so that when I'm between her legs eating that sweet pussy, her eyes have nowhere to look but at me. A realization crosses her face and then a softness comes there. I know what it is.

I've been considering the logistics of this since last week when I made her come with my hands. The reason Gabi hasn't been able to come is that she drifts. Her mind leaves what's happening and moves to a different subject, taking her from the edge so she can never cross it.

Last time, my voice helped.

Obviously, I can't talk to her this time—my mouth will be otherwise occupied.

So instead, we're going to try visual concentration, among other things.

"You're going to watch me, Gabi." My hand goes down between her legs to touch her as my face gets close to hers. Her breaths pant on my lips, wet with her. Her eyes drift shut with pleasure. "You're going to watch me while I eat your pussy and make you come on my face."

"Oh," she says.

"Yeah, oh." God, and there it is again. Even though my cock is harder than I can ever remember it being in my life, I'm laughing. Not at her. But because of this gorgeous woman in front of me.

I move down her body once more, licking her nipples as I pass, my tongue circling her belly button until I'm back at her wet center.

"Keep your eyes on me, Gabi. No matter what happens, you look at me. You feel what I'm doing to you. You start to drift, you tell me. We'll work on it together." She nods. I use a thumb on either side of her to reveal her pretty pink pussy. "Gorgeous." The word is for me, but she clenches in response.

My cock does too, a silent conversation between her pussy and my dick. My dick that cannot wait to be cordially invited inside.

God, that sounded weird.

Maybe she's rubbing off on me.

Focus, Brandt.

I dive in.

First with my tongue, entering her, and she squeals a sound of satisfaction. I smile against her pussy.

"Holy shit, Vic!"

Yeah, kitten. You keep my name right there on your tongue and I'll keep you on mine. Her hips buck, moving to get me where she wants me, but we're on my time now. I move a hand to her hip, pressing down to keep her in place.

She grunts out a noise that sounds like a pout, and when I move my eyes up, face still in her cunt, I see she is, in fact, looking down at me with a pout. I laugh against her and her eyes go hazy.

That's it, baby. Trust the process.

I move my point of focus from her entrance to her clit, circling it slowly with my tongue.

She yells.

Yup, seems that anyone who has ever done this in the past had no fucking clue what they were doing.

"Oh, god, Vic. This is so hot," she says under her breath, and when I look up at her, her eyes are locked to mine, fire burning there.

She likes watching.

Fuck yeah.

As I circle, varying directions and pressure, teasing her before giving her what she wants, my mind drifts to the many ways that "watching" can be added to our lesson plan.

I know I would fucking I love to watch anything she does.

I give in then, circling my mouth on her clit and sucking, lightly, not too much to start.

Her hand moves from her side and then hovers over me. *Hesitating.* Hesitating as I suck her clit, her hips moving to pull me closer.

The hand falls to her inner thigh, pulling herself more open.

She's perfection.

How has no man ever put the effort in until now?

How did I get this fucking lucky?

Who knows?

But as I reach up for her wrist, I decide I won't look too closely at my luck. Because no matter what happens in the next month, Gabrielle Mancini is mine.

I move the hand to my head where she was hesitating, and instantly her fingers tangle into my hair then push me down, closer to her.

Fuck yes.

I groan my appreciation as I move my hand to her entrance, a single finger circling her. I didn't do this last time, staying out and just focusing on her clit, but when she begged for it, I was dying to know what she feels like there.

"Oh, god. Vic. Yes! Please. I need more."

I go in.

She instantly clamps on my finger, muscles fluttering, and the mere thought of this finger being my cock inside of her has me rubbing my hard-on into the bed like some kind of preteen boy.

"Yes, yes, yes," she's chanting, panting with each word, moving her hips in circles as her fingernails dig into my scalp and push me further into her pussy.

Never has eating a woman out been so unbearably exquisite.

I need her to come on my face.

The finger inside her crooks, grazing her swollen G-spot softly, and she bucks her hips up. "Holy shit!" I smile against her as she grinds my face onto her. She's close; I can tell. So fucking close she just needs...

And then the hand loosens its grip.

Not a ton, just a tiny fraction. Enough for me to notice, though.

My eyes look up at her.

Hers aren't on me any longer.

They're looking to the door but not seeing it.

I lost her.

Shit.

I move my mouth.

"What? No!" she says, and there's real panic there, like she genuinely doesn't want me to stop. Comforting, at least. I'm not offended either way. No, this is just her mind getting in the way. With my mouth otherwise... occupied, there's nothing else to keep her here with me, keep her focused.

"All good, baby," I say, crawling up her body.

"Vic, really, what are you—" I push a strand of hair back and look her in the eyes.

"What was it?"

"What?"

"What made you lose focus?"

"I didn't—"

"I already know your body better than you. I'm learning your mind. You lost focus." There's hesitation. And then a blush across those tan cheeks.

"It's not you, I swear. I—"

"I know it's not. But to help you get past this, we need to work on what's getting in the way. I don't blame you. I don't even care, not really. Just means I get more time playing with you." I give her a wink for good measure, and she looks at me, taking me in and dissecting my gaze.

"You mean that, don't you?"

"Of course, kitten." It kills me to know men before me saw her mind as a shortcoming instead of a boon. Instead of beauty. It also kills me that there were men before me, but that's a mental topic to dissect another time.

Not today.

Maybe never, if I can avoid it.

"The sound," she says in a whisper.

"What?"

"The sound. That's what got me. Distracted me."

"The sound?"

"You know... of you..." She tilts her head down. "Down there."

It takes everything in me not to smile at her.

God, she's so fucking sweet. One minute she's a damn sex fiend, grinding on my face; the next, she can't even say I was eating her pussy.

"Got it." I think about this. "I've got an idea." I get out of bed.

"Vic, what—"

"Two seconds," I say then run out of my room, grabbing what I need before running back, adjusting my still very hard cock. Her eyes move right to it and fuck, she licks her damn lips.

"Quit it, kitten." Confusion washes over her face because she doesn't even know it. She doesn't even know the power she holds over me. I tap a few times on the tablet before loud waterfall sounds come out of my iPad, and I nearly jump back into bed.

"When you start to lose it, when you drift, focus on that."

"What?"

"Focus on the white noise. And then focus back on me." My lips start their descent for a third time, kissing between her breasts, over her soft belly, back to my new favorite place, still glistening with a mix of her and my spit. Fucking beautiful.

"Vic, I don't think—" I slip a finger in but keep my head up, keep looking at her. "Oh god. Yeah. Like that." Her eyes glaze over.

"You like that, kitten? You like me fingering your pretty pussy?" She nods with hooded eyes, the movement slow and disconnected from reality. "You want another finger inside?" Those eyes widen again, and her mouth falls open as she moans her confirmation. Another nod. Shit, this woman might be the end of me.

I do as promised, sliding another finger inside. She's so fucking tight, though her wetness lets me slide in easily. "Oh shit, Vic!"

My name on her lips is my new favorite song. I wish I could record it, make it my ringtone, my alarm clock, my doorbell.

I drop back down and return to what I was doing.

Her hand goes back to my head and pushes hard. She's already close. Her hips are bucking now, consistently riding my face, riding my fingers, and shit, I want to fuck her. I want to be inside of her. My eyes drift up to meet hers but they're closed, her head tipped back, and I think... I think... I move my fingers deeper, crooking them to press as I suck hard... and her back arches, a scream tearing from her as wetness gushes from her onto my face, onto my fingers.

She came from my mouth.

Another win.

I continue to pump in her, to gently lick through the aftershocks until her breathing starts to even out.

"Holy shit."

Now I let myself laugh as I move up again so I'm lying next to her.

"Good?"

"How do you keep doing that?" She has no idea what she's doing for my ego at this moment,

"Learning your body, learning your cues. Taking my time. Add in some killer chemistry and a perfect student, and we're combustible, baby." Her eyes warm as she hitches a leg over my hip, her center brushing my very hard cock still encased in underwear and sweatpants.

"Now it's my turn."

"Gabi, you don't have to."

"Oh, trust me, I know." I laugh. She's also funny as hell. "If I didn't want to, I wouldn't, Vic. Do I seem the type of woman to do what I don't want to do?" She doesn't. "I'm not. And I really, really want to make you come tonight, Vic. I've been..." Her eyes move, looking away.

"Been what?" I ask before I can even hold the words back, needing her to finish that sentence before she gets sidetracked.

"Thinking about it." The words are low and embarrassed. *Oh no, baby. Nothing to be embarrassed about.* I've never heard anything hotter come from a woman's mouth.

"What have you been thinking about, Gabrielle?" My voice has gone gruff, ragged with the thought of Gabi daydreaming about getting me off in any way, shape, or form. Jesus, I'm so fucked.

"I..."

"Don't be embarrassed. Tell me." As I say this, I move my hands to my hips, pushing my boxers and sweats down. If she wants this lesson, I'm more than happy to give it.

"This."

"What's this, baby?" I take her hand and move it to where I'm achingly hard. She's tentative when she wraps her hand around me.

"Holy fuck," she whispers under her breath, and my dick twitches in response as if she were speaking directly to it. Which, I guess she was.

"Gabi," I say, warning in my tone. I want this. I want her to tell me what she wants to do. I want to keep her on task. Something tells me she needs it.

Something tells me that the only reason other men have failed when it comes to Gabi is that she enamors everyone she meets—there's no way a man can get into a bed with Gabi, see all the beauty that she is, hear her words, feel her hands, and not lose his mind.

But in order to handle this woman, you need to stay on earth, and you need to work to keep her here with you.

"This. I want to touch you." I move my hand on top of hers and slowly start moving both of our hands up and down. Holy shit, that's amazing.

"Yeah? How?" I can barely speak, and this just started.

"Like this."

"Words, Gabrielle. Use them. Tell me what you want to do." She hesitates. I move my face to her neck, burying it there and licking her rapid pulse. "You like my words, baby. Like when I talk to you. Ever thought I might like the same?" That pulse increases along with her breath.

I wonder if maybe she'll tense up, panic, get into her head. This isn't just outside of her comfort zone. This is in another universe.

But as always, she takes me by surprise.

"I want to jack you off. Make you come with my hands." I groan, deep and loud, and when I do… her hand grips a little tighter. An impulse. Fuck.

"Yeah, kitten, like that," I say, moving my hand from where it was, helping her to move some of her hair behind her shoulder. I want to see her. I need to see her. Wide eyes, open mouth. Even though she just came, she's turned on.

Our next task should be coming at the same time.

Sixty-nine.

My dick twitches.

Her pace increases, thumb moving to graze over the head. For a split second, I wonder where she learned the move from, who taught her that. Which man in her life showed her he liked that and she's replicating it on me?

But no. Somehow, I know that every man before me taught her nothing. Guided not one bit. They wouldn't need to; the promise of her is enough to make any man come like a teenager. Gabi is working on some kind of sex goddess instinct.

"Why do you call me that?" she asks, a whisper pulling me from my mental bubble.

"What?"

"Kitten. Why do you call me that?"

"You are one."

"What?" Her hand stops. She's losing it, losing focus.

My hand goes back to hers, helping her but finishing her thought, so it doesn't get stuck there, distracting her further.

"You're a kitten. Sweet, Cuddly. I want to protect you. But you pounce, and you have claws. Like to play." I take a deep intake of air as she tightens, brushes her thumb over the head which has beaded with pre-cum. Her breath hitches in turn. "You're a kitten, kitten."

"Oh." That's all she says.

But it's fine.

I'm close.

So fucking close.

And I need to ask one last question.

"In your daydreams, where do I come?"

"What?" Another clench on my dick, the hand moving faster now. She knows.

"Where do I come, kitten? You've got me too fucking close; I'm going to come. Where do you want me to come?"

"But it's only been a minute or two." I almost laugh. If my balls weren't drawing up, I would laugh. But right now, I'm in the odd position of trying not to freak her out by coming all over her.

"Been thinking about this for months, Gabi. No one but you since you came into my ER. Now, where should I come—a towel?" She's quiet for a moment, and I'm about to move, grab something, but then four words leave her lips.

"Come on me, Vic." My breathing stops. "I want you to come on me." No need to ask twice, I explode, months of pent-up sexual frustration I didn't realize I had inside of me landing on her stomach, painting her tan skin with white streaks as I let out a deep, animalistic groan of her name.

My orgasm trails out, and I work to catch my breath, eyes closed, but her next words have my eyes snapping open and staring at her.

"Holy shit, that was the hottest thing I've ever seen. Hotter than any of my daydreams, for sure." Her eyes are wide, her full lips pouted, and fuck, she's cute.

All I can do is lean forward and kiss her.

TWENTY-THREE

-Vic-

The incessant drive to see Gabi is slowly leaking into my bones. It's been only two days since I had her last and the texts back and forth aren't cutting it. I need to have her.

I told myself I'd stay away. Give her room to breathe and let her come to me. The way it's gone with every woman I've ever dated in the past ten years. I date them. I let them call the shots. Let them decide when we'll meet. I let them reach out, let them be the eager one.

After our last lesson, our sleepover, our conversation the following day, I need this space. I need this breathing room. I need this reminder that I'm the one in control. But all I want to do is call her, go to her apartment, lock us in for days until I get her out of my system.

Though, I'm assuming that's the issue. It's the only outlying metric that would explain why I feel this pull to her. We haven't had sex yet. We've done things—great things. Amazing things, even. But that last step is typically what keeps me from becoming a simp, from reaching out, from making the first move.

While I'm not against being the one to reach out, I just haven't ever felt the need to give a woman that kind of hope, give her the wrong idea. For Gabi, it's the opposite: I don't want to scare her off.

She's Gabi—independent and high-strung and stubborn and in her head. Something tells me if I push too hard, it will scare her into deciding this is too much. Too much work, too much effort, too much complication, too much commitment for something that's just supposed to be a learning experience.

So for two days, I've been telling myself to wait, to be patient. She'll make that move. I need to play it cool. Except, it's not working. Tonight, I'm off for the night and she's going to be sleeping in bed next to me—the only question is her bed or mine.

I've made my decision.

It's time for our next lesson. Should I have planned it better considering it's nearly five already? Yeah. But in my defense, I haven't done the girlfriend thing in some time. I was also trying my best to avoid her. Avoid this... ache.

Is Gabi my girlfriend?

I block that question from my mind. Instead, I send her a booty call text.

That phrase alone churns sour in my stomach.

> I'm off tonight. You free? I think it's time for another lesson.

The reply comes quickly as I'm packing up my bag to leave the hospital for the night. I love that about her—she doesn't play games the way other women do. She doesn't wait for some predetermined amount of time to answer to avoid sounding too excited to talk to me.

> I'm going on a date, sorry. Tomorrow?

Well, maybe she's not excited.

Also, what the fuck.

She's doing what?

We're together now. She's mine. I mentally comb through our conversations, our agreement to this crazy deal I made with her to see if at any point I outright told her we would be exclusive during this crazy as fuck arrangement.

But I can't find one.

Shit.

Then again, never would I have thought that sweet, not innocent (the outburst at the bar taught me not to use that word) but inexperienced, kind, and caring Gabi would go off on a date with another man while seeing me.

The fury running through me takes me off guard too.

Not fury at Gabi. Not really.

Fury at whatever man thought to even look at her.

Because she is mine. For however long this thing lasts, Gabrielle Mancini is mine.

Walking out of the hospital, I dig in my pocket to bleep the locks of my car as I hit call on my cell.

It rings and rings.

"Hey, you've reached Gabi. I can't come to the phone right now. Leave a message and I'll get back to you as soon as possible. Thank you!" her happy chirp says before an automated voice gives me instructions for leaving a message. I don't.

> Gabi, text me. Now.

I drive to my apartment in a frustrated rage, not seeing stoplights or little old ladies and wondering if an officer will come to my door at some point. That would be fun to explain.

Well, you see, officer, I didn't see that stop sign or your lights because all I could think about was my girlfriend, who isn't really my girlfriend, but she sure as fuck feels like my girlfriend going on a date with another man.

Something tells me that wouldn't keep me out of handcuffs.

Or maybe even a padded room.

When I walk into the apartment, stark white with a big black TV screen right across the room, I kick the door shut and throw my bag onto the expensive leather couch that perfectly fit two bodies side by side before flopping into it.

It's too big for one body.

Gabi was right.

This apartment is boring as fuck.

Maybe I should let Vivian decorate after all.

Or maybe Gabi.

I could see her mixing her crazy prints and whimsical style around here, bringing some life to this apartment.

Something about having her explosion of color and life and joy has me realizing how... dead my life has been. Free of any form of excitement or interest.

Thinking of Gabi reminds me to sit up and recheck my phone.

Nothing.

Fuck that.

I call again, throwing all concepts of calm and relaxed out the window.

I get her voice mail again. This time I leave a message.

"Gabi, answer your phone." I think that says everything I need to say. I pace to the kitchen as my phone beeps in my hand with a message.

Finally.

> What's up? I'm on a date.

Is this woman for real? There's no way in hell she's this obtuse that she doesn't understand the urgency of this. Doesn't understand how much she's tearing me apart. Then the question hits me: is she... Is she playing games?

There's no way. If there's a person on earth who I could trust not to be playing games, it would be Gabi. Because… she's Gabi. She doesn't need to play games. She tells it like it is every time, whether she means to or not, her big beautiful brain refusing to filter anything out.

It's my favorite part about her.

> Are you serious right now?

> I can't keep texting you. It's incredibly rude.

I call again. It rings once before it goes straight to voicemail.

> Did you just fuck you button me?

> I'll talk to you later, Vic. I can't be doing this right now. It's so unprofessional.

Unprofessional? What the fuck does that mean?
I call again.
This time it doesn't even ring before it goes to voicemail.
Either she blocked me or her phone is off.
I don't think she had enough time to block me.
And if I find out she's on a date with some stranger and turned off her phone, I'm going to go ballistic. Because while I might not love the idea of her going on a date, I hate even more the idea of her being so fucking unsafe.

I should call her friend Cassie.
I don't have Cassie's number.
I could call Ben—he's friends with her fiancé. I could get the fiancé's number and then get Cassie's number.

Shit. That's excessive, though, right? I take a deep breath, breathing in common sense and exhaling my irrational thoughts.

Gabi is smart. She's smart and wouldn't do something so dumb as to endanger herself.

I walk to my kitchen. I need a distraction. Food. I could make food. Let's do that. I pull out eggs and milk, vegetables, and cheese for an omelet, but my blood is burning in my veins. Each movement of my body fuels my frustration and anger at Gabi. *I'm on a date.*

She's on a date.

With a man who is not me.

Potentially with a phone that's off.

What is she thinking? My mind drifts to the women who come into my ER after being assaulted on a date they thought would be normal. That could be Gabi. She's trusting. She's sweet. She's too kind for her own damn good.

As I eat, my eyes drift to my phone incessantly, fumbling every few minutes to make sure the ringer is on loud or double-checking if I missed any messages.

When my dinner is eaten and I still haven't heard from her, I realize I can't do this all night. I'm going to drive myself insane.

I know where she lives.

And without a second thought as to how much of a psycho this makes me or how much this crosses the line of "just teaching her things," I get into my car.

If my mind was on autopilot on the way to my apartment, it's on another planet driving to Gabi's. Once there, I'm shocked how easy it is to get the sweet receptionist at the lobby to let me in with just the knowledge of what Gabi's apartment number is. A smile and a few compliments were all it took before I was taking the stairs to the fourth floor and standing in front of a door with a mat that says, "I'm so glad you came. That's what she said." In any other circumstance, I'd smile and shake my head because it's so Gabi (*and so ironic, all things considered*) but I can't think of anything but Gabi on a date with another man.

So instead, I stand, waiting for her.

We have a lot to talk about.

———

Nearly two hours later, it happens. I'm leaning against her door, still waiting like an absolutely crazy person, shifting my phone in my hand over and over absentmindedly when I see her walk around the corner of the hallway.

Well, her hair.

Then her.

She's in a tight white tank top and jeans that hug her curves and she almost looks... average.

It rubs me wrong.

Not only is she going on a date with some man, but she feels the need to dress like every other woman on the street while meeting with him?

She is not that. She is not some average, everyday woman. She's so much more.

A man who makes her feel like she needs to hide that shine? My fingers curve into my palm in agitation.

My eyes keep moving, though, past the look of surprise to the stutter-step she does when she finally sees me.

She's in clunky wedge heels that give her at least four inches, with black and yellow stripes and little bumblebees on the clasps. When I look back up, eyes hungrily devouring her body in her tight outfit, the front curls that always fall into her face are held back with a little clip that looks like a bee.

Not full-blown Gabi, but it's better than some catalog version.

She stops walking about five feet from me and stands there. I straighten, standing in front of her door with my arms crossed over my chest.

"What are you doing here?"

"Why is your phone off?" Her nose scrunches up in confusion. Cute. She's cute. I want to stay irritated with her, but she's too fucking adorable.

"What?"

"Your phone. I've been trying to call you. It goes right to voicemail." Her eyes move to the side. "Or did you block me?"

"I should have." Frustration and indignation cross her face, and her hands go to her hips.

"Excuse me?"

"I should have blocked you. I can't believe you did that! Calling me and texting me like that."

"So your phone was off?"

"What?"

"Your phone. You turned it off?"

"Yes, Vic. You wouldn't stop calling and texting me. You were out of line."

"Gabi, you turned your phone off while you were on a date with another man. A stranger, I would assume. You were alone with some man, and you turned your phone off." She opens her mouth to argue, but I keep going. "Do you know what could have happened to you? Out alone with a stranger, a man. No way to call for help because your fucking phone was off." I should move to her or tell her to move to me, but I don't. I do watch her face go softer, just a touch. Recognition or understanding crosses her face.

"Honey, I—"

"I do. I work in an ER, Gab. I've seen shit I don't want to remember. Shit that chills me to the bone. Shit that, when I get off shift, I have to call my sister to make sure she's okay."

"Vic—"

"You had no way to reach out if something went bad. If—"

"Cassie was there," she says, moving a few feet closer to me. Now she's close enough that if I reach out, I could hook my arm on her waist and pull her to me. I don't though, lost in her words, in what she just said. Cassie was there.

"Cassie was on your date?"

"It was a work date. Training." A work date.

Her dates.

"You were with Cassie." She nods and steps once more until we're nearly nose to nose. Clarity breaks through. She wasn't with another man on a date—not really. She was at an interview with a man and her boss. Her phone might have been off, but she wasn't alone. She wasn't in danger. I move, my arm finally wrapping around her and moving both of us until her back is to her front door.

"Vic, what—"

"I've been going fucking crazy."

"What?"

"Thinking of you. Out with another man. On a date with another man."

"Vic, I—"

"I realized we never had any conversation about exclusivity." That shuts her up. "So right here, right now, I want to make this crystal fucking clear, Gabrielle. You're mine. That's it. Mine. You don't go out with other men; you don't dress up for other men. You. Are. Mine. Do you hear me?" I expect an argument, because this is Gabi, after all. Instead, I get a challenge. I realize now her breathing is heavy, soft pants hitting my face, those high shoes bringing her closer to my height. But despite that, there it is: that never back down, stubborn challenge.

"Are you mine?" She doesn't get it. She doesn't know.

Gabi has me, beyond a shadow of a doubt. Somehow, in the chaos of this arrangement, she has snared me so deep, I can't see light unless she's around. The earth spins, the universe continues to move, but my world stops until she's back in my arms.

The thought scares me.

But I push it aside when I answer—that fear can't be near me when I do.

"Fuck yeah, I am," I proclaim, and then her lips are on mine, kissing me, making the first move. So Gabi, demanding everything from me and then taking more.

We kiss and I press her into the door, lining her body up with mine, reveling in the fact that she fits. She fits me. Perfect for me in every way.

"We need to get inside," I say, panting against her lips as I grind my hard cock into her.

"Yeah," she says but doesn't make a move, just stays there, her eyes hooded, and her breasts are brushing my chest with each inhale.

"Your apartment, kitten. You've got the keys," I say with a smile, brushing a curl back.

"Oh. Yeah," she says, and then her hands move to the little purse at her side—a daisy purse. A theme. She digs in there and then hands me a bright yellow key with a smiley face painted on it. I'm not even surprised at this point. I smile then take it, unlocking the door and pushing it open as she almost falls through.

But I catch her.

I will always catch Gabi.

A hand goes to her waist, pulling her to me as my other hand tosses the keys to the floor with a loud clang before moving down her arms, grabbing her wrist. I hold it to the wall beside the door, my hips keeping her in place as I move her other hand right next to it. Both hands are over her head, her body pinned in place by mine, and she's at my mercy.

It's a beautiful sight.

And it's a fair trade-off since it feels like I've been at her mercy since the day I met this woman.

What is going on?

TWENTY-FOUR

-Vic-

I BRUSH THE THOUGHT AWAY, pressing my lips to hers again. I kiss her the way I thought about the entire time I was waiting outside of her apartment for her, in a way that would knock thoughts of any other man from her mind indefinitely. A kiss to remind her whom she belongs to.

Me.

She belongs to me.

But she plays along with my kiss, going with it, tasting, nipping, panting with the same inexplicable need I feel deep in my bones. Her hips move to grind against me, needing more, needing skin on skin, needing release.

I pause, putting my forehead to hers.

"I want you to suck my cock, Gabi." I'm breathing in her air, and her hands are still pinned above her head. "That's your next lesson."

Unless she says no...

Her eyes move away from mine. "I don't... I've tried it." She's panting, pinned against the entryway because we still haven't gotten far despite how long it seems we've been here—both an eternity and a moment in time.

"You don't like it." She shakes her head. "Why not?" It's not that I need her to suck me off. Have I been daydreaming about having her full lips wrapped around me for fucking weeks now? Yes. Undoubtedly. Am I dying to eat her while she sucks me off? Absofuckinglutely. But there is more than enough ground to cover with Gabi. We don't need this. I won't push it.

But there are many things I'm sure she thought she didn't like. Things she thought she couldn't do, even. Orgasming is one. Having a man eat her sweet pussy is another.

She shrugs and tries to look away, but I put a hand on her cheek, turning her face until she looks at me. "Why, Gabi?"

"I... It's strange. It's like... right there?" she says it like a question for me rather than an answer.

"My cock?" Her cheeks burn.

"Not yours. But generally—" My brain explodes.

"Tonight is not the night to talk about another man's cock."

"I wasn't—"

"No day, really. There is not a single day I want to hear my girl talk about another man's cock." "My girl" sounds really good. "But tonight I spent hours outside your apartment like a fucking stalker, thinking you were on a date with another man." There's a short pause before she nods, quick and concise, like we reached a business agreement, her forehead rubbing against mine with the movement.

"Got it. No cock talk."

"You can talk about my cock all you want," I say, grinding said anatomy into her. It's crazy that I'm this hard and we're having an entire, barely related conversation. It's like it's a Saturday morning and she spent the night, rather than she's pinned to a wall in front of me and I'm hard as fuck, not having had her in days. "Why don't you like giving blow jobs?" She rolls her eyes and sighs, the classic Gabi one that makes me smile.

"It's weird. It's... one-sided. I don't mean that in a rude way, like I always need reciprocation. It's just the position, the way it is, it's..." Another sigh. "Plus, it's kind of boring." *Ding ding ding.*

"Your mind wanders." I get it. Her mind wanders to unrelated subjects as it likes to do, but it happens while there's a cock in her mouth. I can see how that would be... unpleasant. She nods.

"I drift off and then come back and I'm choking on a penis. Not... sexy." God, how am I laughing right now?

"There are ways around that, kitten," I say once the mental image subsides. My voice drops and her eyes go wide.

"There are?"

"Oh yeah. Have you ever touched yourself while you sucked a man off?" Her head shakes, the movement slow. I could have guessed that. "Has a man ever eaten you while you sucked him off?" Her bottom lip drops, mouth going slack, eyes going hooded. She shakes her head again, in the same dazed way.

"We can keep you in the moment, kitten. We can make it enjoyable for you." I'm not going to push one way or another, but—

"I want that."

Perfection.

She's perfection.

I smile at her before stepping back. Her knees are weak, and my arm goes around her waist, holding her in place while she regains her balance. I rearrange myself and her eyes go to my hardness before she licks her lips. It's unintentional, not a planned move, but it says everything I need to know.

She wants this.

"Come."

"I'd love to," she says with a smile, and I can't help but return it.

Sex shouldn't be this fun and light, should it? I've never laughed so much as I do with Gabi, ever, much less when my cock is hard and I'm dying to get her naked.

"Show me to your room. Start undressing as you do—I've been outside for hours thinking about that body." She smiles again, no longer shy, but teasing.

"Only if you do too." With that, I cross my arms behind my head, tugging off my shirt and tossing it to the ground. Kicking off my shoes and, with my hands on the fly of my jeans, I look at her, anticipating her move. She just smiles again, spinning away from me and sauntering off towards her room. I almost call after her, but then she tosses the silly flower bag to the ground as she keeps walking, crossing her hands over her front and slowly creeping her tank up.

I stand there, frozen, hands on the zipper of my pants as an inch of tan flesh is revealed.

But then she stops, hair moving as she turns her head to face me.

"You coming?" The smile is there, the tease. This fucking woman. I shove my pants down before following her as she tosses the white tank to the ground and disappears through a doorway.

I'm in my boxer briefs and nothing else when I reach her room. It's exactly what I'd expect—a chandelier covered with colorful scarves that throw off sultry light, fake vines wrapped around curtain rods, and a frilly pink bedspread. My feet sink into a plush shag rug that takes up almost the entire room and when I look at it, I notice it's white with little sprinkle shapes on it. Gabi. So Gabi.

But I don't have time to take too much of it in because when I reach her room, she's sitting on the bed, no top, bent over as she undoes those yellow and black shoes. It takes my breath away, all that bare skin, bent over on her girly bed in this crazy room. I push down my boxers, the last piece of clothing, before I lean against the door frame and watch. My hand goes to my cock, already hard just from kissing her, and strokes as I watch. One shoe. Two shoes. Then she stands a bit to wiggle the jeans down, taking her underwear with them, and I stroke a bit faster as I watch her ass jiggle with the movement. *Fuck.*

I must have made a noise because she stops with her jeans at her knees and looks up at me, then at my hand.

A moan comes from her.

If I didn't have a plan, if I didn't need to drag this out, I'd fuck her right there. Flip her over, bend her on that bed, and slip inside.

I know she's wet already.

But I stick to my plan and continue to stroke, locking eyes with her as I speak.

"Take off your jeans then sit on your bed." I expect her to argue, but her hands just move down her legs, pushing the jeans down and kicking them off before her ass is back to the edge of the bed where she sits, waiting for her next command. I move then, standing about a foot in front of her.

"Open your legs, Gabi." She does. I keep stroking, tugging harder when I see she's already glistening. Fuck, that pussy is beautiful. "Move your hand to your clit, baby. Touch yourself." Again, I expect her to argue. To get shy. Anything. But as always, she shocks me, a hand moving up her inner thigh until it's right where I told her to go, circling her clit, dipping in to grab some of the wet, then continuing.

It's amazing to hear her moan, to see her move the other hand back to support herself in her bed, and watch her start to feel it. This woman who, weeks ago, told me it was impossible for her to come is now clearly close to the edge.

"That's it, kitten. So pretty, watching you play with your pussy for me." I continue to jack myself, grazing the tip with my thumb before moving back down, over and over.

"I want..." she says, the words breathy.

"What do you want, baby?" This is what I'm waiting for. Her to make that move. If she's never ready, I'll let her make herself come, watch that show, then come on her tits because shit if that isn't a version of something I've been dreaming of. But she tells me.

"I want your cock in my mouth, Vic." I don't think I've ever heard more beautiful words.

"Alright, baby, you can suck my cock," I say, smiling. Again with the smiling and laughing during sex. I take a step forward and fuck if the angle isn't perfect. "I'm gonna slide into your mouth, Gabi, and I'm gonna talk to you. I want you to keep fingering that puss of yours, yeah?" She nods, her pants hitting my dick in the most erotic caress.

But of course, she has one more thing to say to completely annihilate my mind.

"I want you to come in my mouth, honey." Holy fucking shit.

"What?" I pause, frozen, my hand on my dick that I was about to guide into her mouth.

"My mouth. I want your cum, Vic." Could this woman be any more perfect?

"You sure?"

"Oh yeah," she says with a smile but then gasps and moans because she must have hit herself just right. I make a decision then.

"Here's what we're gonna do. I'm gonna slide my cock into your mouth and you're gonna suck me off while you touch yourself to stay grounded. I'm gonna fuck your mouth, Gabi, and I'm going to tell you just how pretty you look doing it. Then when you're close—really fucking close, baby, get yourself almost there, we're gonna move to the bed, and you're going to suck me off while I eat your pussy until you come, yeah?" She moans, deep in her chest. "I need you to answer me, Gabi."

"Yes, Vic. I want that. Please." I don't need any more encouragement. I bury one hand into her curls, move a step forward so that my legs hit the bed, and guide my cock into the warm, wet heat of her mouth.

"Fuuuucccck," I groan out, feeling her tongue run down the length as she sucks gently. I use my hand to move her head back and forth, slowly, not going too deep. She said she's never been into this— I don't want to put her off it forever, especially since this is my version of heaven.

"Fuck, Gabi, seeing your lips on my cock, fucking your mouth— nothing better." She sucks again, her tongue grazing the spot right under the head as I pull out before I push back in. "Just like that, kitten. Fuck, you're good at this. Would do this all day, have you suck my cock like this all day if I could." She moans, pushing her head further into my hips, trying to take more, but I use my grip on her head to slow her.

"No, baby. Keep this easy today. Not too much. Need you to enjoy sucking me off because we are definitely doing this again." She moans once more, the vibrations going up my dick and to my balls that are pulling up with the pleasure.

I'm not sure if I can last.

Fuck, I need to last. Distraction. I need a distraction. Funny how this all started because Gabi is too distracted, and now I need one to avoid ending this too quickly. No wonder men before me couldn't make her come—she's too fucking good.

"How's that pussy, baby? Is it nice and wet for me? I can't wait to eat it, have you grind on my face when you come." The wet sounds from between her legs get louder, and the only downside of this plan is I can't watch.

Maybe that should be a lesson.

Watching.

My dick twitches at the thought.

"I think we should do that next time," I say, thinking aloud. "You watch me jack off while I watch you make yourself come. It's a sight I'd love to see, baby." And then, thank fuck, she uses a wet hand to push on my thigh. Wet with her. Fuucckk.

"Now, Vic. I need..." Fuck yeah, game on.

"I'll take care of you, baby." Part of me wonders if we might be over the hill of distractions, if maybe we're so in tune with each other that I know how to keep her here on earth and she knows how to stay here with me. That was a lot quicker than I thought it would be.

Not that I'm complaining.

My hands go to her waist, and I toss her up onto the bed before I get in behind her, lying on my back with my head near her knees, feet to the bed, and legs cocked, so she has room.

"Climb on, baby. Put your cunt on my face and my cock in your mouth." Again, she surprises me when she does as I ask, straddling one leg over my chest and then moving back until that wet pussy is hovering over me as she bends. I'm impatient, though, my hands going to her hips and pulling her down before I'm even in her mouth.

She moans, but it's quickly smothered as my cock slips in, silencing her. She's soaking wet, her clit swollen from her playing with herself, her hips rocking on my mouth with intuition. Even if she's never done this, even if she's nervous or self-conscious, her body knows what to do. What it wants.

I suck on her clit, and she takes me deeper, so deep I feel myself slip down her throat as I pull her hips down closer to my face. I try to move my hips back into the bed, so she isn't doing too much, but fuck if little hands aren't mimicking my actions, pulling my hips closer to her so she can continue to deep throat me.

It's unbearable.

Pure torture.

What my wildest dreams are made of as I start to fuck her face to the same rhythm she has set as she grinds her pussy on my face over and over, taking what she needs rather than waiting for me to give it to her.

I moan into her cunt and slip a single finger into her, and that's it. I feel it both as she clamps down on my finger and when she moans and takes my cock deeper still into her mouth.

She's coming.

She's coming, riding my face, my finger in her pussy, my cock in her mouth, and the sounds she's making, the way her entire body is shaking, she's loving it.

That's all it takes for me to dig my finger in deeper, pressing on her G-spot to draw out her orgasm as I explode down her throat, fucking her in light pumps until I'm spent.

And what feels like both moments and hours later, her pussy still in my face and her head on my thigh, my cock having slipped out after she swallowed me down, I hear a giggle. I push her off with a gentle roll and look down to see a gorgeous smile on her face.

"I totally want to do that again," she says with a laugh, and if she wasn't already mine, I'd do whatever I could in my power to make it that way.

TWENTY-FIVE

-Gabi-

I am not a morning person.

So much so that when I was in high school, it was near impossible to wake me up. One time, the summer before freshman year, my dad got so fed up with me sleeping in until noon that he had my brothers carry me from my bed and toss me into the pool.

I was so mad I went on a hunger strike for a week, forcing me to enlist my best friend Paige to sneak in food through my bedroom window.

Waking up in my bed on Sunday morning, face snuggled into the broad chest of Doctor Victor Brandt, I can't wait to face the day. His hand moves down my arm, cluing me in to the fact that he's awake too, and we move to face each other.

"Hey," I say, my voice croaky with sleep.

"Morning." He gives me a small smile, eyes sleepy and voice groggy.

"What are your plans today? You working?" I ask, smiling as he moves the loose curl that fell from my sleep ponytail. He watches his fingers as he tucks it back behind my ear, but I watch him. He's so fucking handsome, especially like this, barely awake and smiling at me.

"We're going to your parents', right? Gia made her demand." My stomach drops, and my heart stops.

"What?"

"Sunday dinner? At your parents'? That's still happening, right?" I nod.

"It's every Sunday."

"And I told Gia and Nicky I'd be there. Don't want to disappoint my number one fan." He smiles again, white teeth flashing. He's got a good smile.

Focus, Gabi.

"But you don't... You don't have to... You're busy..." Part of me wants him to bail. Part of me knows that Vic coming to family dinner could very well be the last straw in his putting up with me and my chaos. The other part thinks it could very well be the final straw on the scale that's precariously leaning in my heart.

"I rearranged my work schedule. We're good." I stare at him.

"My family is absolutely crazy." A smile. "Like, insane." He stays silent still. "If you think I'm out there, my family is why I am the way I am. And they'll all be there—all my brothers, Gia, Ant, the nephews, and Sammy... It's the law of Gemma Mancini. She raised five assholes to be complete momma's boys so they'd stay close and never leave Jersey."

"Why do you go, then?"

"What?"

"You said your mom raised your brothers so they're conditioned to stay close and come every Sunday. Why do you go if just the thought of joining in is putting you into a panic?" I sit on that for a moment before sighing.

"Because as annoying and fucking nuts as they are, I love my family." He continues to stare before I roll my eyes. "And because my dad did the same for Gia and me, making us daddy's girls." Vic smiles, like he knew the answer all along, and I want to glare at him, but I smile too. "He goes crazy if we miss, calling and insisting we tell him where we are so he knows we're safe, asking if he needs to send Mom over with soup or the boys to kick someone's ass."

"That's how dads should be," he says, and for a split second, I can almost see it: a brown-skinned little girl with a mop of dark curls sneaking into bed in the morning between us, Vic refusing to tell her no and me rolling my eyes.

The thought itself almost hurts with how beautiful it could be.

How beautiful it *can't* be.

I can't stay in this bed with him, daydreaming about futures that will never happen.

That I don't want to happen, I remind myself. Vic is the easy, fun first time. Nothing more.

I nod to myself, making Vic smile bigger before I roll, escaping his arms and nearly falling to the plush rug beneath my bed with my effort. Vic laughs.

"What was that?"

"I'm starving. You want breakfast?" I lie, grabbing the short silky robe hanging on my closet door and slipping my arms through. He stares at me and I think for a minute he'll call me on it, ask where my mind is, try to decode me. But then his phone rings—saved by the bell. Leaning over, he reaches to the bedside table and grabs the sleek phone (not in a case, which, in my opinion, is insanity and probably a red flag) and then groans.

"Work?" I ask, nearly hopeful—work could mean he can't go to family dinner.

"Worse. My mother." My eyebrows furrow in confusion as he continues to stare at the screen. "Probably a potential date attack."

"Answer it," I say with a laugh. "I'll go try to find food for breakfast." He gives me a look telling me he's thinking about not answering it, but I do my best at replicating Gia's stern mom look. It's his mother, after all. Finally, it seems to work when he smiles, nods, and swipes to answer.

"Hello, Mother," he says, flopping into my bed and making me smile again. He would call his mom "Mother."

I make my way to the kitchen, where I scrounge for food. Sugary cereal for the boys. Milk that smells not quite right.

English muffins. Those should do. I use a fork to separate them, popping them into the toaster and opening the fridge to grab condiments. Jelly, peanut butter, butter, honey... I have no idea what Vic would want.

Walking back to the room to ask, I stop in my hallway, listening.

"No, Mom, I don't need you to set me up," Vic says into the phone, pacing but facing the headboard, not the doorway.

I should leave.

Or make a noise.

Anything besides standing here and listening.

But I've never been one to listen to my own advice.

"Yes, I told you, I'm working with a matchmaker. A real one. No, seriously!" He pauses. "I'm not giving you her number. She doesn't need your advice." I stifle a laugh. "No, I'm, uh... I'm already matched. I got my first match. She's sweet... Yeah, I like her a lot." My entire body goes into a state of warm prickles: half panic, half pleasure. Calm down, Gabi. He's just saying that to get her off his back. He makes a sound that is essentially an audible eye roll. "Yes, Mom. I'm actually going to her parents' house today, meeting them." He moves the phone from his ear, cringing. "God, Mom, stop. No, I'm not inviting you. And no, you don't have to meet her. It's... It's not that serious. You don't have to meet her." The warmth goes to ice. I don't hear the rest of the conversation, moving into my head, my safe place.

I don't know why that burns. Why his not wanting me to meet his parents guts me a bit.

Liar, my inner voice says, but I bat her away, thankfully returning to the land of the living as Vic swipes his phone off and turns to me.

"Hey," he says, smiling. Not annoyed that I'm standing here. Just smiling.

"Uh, what do you want on your English muffin?" I lift the butter and jelly I brought here to show in my silent question and he laughs.

"Both," he says, walking towards me, and we both head to the kitchen, his hand on my lower back as the muffins pop up.

I think about offering to meet his parents, but I can't get the words out. All I keep hearing repeated over and over in my mind is, *"It's not that serious."* The reminder of what we really are.

And what we're not.

TWENTY-SIX

-Vic-

As per Gia's demand, we're on our way to meet Gabi's family for Sunday dinner.

I think we might die before we get there.

It turns out, sweet Gabi is an insane driver.

She has a lead foot, both on the gas pedal and the rarely used brake. When she does use the brake, my entire body jolts forward, a hand reaching out to steady myself on the dashboard.

Before we got onto the Parkway, she completely blew through a red light that had turned red a full second before we hit the intersection, more than enough time on yellow to slow and stop. When I told her this, she told me she had places to be and, "Yellow means speed up to make the light."

And now she's losing her damn mind.

"Jesus fucking Christ, you moron, get the fuck over!" Gabi shouts at the car in front of us, her hand gesturing to the right lane with full-blown anger. I stare at her, shocked as she switches back to calm, slipping right back into the conversation we'd been having before her outburst. "Anyway, so fair warning, I have five brothers." I don't respond, instead staring at her until she glances my way. "What? I already told you that, right?" Now she looks confused.

"What was that?" I ask, staring at her with a slight smile I can't seem to fight when she's around.

"What was what?" Then she lays on her horn, the sound loud inside the small car. "Get out of the fast lane, you dumb ass! Fuckin' Pennsylvania drivers! No fucking idea how to drive!"

Once again, I stare at her.

At sweet, quiet, relatively reserved Gabi.

"That."

"What are you talking about?" Her eyes are on the road as she hits the horn again. "Nice blinker, buddy."

"Gabi, do you need me to drive?" She looks over at me, clearly no idea what I'm talking about. I point to the road, redirecting her gaze. "Please, watch the road." Gabi does as I ask before responding.

"What? No. Why?"

"Because you seem like you're about to have a panic attack."

"What? No."

"Babe, you haven't gone more than a full minute without screaming at someone."

"We're on the Parkway. It's what you do." I look at her with my eyes wide. Her face shows that this is not a joke—she really thinks this.

"No, kitten. It's not. It might be what you do, but normal people? No."

"Did you just see that guy?" she shouts, moving her hand at a red car that cut in front of her. "See?!" And then I'm laughing, a real, genuine, body-shaking laugh, because in one million years I would never have thought that sweet Gabi, assistant to a matchmaker, virginal lover of romance novels, dresses like a preschool teacher, would have serious road rage.

"Next time I drive," I say as my hand reaches for the handle above the window, and I pray it's a short drive.

Thankfully, it is and we park in front of a large home on a cul-de-sac filled with cars. When we park, she continues to stare out the windshield. Her color has dipped, a nervous pallor on her skin as she starts talking.

"Okay, so, reminder. I have five older brothers and one sister. I am the baby."

"Got that."

"And I have a dad." I bite my lip to avoid smiling since I think smiling here would annoy her, but she's not even looking at me.

"Got it."

"My mom will probably kiss you when you walk in the door. If you can, just accept it. Trust me, it makes everyone's life easier. But if you're uncomfortable, tell me now and I'll stop it before it happens." She's wringing her hands over her skirt, this one with little goldfish on it, a Celine Dion tour tee shirt on top. She's nervous.

Nervous.

Gabi, nervous. And not about anything sexual, which is the only time I've ever seen this side of her.

"What's wrong?" I ask, grabbing her hands. Finally, she looks at me. Her eyes are wide with anxiety before she sighs.

"My family is... a lot."

"So is mine."

"Yours means well." Of course, she has no idea since she's never met my family.

"I'm sure yours does too." I've met Gia and Ant. They're friendly, a little loud and chaotic, but nice.

And they clearly love Gabi.

For some reason, when it comes to her family, that's all I care about.

"They do, but also... they're insane."

"Insane how?" Her eyes flit over my shoulder, going wide.

"You'll see soon enough," she says with a strange mix of a cringe and a genuinely happy smile before my door is opened and a dark-haired Italian man is standing next to me.

"Gabs!" he says, clearly happy to see her as he squats beside me to look through the car at Gabi.

"Hi, Gio," she says, opening her door and stepping out.

"You let her drive you here?" the man, her brother I assume, asks with a tip of his chin toward his sister.

"Uh, yeah."

"Bad decision. My sister is a horrible driver," he says before standing and grabbing his sister, who has walked around the front of the car. He's at least an entire foot taller than her, dark hair brushed back with the sides neatly cut. Gabi stands next to him in the grass, her Converse giving her zero height, an arm slung around his waist and her head pressed to his side.

They're close.

"Gio, this is Vic. My..."

"I'm her man," I say, grabbing his hand and shaking it. It's a tight grip as he appraises me with skeptical eyes.

"Gio, don't be a dick. He's got five more of you to meet."

"Dario and I have a bet going on if he'll come back after this." Gabi rolls her eyes, letting go and slapping his chest.

"I said, don't be a dick, G."

"Did you warn him?"

"I tried. He doesn't get it," Gabi says, grabbing my hand as we head up the walk.

"You should have believed her," he says over his shoulder to me, a smile on his face, and I'm beginning to wonder what the fuck I got myself into.

Walking into what I've been told is Gabi's childhood home, it's loud.

There's a staircase to the right and I hear feet running around above us, so I assume there are rooms or a playroom upstairs. Giggling accompanies the footsteps. Kids. The nephews I already met and maybe the niece I haven't yet.

"My Gabrielle!" a voice says from the kitchen as we walk in that direction. The kitchen is huge, with a living room to the right and a dining room already set with plates and utensils to the left. It's not modern and open with clean lines and stark light colors. Instead, it's homey, lived in. It screams Italian American with signs all over the kitchen with words like "Mangia!" written in bold letters, an intense number of large glass lidded jars with at least a dozen different types of pasta on shelves in the corner. The cabinets are dark wood, all with golden yellow and red accents.

Somehow, although I had zero expectations coming here, it's exactly what I expected after talking to Gabi and meeting her sister.

"Hey, Daddy," Gabi says, words directed to an island where a man with a thick head of combed back salt and pepper hair sits on a stool, his arms out.

He looks exactly like an older male version of Gabi, but taller. She drops my hand and walks to him, coming to his shoulder despite him sitting down. But the face—it's the same as Gabi's.

"Pop, Gabs drove here," Gio says, walking in behind us, clearly finding this humorous.

"You let her drive?" another male voice asks, coming in from the dining room. He looks identical to Gio. The twins. This must be Dario.

There are five Mancini brothers from what Gabi quizzed me on this morning while we ate breakfast. Dom is her oldest brother, two years younger than Gia, eight years older than Gabi. He has an eight-year-old daughter, Sammy. Next is Nico, followed by the middle Mancini kid, Enzo. Six years and four years older than Gabi, respectively.

The twins, Gio and Dario, are two years older than Gabi.

Mr. and Mrs. Mancini spent ten years having kids near-perfectly spaced out. It's really a feat to commend if you don't stop to think about how completely insane this house must have been.

"You made it here alive?" A third man walks in, dragging a small body with him that's clinging to his leg. I know that small body, at least.

"Doctor Vic!" Nicky screams, leaving what I assume is an uncle and running to me.

"Hey, bud!" I say, giving him a high five.

"Look at all of my signatures!" There are scribbles all along the cast, the cottony part near the fingers stained in what I can only hope is chocolate.

"For the love of God, Nicky, please do not show the doctor how absolutely disgusting that cast is," Gia says, walking in with a fourth dark-haired man. Not her husband—this must be the oldest brother. Dom.

"Totally fine. I've seen worse."

"I promise that's chocolate from s'mores. Not... anything else." Gia smiles before coming up to me, kissing each cheek before moving back. "Glad to see Gabs hasn't scared you off yet."

"She might have if she drove him over. Gabi drives like a fuckin' maniac," the final brother says, walking with a blonde-haired girl tucked under his arm. Sammy, Dom's daughter.

"Can we stop talking about my fuckin' driving?" Gabi says with her hands on her hips. Gone is my sweet Gabi, who was nervous and wanted to run. In her place is a full-blooded Italian princess the likes they make movies about, the youngest in her family, outrage and frustration rolling off her.

"Gabrielle Nicolette!" a woman shouts from where I didn't see her. She's tiny, like Gabi and Gia, and now I see where Gabi got those wild curls. She stands at the stove, a colossal metal pot in front of her that she's stirring, a sauce-speckled apron protecting her clothes. Not sauce—Gabi was particular in telling me that in her house, it's called "gravy." Her hair is huge, crazy, and wild, dark like Gabi and Gia's, but sprinkled with streaks of grey.

"Watch your mouth, Gabrielle," her father says with a look fathers save for daughters—a mix of soft and stern with laughter at the edges.

"Why didn't you say anything when Nico cursed?" Gabi asks, glaring at her father. He just looks on with just the softness now.

"Because he's a boy, *patatina*."

"Daddy, that's ridiculous," Gia says, and from the look of near everyone in the room, this is a constant and irritating conversation.

"Might be ridiculous, but that's the world, *polpetta*, and it's the truth." Gabi's mother turns from where she had returned to stirring, the saucy spoon held high in the air and pointing at her husband.

"Don't spin that shit in my kitchen, Vincent." So that's where Gabi and Gia get the fire. I stand back, quietly observing as what I can only assume is a common occurrence unfolds. No one seems phased by it, at least.

"Who bought you this kitchen, *mi amore*?"

"Try that again and you'll be livin' in a fuckin' hotel room. Won't matter who fuckin' paid for this kitchen. This kitchen, mind you, that I keep clean, make you all your damn meals in, raised our babies in, while you sat on your damn chair and ate prosciutto and bruschetta I laid out for you."

"Gemma—"

"You'll lose, Vincent Mancini. You play this game, you'll lose every time."

It seems volatile in the kitchen, but all seven faces in the room are understanding, if not bored. I lean into Gabi, who has made her way back to me.

"Is this... okay?"

"Oh, this is how they always are," Dom says, a smile on his face. He's the first brother so far who hasn't given me a death glare at my hand on Gabi's waist.

"You get used to it," Gabi says in agreement under her breath.

"They're always fighting," Nicky says about his grandparents.

"Okay, sit for dinner!" Mrs. Mancini says, and without even the tiniest argument, the room shifts towards the dining room.

This is going to be an experience.

TWENTY-SEVEN

-Gabi-

"So, Gab, how's work?" my mom starts. This is how most family dinners go. Each kid gets their inquisition, starting from oldest to youngest. My siblings have already been through the exchange, and at this point, most of the garlic bread is gone.

"Good," I say. I leave it at that for now. Depending on my dad's mood, more questions will be asked. I went to school for business administration so an assistant to a small business owner is pretty on-brand. But when I told my family that after jumping from job to job that I didn't exactly love, I finally settled on the assistant to a matchmaker... well... there were a lot of questions.

"And how's Cassie? How's the wedding planning going?" Okay, safe. This is a safe topic.

"Good. We're closing in on the one-month mark, so she's running around crazy."

"With that family of hers, I'm sure she's stuck doing a lot of it herself." I nod. She is, though Luke's sisters and mom have been a tremendous help. "I hope you told her we'd be happy to help." I nod again.

"I did. You know Cassie, though. Loves to do it all herself."

"Hmm. I'm sure Lucas's mom is excited for some grandbabies." About two months ago, Luke, Gabi, and Luke's similarly crazy yet blissfully smaller family came for Sunday dinner at my parents'. My mom and Mrs. Dawson instantly hit it off. This is not a surprise, since my mom loves near everyone and loves any way she can wiggle herself into her children's lives.

They now have coffee together every other Tuesday.

That's my mom for you.

"I think they're taking their time," I say, non-committal and nonchalant.

This is a minefield.

I must tiptoe gently.

My eyes go to Gia's, which are already on me. She knows too.

A fucking minefield.

When her head turns to Vic, I can hear the ticking, loud, like that atomic clock or the grandfather clock my grandparents had that would chime every hour on the hour so loud it shook the house...

"I can't wait for Gabi to give me some grandbabies."

Tick, tick, boom.

She's been set off.

Shit.

"Mom—" I start.

"You literally have three grandbabies, Ma," Gia says with exasperation in an effort to diffuse. She's a good sister. I'm going to keep her.

It's useless, though. We all know it.

"What, I can't want more?" she asks Gia but keeps her eyes on Vic. I look at him, expecting to see the deer in headlights look my brothers get; the look Ant had for nearly seven years until he finally got Gia pregnant six months after they tied the knot, but nope. It's not there.

It's like he expected this. Maybe even like he's experienced in this.

"A mother can't want more babies?"

"You had seven children," Gia says with a sigh.

"You think I did that for shit and giggles? Hell no. I did that and raised you hooligans right so that I'd have grandbabies."

"If we were so shitty, why would you want grandbabies?" Dario asks.

"Because I couldn't spoil you and send you home. This was your home. I had to deal with your shit day in and day out. But babies, I can spoil rotten then send home and sleep in peace."

"No shit," Ant says under his breath, and my brothers and I take in a hiss of breath.

"Antonio Russo, you zip it or I'm calling your mother," my mom says to her son-in-law. He shuts up. The only mother I know who is more intense than my own is Ant's mom, Gia's mother-in-law.

Another crony of my mom's, a friendship was cultivated just weeks after Gia started dating Ant in middle school. I truly hope whoever I marry, my mom hates his mother and I don't have to deal with this. Her head turns back to Vic.

"So, do you want kids, Vic?"

"Jesus, Mom!"

"Mom, that's rude!" Gia says, helping out.

Five manly voices laugh. A lot of help my brothers are. I glare at Dario, who is across from me, quickly jotting his name and offense into my mental tally of shit I need to pay my brothers back for.

The list is very, very long.

"Auntie Gabi would make a good mommy," Sammy says, and while that's sweet, she's adding fuel to the fire. Bless Dom for giving her "the look."

For that, I cross off the time he tied my Barbie to a bottle rocket when I was seven.

"She would. I need to know how long of a wait I have," my mom says.

"Eventually," Vic says. "I'd like kids, eventually. Once I'm settled and work evens out and I'm married." I look at Vic and try to give him a thumbs up with my eyes. Good answer.

"Don't mind my wife. She's nosey and a pain in my ass."

"Vincent!"

"You are."

"Jesus, here we go," Gio says, leaning back in his chair.

"No worries, Mr. Mancini. My mom is the same way, always asking my sister and me when we'll give her grandkids," he says, the perfect selection.

"See! It's not just me!" All seven of us Mancini kids roll our eyes, knowing our mother takes "normal" mom behavior and blows it out of the water.

"Drives my sister and me crazy, but I know she means well." And then a miracle happens. My mother nods. She nods and then proceeds to pick at her plate.

The inquisition is over.

The bomb diffused.

I look at Vic before I whisper under my breath. "Are you magic?" Dario, who is close enough to hear it, laughs so hard that we all end up joining in, even if most don't know why he's laughing.

After dinner, my siblings, Vic, and I are sitting out on the back deck with wine while my mom spoils the grandkids with ice cream sundaes and my dad takes a nap in his lounger.

This is how Sundays go.

And as annoying and frustrating and crazy as my family is, I love it. We all do. It's why we all willingly come to Sunday dinner each week.

I love my family.

"So, how did you two meet, by the way?" Dom asks, and my sister's head moves to me, a silent, judgemental laugh on her face.

I hate my family.

"Vic helped when Nicky broke his wrist," Ant says.

I adore my brother-in-law.

"Oh, no, they knew each other before that," Gia says with a sickly sweet smile, one all of my siblings know as Gia's big-sister-teasing-mode-activated smile.

I despise my sister.

"Oh, Gabi looks like she wants to barf!" Nico says. "Story time!" I down the wine in my glass. Gia grabs my empty glass and refills it with the bottle next to her. I glare at her but nod in thanks all the same.

It truly is a love-hate relationship.

"He was at the ER when she broke her wrist," Gia says.

"That's not interesting," Enzo says. "Why do I feel like it should have been more interesting?" Please, for the love of god, change the subject. Anyone. Please. I look at Vic, but the man is smiling.

Let's add him to the list of people I hate.

"Oh, there's definitely more to it. Look at her face."

"G, do you know?" Enzo asks.

"Of course I know. She's my sister."

"What's there to know? She broke her wrist," Dario says, his ever-present confused face on.

"Do you know where she broke her wrist?" Gia asks, a devious smile in her voice. My face burns. *Oh god, oh god!*

"Her apartment?"

"In her shower," Gia says, and everyone gets quiet. No, no, no! I'll never live this down. Never ever, ever. I'll be 80 and my brothers will be giving me shit about this.

"Gia, shut the fuck up!" I shout, but that's my fatal mistake. I should have let it go, played it off. By yelling at her, I might as well have admitted my sin.

Ribbing ensues. My brothers laugh with one another over the fact that I clearly fell while... servicing myself.

Or attempting to.

And failing, obviously.

"Oh, my god," I say, burying my face into Vic's shoulder. I want to melt and disappear. I want a time machine to go back to an hour ago so that I can punch Gia in the face. That way, she wouldn't be able to talk for the rest of the night, holding an ice pack there.

"It's all good," Vic whispers into my hair, smiling. "I'd tease my sister the same way."

"About your sister masturbating?"

"I know nothing about my sister's, ahem, self-care habits, and I like keeping it that way."

"Exactly."

"But if I did somehow find out, I would hands down give her shit about it." I want to die.

"This is so embarrassing."

"It is, but in a good way. Your family is cool." I roll my eyes, but thankfully the laughs have simmered, and the conversation begins to change. Probably because my brothers are realizing that falling in the shower means I was masturbating, but also, do they want to ask questions about their baby sister masturbating? No. No, they don't.

We're close, but we're not that close.

Gag.

Vic gets pulled into a conversation about baseball, opening games having happened last weekend. My parents' house is plastered with little league and college ball pictures from my brothers, a Yankees' flag flying proudly on the front porch where some would have an American flag.

Then, my mind runs off as I stare at the trees surrounding my parent's property, the moon shining through. It's a gorgeous night out, not too hot, not too cold, a fire in the metal fire pit before us.

I could get used to this. Family, great weather, a full belly, and… Vic holding me.

I fall back into the conversation at hand, my mind melting into the conversation with a question.

"Why is the stitching red?" I ask, my voice soft as my eyes are still fixed on the sky. The wine is making my filter slower.

"What?"

"On a baseball. Why is the stitching red?"

"Here we go," Enzo says.

"Here we go?" Vic asks, my hand in his lap, his thumb absent-mindedly rubbing. A comfort. I like it. More than I should.

"The questions." Vic stays silent. "You had to have noticed the questions."

"I don't know what you mean," Vic says, being the gentleman he is. Gio helps him out.

"Gabi asks questions. Non-stop. About dumb things. Drives us all crazy. She has since she was Nicky's age. Younger, even."

"As soon as she could talk," Dario says with a laugh. I flip him off and roll my eyes.

"She notices things. Has questions. It's normal. Admirable, even," Vic says, and my hand squeezes his. He's a good guy. Gia looks at me with wide eyes and a smile. She gets it. Good guy.

"She's annoying," Enzo says in that irritated big brother voice typically reserved for brothers in movies half his age, full of exaggeration. Of all of my brothers, Enzo and I butt heads the most. Vic's hand holds mine tighter.

I don't think it's for my comfort, though.

"What?"

"She's annoying," he repeats like Vic's an idiot who didn't finish middle school instead of a man who is a literal doctor. I wonder if that's his second or third glass of whiskey in his hand. "She's always saying random shit that makes no fucking sense. Pop's the only one who endures it."

"Enzo, man—" Dom starts.

"She's not annoying," Vic says, interrupting. Everyone is quiet, eyes to Vic. "She's smart. Her mind is exquisite. Anyone who looks at the world around them and doesn't just accept it but instead questions it? That's beautiful." He pauses, but he doesn't look at me, despite my eyes being locked on him. If he looked at me, though, I don't know what I'd do. Stop him? Kiss him? "A man who finds that annoying? Probably doesn't notice a single good thing in front of him."

My gut is in my feet. Of my brothers, Enzo is also the most combative, the least filter to his words. We're similar in that way.

"That's because you're fuck—" Vic stands, dropping my hand.

"Vic!" My eyes are wide, moving from Vic to Dom to Gia, trying to figure out what to do.

"I'd suggest you shut the fuck up," Vic says, eyes locked on my brother.

"Enzo, man, you need to go inside," Dom says. He's standing now too, and so is Nico, my oldest brothers, the ones who always protected me the most.

"Fuck, Dom, you're taking some random dude's side?" His eyes are glazed. He's drunk.

What is going on?

He might be rude and quick to snap at people and have zero filters when it comes to kindness and societal norms, but this... This isn't him.

He's not the "get drunk and try to fight his brothers and make his baby sister cry" type.

"I'm taking Gabi's side, man. What is up with you?"

"What's up with me?"

"Yeah, Zo. What is up with you? You've been like this for fucking months."

"Fuck off, golden boy." It seems his anger has moved from Vic to my brother. Vic is still standing, hands in fists at his side, forcing me to stand slightly behind him, but Enzo's outburst is not about me anymore. I can see that. We all see that. This is something... different.

"Man, you need to chill the fuck out."

"Fuck this," Enzo says, standing before he's off, walking through the sliding glass door, slamming it shut in a way that seems to rattle the entire house. Through the windows, I see my mom's face go into shock, my dad's go red as he yells at Enzo's back.

"Does someone have his keys?" I ask, my eyes stuck on the glass. He's an ass, but he's still my brother, and I would never want him driving home like this.

"I drove him here," Nico says, and he's playing with his car keys in his hand. At least there's that.

"Jesus, what the fuck was that?" Gio says after a few long moments of silence.

We all just stare, unsure of what to say.

"Vic, gotta say, takes balls to stand up to this crew like that," Ant says. Ant went through his own initiation phase long, long ago, when he was dating Gia. I don't remember it well since I was six or seven during the worst of it, but I've heard the stories.

Even though Gia is the oldest, Dom and Nico were old enough to make his life hell, the same as my dad.

"Gabi doesn't need anyone making her feel like she's different or annoying. She might be your little sister and annoying to you by nature—" He looks around at my brothers. "—and I get it. I have a little sister. But I'll tell you now that I won't stand for that shit as long as I'm around." Something in me breaks. Something small and almost unnoticeable but irreparable all the same.

And with his words, words that could have caused a backlash on a bad day, my four remaining brothers, my brother-in-law, and my sister all nod and smile.

It seems they've accepted Vic.

TWENTY-EIGHT

-Vic-

The drive home from the Mancini's house is quiet.

After the chaos of Enzo snapping at Gabi and storming out in a rage that, to my small knowledge, didn't seem related to Gabi herself, things settled back into sitting around the fire, drinking and laughing. Mrs. Mancini brought out a tray of desserts, cannoli, and mini pots of tiramisu and Italian butter cookies that Gabi told me were all from the bakery down the street owned by their grandmother's best friend. A place they all grew up going to, getting cakes for every birthday and cannoli for every Sunday dinner.

Apparently, having a guest called for adding to the order.

Not long after, the siblings started to scatter. Nico took home a still silent Enzo. Gia and Ant rounded up their boys and headed out. Sammy kissed me on the cheek before running off with a blush, and then Gabi and I followed closely behind. I thanked Mrs. Mancini for dinner (who gave me a kiss, as per Gabi's warning) and Mr. Mancini gave me another firm but less angry shake before telling me it was nice to meet me, and that they hope to see me again.

In that family, I feel like that's a win—an invite back is the golden ticket.

I insisted on driving home, blaming Gabi's two glasses of wine and definitely not bringing up that her driving terrifies me. As we drive, she's in her head. Embarrassed. I can nearly see the thoughts running in her mind right alongside the shine of the headlight from oncoming traffic brushing over her face.

"Your family is cool." She nods. "Crazy, but cool."

"They're obnoxious."

"They love you." She sighs. I don't think she can argue that. "Who are you closest to?" She looks out the window, turning her head from me.

"Dom. And Gia because she's the only other girl. Gia and I help Dom a lot with Sammy. After she was born, I spent a year living with him, taking care of her while I did school online."

"I didn't know that." It seems there's so much I don't know about Gabi. So much I want to know about her. "Where's her mom?"

"Who knows? She ran off. Dumped Sammy at Dom's house and said she'd be back in a week. Said she needed a break. Dom didn't even know Sammy was alive. She was two months old and her mom was a one-night stand or something like that. I don't ask questions about my brother's sex life." She makes a disgusted face I can't help but laugh at. It reminds me of my sister. Vivi would love Gabi.

She will *love Gabi,* I correct my thoughts. I might not want Gabi to be subjected to the crazy that is my mom and sister just yet, for fear of scaring her off, but if things go the way I see them going, it will happen.

"He had nothing ready, of course. He was 26, still a bachelor. Single and living life. He called me in a panic—I was 18. Gia and Mom and I ran out, got everything he'd need. Thought they'd work on custody or something—if he knew Sammy was alive, he would want her in his life. But... her mom never came back. So he went to court and got full custody. It was chaos. And then he was a full-time single dad. But he worked. He didn't want to put her in daycare.

Hell, he couldn't afford it. Do you know how much daycare for an infant costs in New Jersey?" I shake my head no. "It would have equated to over half of his yearly salary." My eyes bug. Jesus. How do people afford that? "He wasn't making a ton but still. Too much to qualify for any kind of child scholarship or financial aid. I'd just graduated from high school and had no idea what I wanted to do with my life. I didn't want to waste a year of college tuition only to change my mind. Two years before, I saw Dario make that mistake. So I was his nanny for a year. I lived with him while I took some online classes and figured out what I wanted to do. Gia was pregnant with Gino or she would have insisted on taking turns." Even though she's still looking out the window, I see her cheeks move into a smile. "It was a good year, though. I love that little girl. She's so sweet. And Dom is a great dad. I still watch her sometimes. Sometimes I take on all three, though not too often. They're a lot."

"You're a good sister."

"They're annoying and mean sometimes, but they're good brothers." She sighs. "You definitely won them over tonight. Thanks for that, by the way. You... you didn't have to."

I did.

I did. And the fact that she doesn't see that is near infuriating.

Instead, I say, "It wasn't a big deal." She doesn't buy it, quietly looking out the window, watching the green signs on the Parkway as I take us home.

Long minutes pass before I speak again, both of us trapped in our own minds.

"New Jersey used to be separated into East and West Jersey." Her head turns to me, confused.

"What?"

"There was East and West Jersey." The headlights flash on her face, showing furrowed brows, but I keep my eyes forward. I'm not sure why I suddenly feel shy or embarrassed. I wonder if this is how she always feels.

If so, I'm making it my mission to change that.

"Okay?" She's confused.

So am I, to be honest.

I'm confused about why I went and found out this random bit of information. But I needed to. It tugged at my brain for a few days until I sat down to learn it.

"So, from what I could find, West Brunswick technically crossed over into what is now Somerset county. Or East Jersey at the time. The Plainfields and the Brunswicks were all territories owned by wealthy families before they were turned into separate townships. And, for a brief moment, West Brunswick was a small, unincorporated area they eventually turned into Franklin. But have you ever looked at it on a map?" I ask, glancing her way. Her eyes are on me now, wide and confused.

"No?"

"I did. When you look on a map, North Brunswick and South Brunswick are essentially just west of East Brunswick. It doesn't make much sense, but... there it is." She continues to stare at me, her gaze burning on my face as I drive, locking my eyes to the road.

It's no longer because I'm driving and need to be safe—it's to avoid looking at her.

"You looked that up?" Her words are so low I almost can't hear her.

"What?"

"You looked up why there's no West Brunswick?" I nod.

"Yeah."

"Why?" Her voice is breathy. I look at her finally, unable to resist. There's awe there.

Beneath the confusion, there is awe. Her eyes are wide and sparkling in the dark.

"You wanted to know." It's the only answer I have.

"Why not just wait for me to look it up?"

"I figured you'd forgotten."

"I did." She doesn't say more than that, just stares at me as I drive. I wait for her to speak, but she doesn't, just stares at me. In the dark, I can't tell if her mind is here on earth or in some Gabi universe. Either way, as we turn into the parking garage for my apartment, I whisper my thoughts.

"That means something to you." There's a long pause, a beat where I'm unsure if she'll respond. But then she does.

And when she does, her voice is low and breathy, filled with meaning. "Yeah, Vic. It means something to me."

TWENTY-NINE

-Gabi-

We arrive at Vic's place and for the first time in what feels like years, I look around and take it in. It's still stark white with black but there, in the corner, in a frame I recognize from a pile of empty black ones I saw stashed in his medicine closet, is a drawing.

One Nicky made for Vic while he was in school. He had me give it to Vic, and I figured he just tossed it in a junk drawer.

As I walk over to inspect it and make sure I'm not seeing some kind of mirage, I'm stunned by more color. A painting on the wall. Golds and whites and creams swirled together into a pretty mess, framed meticulously and hung over the couch.

"When did you get this?" I ask, confused.

"It came the other day. They hung it for me."

"Where'd you get it?"

"That auction you sent me a link for?" He's flipping through papers on his counter—mail, I think. He's absentminded, like he doesn't care, but I'm thrown off. I sent him the link for an auction here in Ocean View, raising money for the art department at the high school where Dario works.

"You're decorating?" There's a teasing smile in my voice, mixed with copious amounts of shock. That makes him look up as he's ripping up junk mail. He returns the smile.

"Yeah. You were right. It's like a shitty art gallery here. Boring." I move my eyes from him to the painting. "Don't tell my sister or my mom, though. They'll go nuts and start decorating. Getting throw pillows and vases."

"What's wrong with throw pillows?" He's coming my way now.

"They have no true value."

"It's a pillow, Vic."

"No, it's not. It's usually a weirdly uncomfortable decorative piece that you're supposed to convince yourself is comfortable, but it's not. The fabric is usually rough and dumb, and the corners are hard." I laugh.

"Aren't I supposed to be the one that rambles angrily about strange topics?" I ask with a smile.

"I'm sure you have opinions on throw pillows."

"I do."

"And?" I sigh.

"I hate to admit, I agree." He laughs, wrapping an arm around my waist. "We should start a pillow brand. Comfortable throw pillows only. Function over fashion."

"What's your take on throw blankets?"

"Depends." His lips are brushing mine and my voice is breathy. My mind wanders from the topic at hand and is moving to the feel of his warm body on mine. "Sometimes they're great. Sometimes they're all holey, and it doesn't even keep you warm. The point is to be cozy."

"Got it. Cozy throw blankets only."

"Tight-knit," I say, but my mind is already in the quiet place, my body submitting to his. "Hey, Vic?"

"Yeah?" he asks through a kiss, soft and sweet and slow.

"I'm ready." The words are a whisper, and if he didn't lock his body, if he didn't stop completely, then I'd think there was a chance he didn't hear me.

But he does, so I think he did.

"Ready?"

"I'm ready, Vic." There's a long pause. I don't need to elaborate. He knows.

"Are you sure?" I wait a moment, too, because knowing Vic the way I do now, I know if I answer instantly, he'll question it. So I think.

Am I sure?

Do I want to give this last piece of me to this man? This piece that, despite my best efforts, has been kept safe for 28 years?

Is it time?

Do I trust him?

Shit, do I trust myself to know what the fuck I'm doing?

The answer to all these questions is the same.

I knew as soon as he stuck up for me. Hell, I think I knew that first day when I dumped out my thoughts under the haze of painkillers and adrenaline. And I definitely knew the day he took care of me when Nicky got hurt.

And I knew with every moment that he took the time to teach me, show me, and help me learn myself. The fact he put in the effort, took the paces, refused to rush it.

I knew.

So I give the only answer I have.

"Yeah, honey. I'm sure."

He breathes, and then his lips are on mine. Sweet. Tentative. Nervous.

God.

Then we're kissing, tasting each other, relearning each other, knowing this is it, this is the last lap.

My gut pinches at that thought, and I throw it away.

I can't have that right now.

Breaking the kiss, he takes my hands and leads me to his

bedroom, still the same black and white all over, but now for some reason, it's cozy despite that. Home. After nights spent here, memories made here, it seems like... an extension of Vic, from that first day when I woke up hungover and in a strange man's shirt to now, where that strange man's fingers are helping me take my shirt off as I push my skirt down.

That makes me giggle.

"What?" Vic says, smiling as he works on his clothes. I think we're past the point of a seductive striptease, the mindset of sex-hungry teens taking over. Clothes off, into the bed.

"I was just thinking how, just a month ago, I woke up in a strange man's bed. Now that strange man is about to deflower me." He laughs too, a big laugh cutting through the tension I didn't realize needed cutting.

Is that normal? Laughing so much when you're about to have sex? I feel like all I do is giggle and laugh around Vic. Before I can question that more, though, my panties are off. I'm moving, lying in his giant bed with the boring white duvet cover and watching him finish undressing, dark skin revealed inch by inch.

God, he's gorgeous.

"Yeah, well, before I get to the deflowering, I need to acquaint myself with your body," he says, those white teeth coming out as he joins me on the bed, moving so he's kneeling between my legs.

"Yeah?"

"Oh, yeah," he says, a thick finger moving up my inner thigh, the feeling causing flames to chase the skin as it moves. "God, you're soaking already." A finger slips inside me without hesitation. My back arches with a moan as it moves, swiping that spot inside me that has my belly heating.

"I wonder if you'll always be like this, so ready for me, responsive to me." I don't let his words sit in my mind too long, letting them flow the way he's taught me to, avoiding distraction.

Something tells me I could overthink and dissect those words better than anyone.

"Maybe," is all I say, the words coming out breathy and needy as his thumb brushes my clit.

"I'll make it my mission, Gabrielle." And then another finger moves into me, stretching me, fingers scissoring in a way he hasn't done before but that has my entire body feeling too hot, too warm, too sensitive.

"Ahh!" I shout, bucking my hips to get more. "Vic!"

"I know, kitten. You'll get it. I need to get you ready first. Want this to be good for you." He knows me and my body and mind so well, words aren't necessary. I let my body speak. I use my hips to ride his fingers, bucking to get his thumb to circle my clit, moving my leg to wrap his body, to get more.

A third finger slides in, and I'm so blissfully full. Words don't work as I watch his eyes glued to where his fingers are fucking me, watching all three disappear and reappear, watching my hips move to ride them.

"Almost ready, kitten. Just one more..." He has a wicked smile, and I should question him, but I trust him. I'm glad I do when he moves back, fingers buried deep, and his mouth circles my clit, sucking hard.

My hips buck, and a deep, primal, needy sound falls from me as he builds that pressure, the water beyond the dam rising until it almost, almost...

And then he's out. Off of me. Leaning over to his bedside table and rustling. I mewl like the kitten he's named me, but then he's back, kneeling between my legs, a silver packet in his fingers.

It's time.

He stares at me, eyes roving down my body that won't stay still, so needy, sensitized.

"Are you sure?" he asks. I don't even hesitate. Not for a moment.

"Yes, Vic." He groans gently at my response, palming his hard cock. The sight has my hips bucking again, trying to rush through this, to get to what I absolutely need at this moment.

As he opens the condom, grabbing it between his teeth and

tearing it in a way that makes my mind go fuzzy with lust for a second, I remember what I need him to know before we do this.

"Vic, I don't want—" He stops all movement as he's rolling a condom on. My eyes are locked onto his cock, and holy shit. "Holy shit."

"What?" His face is one of panic.

"That!" I say. I can feel the skin of my face stretching as my eyes go wide. "That thing is way too big!" He sits back on his heels, and then, the asshole he is, he finishes rolling the condom to the base and starts stroking it. I bite my lip and forget what I was saying.

"You've held it before, Gabi."

"Holding it is different from it going *into my vagina!*"

"It's been in your mouth," he says with that same cocky smile.

"Yeah, but that doesn't hurt."

"This won't hurt either."

"You can't promise that!"

"You're good and ready, kitten. You want me to keep getting you ready?" He looks down at my pussy that I know is dripping wet already. Well prepared for... that. Despite that, I think about it because, in all honesty, I wouldn't hate that. He interrupts my thoughts about extended preparation. "You were made for me, Gabi." My breathing stops. "It'll fit, and it won't hurt, not that way. You were made to take my cock, kitten." His eyes have gone dark, moving from my pussy to my tits rising with each labored breath, to my lips parted, to my eyes.

Holy shit, that was hot.

"Okay, Vic," I say, and he smiles at me, moving back so he's got a hand on either side of me in the bed.

"What were you saying before?"

My mind is hazy.

I was saying I wanted him to fuck me, right?

Get this thing over with

Get onto the fun part.

I was saying—

"You said, 'I don't want,' and then you had a panic attack about whether I'll fit in your pussy." Said pussy responds with a clench. This man and his mouth.

"I uh—"

"What don't you want?"

"Please, Vic. I—"

"I need you to talk to me, kitten. What don't you want?" A moment of embarrassment crosses me, but then I remember that I'm about to lose my virginity at 28, so I've really crossed all embarrassment hurdles at this point, ya know? Shit, I met this man because I tried to masturbate in the shower and broke my wrist.

"I don't want slow and sweet." My words come out in a whisper.

"What?"

"I don't want a sweet first time. I want it good. I want... us." He smiles. He smiles big, that smile I love with his white teeth and his dark skin stretching around them.

God, I could fall for this man based on that smile alone.

I knock it out of my mind.

That's dangerous territory.

"What do you want, Gabi?"

"I—" My face is burning.

"After all we've been through?" he teases, and it feels good. It feels normal. It feels less scary. So, I open my mouth and let fly.

"I want rough. I want... hard. I want it all, Vic. I want... you." Because if I only get this once with you, I want it all. I want to remember this for the rest of my life. I don't want sweet because I think if I get sweet, I'll fall and shatter irreparably, broken for any other man.

I don't say that part aloud.

Partly because Vic's head has dropped next to my head and he's groaning into my ear.

"Fuck, Gabi. Fuck. You can't say things like that."

"Why not?"

"Why are we having this conversation now?" He laughs. "I'm naked, ready to fuck you—"

"Then do it!"

"We need to cover this."

"Then do it, and then fuck me!"

"I don't want to hurt you, kitten." He's sweet. I love that about him.

Stop, Gabrielle Nicolette! Stop!

"You won't. Please, Vic. Now. I need this." He looks at me, eyes telling me things neither of us will say aloud, maybe ever. Then he nods, accepting the silent conversation.

And then one hand is moving from the bed.

He's moving to his cock.

He's lining it up with me.

But first, he rubs the head from my clit to my entrance and back again, up and down, getting himself wet, teasing me.

"Oh, my god, fuck, Vic. I need you. Please."

"You feel so fucking good. Not even inside of you, and I could come like this."

"Yeah," I breathe. His eyes lock to mine, despite how heavy they feel. Heavy with lust and need and so much more.

That's why I want hard and rough.

That's why I don't want sweet.

I think sweet could break me.

He's already broken through my mind. The wall keeping him out of my heart is getting flimsier by the moment. That kind of intimacy with this man? I think that would do it.

And I have to wonder for a small moment if this is already too far. If I should back out, if I should say no, because this means something despite what I've always thought and what I've always said.

Shit. It means something. The realization crashes through me.

I don't want it to mean something.

So, I tell myself it doesn't and I do the only thing I can think of.

My hand moves to Vic's ass, pushing gently right as he rubs the head of his cock down and it notches.

And he slides in an inch.

It's thick. I feel fuller than I expected as it stretches me in all directions. But the feeling isn't like when you open your jaw at the dentist and it aches, overstretched and uncomfortable.

The ache instead is in my belly, deep in my belly. A building ache I recognize, an ache I need to satisfy.

"Vic, oh god."

"Jesus, kitten. So fucking perfect. You okay?" I don't want him to be sweet. I don't want him worrying about me.

Maybe I should have lost it to some random frat kid who wouldn't have cared.

But then my eyes meet his and I see everything in them. That playboy curtain is pulled away and in there... he cares. He's worried. He's concerned about me.

And I think it's more. It has to be more.

"I'm good," I breathe. "More." His breath puffs in my ear, the air moving the tiny hairs at the nape of my neck. "I need more, Vic." He growls into my ear, a primal noise I've never heard from him, a noise that has me clamping down—on him now because he's halfway inside of me.

Slowly he moves, inch by inch, until he's seated, filling me in a way I've never felt before.

It's exquisite.

Mind melding.

It's life-changing.

"Mine," he whispers in my ear and this time, it's my heart that clenches. That word.

I know now I'd give away every part of me for him to mean it.

"Made for me," he groans as he pulls back and then bucks back into me, pelvis grinding on my clit as he does. My hands move to his back, holding him close, and I move my face to his neck because I don't want to see it. I can't see it.

I don't think he means I was made to fit him. Not my body, at least.

I think this because I feel it too.

I feel it.

It's so right.

It's so right, it has to be wrong. This can't be. He can't be. It makes no sense.

Part of me wonders for a moment if this is just how it is. What would I know? Maybe sex is always like this, always this perfect and life-changing and beautiful. Perhaps this is what all the fuss is about. Maybe this is why people become addicted, why some people will do anything to get this feeling.

He pulls back and thrusts in hard, and my head snaps back to the bed, leaving his shoulder as a moan leaves me.

My eyes lock to his, his mouth open just a bit as he looks at me, and it's there.

I see what I was afraid to see. Or maybe I was scared I wouldn't see it there—either way.

He feels it.

This isn't normal.

He knows it too.

Something is happening. Something bigger than just two bodies meeting in an exchange of pleasure, the loss of some fictional innocence.

My mind wants to mull over it. Wants to go off to some other planet to stew on this revelation, the way I always have been able to, but his eyes... they keep me grounded. His eyes on me, his body in mine, this melding, and I'm on the earth, indefinitely. That feeling of losing myself I always ache for, the reason I go dancing, the reason I read... I have it. Right now, in this moment, with him.

Then he's moving his hips in small circles while he's planted inside me and everything changes.

My breathing goes chaotic.

My vision goes blurry.

The heat builds in my belly, builds in my lower back.

"That's it, Gabi. I feel you tightening around me. Fuck, so good, so fucking tight. Jesus. Perfection. All mine."

"Oh, god, Vic, Vic. Vic!" I say, chanting his name, a prayer on my lips. A prayer to the orgasm god. A prayer to my body, a farewell maybe, because I think when I come I'm going to explode into stardust, never to become a physical being again.

It would be an excellent way to go.

"Fuck yeah, Gabi. Come on my cock." That's all it takes, his words. As always.

Vic's voice, his words, his command—that's all I need to explode around him, his name on my lips, my vision turning into stars and black galaxies as my head crashes back into the bed. My body arches into his as he slams in deep, moaning my name in my ear as he follows me into infinity.

And for a moment, it's like we're both vapor, traveling together through the world, no longer in our bodies but forever connected.

THIRTY

-Vic-

Today was a bad day. It's Monday night, the day after everything between Gabi and me changed. I woke with her in my bed, wishing I could do this every morning. Wishing this were our typical routine—kissing her hair as I leave, telling her the door will lock behind her and to have a good day with Cassie.

It was the kind of morning that boded an excellent day.

But today was a horrible one.

I'm grateful that those are few and far between, but today was rough.

A car crash.

A child not properly restrained.

That child in intensive care, and when she wakes, she'll be without a mother.

Talking to the father, the husband. Having to explain. Seeing his face.

It's not the sounds that stick with me.

Some doctors remember the sounds: the cries, the screams, the pleading.

I've always been observant. I've always watched faces.

Those are what keep me up at night. The disbelief. The anger. The pain.

No matter the emotion scrawled across their faces, there's always pain.

I walk out quietly, a defeated player in this game. Tomorrow is another day, but not a day everyone gets to see. Every day I'm here, I'm reminded of this cruel reality.

I need to live my life.

I've wasted so much of it.

Arguing with my parents.

Hiding from them.

Living by their standards.

Blowing their standards out of the water.

It wasn't until the past few years I finally gave in to *me*. I finally started to live life for myself, knowing how fragile it is. Emergency medicine will do that to you. Reality check. A harsh one. But part of me didn't understand that giving in to me and fighting what they wanted for me didn't mean I had to avoid every aspect of what they wanted for me, like having a woman in my life, a partner. I fought that for too long.

Sitting in my car, I lean forward, bracing my head on the steering wheel. I hate this. I hate it. I wish every day was broken bones and mild allergic reactions. Panic attacks and kids shoving shit up their noses. Things I can fix.

Days like this make me wonder if my cousin doesn't have the right idea—plastic surgery is dangerous but expected and controlled.

But I live for the unknown. Live for the chaos.

I just need... a home base.

A safe place.

My normal routine of calling up Ben, going to my apartment, and getting drunk off my ass sounds... empty. Not because my friend isn't loyal, wouldn't do it in a heartbeat and stay just a little more sober than me to make sure I'm safe, but because it's a Band-Aid.

This morning I woke up with Gabi wrapped around me and kissed her head, leaving before she was even fully awake. The night before was everything, and so much more.

Knowing there's the potential of that sweetness, that life and energy, and adoration, I know a Band-Aid won't work tonight.

I need more.

Without thinking, without it going through my filter, my hand reaches out to my phone, grabbing it and putting it behind the wheel so I can see it, head still on top. I scroll and then tap, putting the phone to my ear.

It rings.

I wait, breath held.

I don't know what I'll do if—

"Hello?" Her voice is a balm.

"Gabi." It's all I say. All I can say. I think if I say more, the facade will break.

"Vic, what's wrong?" She knows. How the fuck does she know?

Because she's Gabi.

"Can I see you tonight?" No filter. The words tumble out. Maybe I should be embarrassed. And maybe I am, maybe I will be in the morning. But right now...

"I'll be at your place in ten." I breathe. It feels like the first time I've done it in hours, days. "Or would you rather come to my place?" I start to calculate distances. "I'm at Cassie's, but I can be at your place in ten, my place... seven? Maybe eight?" There's rustling on the other end, whispered words to who I assume is Cassie, keys moving.

I forgot she was there, helping Cassie make favors for her wedding. Maid of honor duties. Shit.

"You don't have to leave."

"Already sitting in my car, honey. Just need to know where to go." Of course, the following words don't pass a filter either, but that's okay.

"Have you drunk anything? At Cassie's?"

"Just a Sprite." A sigh.

"Your place. I'll be there in ten," I say. I'm not sure why. Her place is... lived in. Cozy. Comfortable.

And right now, I need that.

"Okay. Vic?" Her voice is hesitant.

"Yeah?" I'm lifting my head now, putting the key in the ignition.

"Are you going to be okay? To drive? I can—"

"I'm good, kitten. See you in ten." And then I hang up before I admit anything more.

I get there in nine minutes, the traffic lights in my favor. I park and head to the front desk where I'm buzzed up before climbing the three flights of stairs.

I need the mental break.

I need the physical exertion.

I need to be reminded that I'm alive.

It's not enough.

My knuckles rap on the door, and I wait.

I count.

Nine seconds.

She was standing close. She was waiting for me.

When she opens the door, her hair has one small ponytail on top of her head, the other half down. She's wearing some oversized band tee that swallows her and a pair of Lucky Charms pajama shorts. I don't even have time to wonder where one gets those. Or why she's wearing them. Or if she went out in public in them.

Her eyes are worried.

"Hey," she says, her voice a whisper.

And I break.

I don't know the last time I broke. Med school?

I stumble forward, pulling her into my arms, my face going into that stupid little ponytail. One hand goes around her waist, another into her hair, and I breathe her in.

My mind barely registers that her arms move, shutting the door behind me before wrapping me up, tight. The hold so tight, it's almost suffocating, but it's what I need. Like one of those weighted blankets kids use for anxiety and security.

Except human and warm.

Alive.

She's alive.

That woman might not be. That child might not be. But Gabi is.

There is sunshine in the world and it is personified in Gabrielle Nicolette Mancini.

Everything clicks then.

I need this woman more than I need to breathe.

Somehow, in this crazy scheme, I fell for her. I fell for Gabi and I fucking need her. Right now is proof in living color.

"It's okay," she says, and that cements it. Not "what's wrong" or "what happened," but "it's okay."

We stand there for long minutes, and I breathe in her citrus scent, her curls tickling my nose, her tiny hands running up and down my back. Just being.

It takes me a few minutes to figure out where I am.

At Gabi's.

I drove here in a daze.

Accident.

Bad day.

I love this woman.

"Can we sit down?" When I say the words, the sound is scratched from my throat like I haven't spoken in years, decades. But once again, she doesn't need to say a word, simply loosening her grip and leading me to the ridiculous velvet couch in the living room.

She tries to sit next to me, not even inches away, but I can't take that. I need her on me, to feel her heartbeat and hear her breaths entering and leaving her chest. I need her here. So I pull her into my lap and hold her there, curled on me, head on my chest, my hand under the thin tee shirt so I can feel her breaths, count her heartbeats on her back.

She's alive. She's okay.

We don't speak for a long time, her chest breathing slowly against mine. Finally, she does, not moving her head to look at me, not moving her body, just in case the answer is no.

"Are you good?"

"Yeah... I'm good. Now." Thanks to you.

"Do you... do you want to talk about it?"

I don't, but I do. I need to.

"There was a car accident today. A bad one. Mother DOA. The child is in intensive care. No idea how she's going to do. I had to... break the news." Her chest moves with a silent shutter.

"Oh, Vic. I'm... I'm so sorry. That's horrible."

"Part of the job." That's what I'm expected to say.

"Stop. I'm sure that doesn't make it easier." No, it doesn't. I'm always prepared for the worst—a small part of my brain knows that something can go wrong at any point and I can lose a patient. But knowing it and having it happen? Knowing someone came to you, was brought to you for you to aid, to save them, and you failed? It never gets easier. Never.

In the morning, I'll be further from it. I'll have perspective, and it won't ache. But right now...

"I need a distraction," I say, using the only words I can.

"What?"

"I need a distraction, Gabi." I pause, staring at her. She's leaned back a bit, legs straddling me, staring at me. "I need a distraction." She keeps staring at me, and it's not lost on me that the tables have turned—I'm usually the one keeping her from her distractions. Now I'm asking for one of my own.

She doesn't question that, though.

Doesn't argue.

All she says is, "I can do that," and her arms are behind my neck, pulling me to her, her lips pressing to mine.

All is right in the world.

Chaos, catastrophe, disappointment, and despair are things I can survive. I can face uncertainty and fear. I can do it all, so long as this woman is by my side to put me back together when I break.

My hands move under her shirt, pulling it up frantically. I need her skin on mine. I need to feel she's here. I need to know she's mine.

She stands quickly and I move my scrub bottoms down until they pool at my feet before she's back on me, straddling me once more as I sit on the couch, hands to her full hips.

"Protection," I say, and a part of me hates that I do. This might feel like high school, the frenzy and the need, but we're adults... and I have nothing on me.

"I'm on the pill," she says. Thank fuck.

"I'm clean."

"I trust you, Vic," she says and then reaches down, grabbing me, guiding me to where she's already dripping for me.

I should say no.

We should skip it—she's probably sore after last night.

But when she starts to lower herself, pressing her forehead to mine, I know it's a lost cause. So instead, I use my hand to guide her, slow her descent. My breathing is erratic, somehow in time with hers.

Like we're one.

"Easy, kitten," I say when she tries to sink down. "Are you sore?"

"I need you," she says, and this fucking woman. My hands tighten, stopping.

"Need to know you'll talk to me. Are you sore, Gabi?"

"Vic, I—"

"Gabi."

"Only a little." She wiggles her hips, trying to get me into her needy cunt now. What started as a distraction for me has turned into a need for her. I love that.

"We do this my way, yeah?"

"Will you fuck me?"

"No." She pouts. Actually, full-on pouts while she's got my cock in her.

That's when I know. That's when I know I'm going to make her mine forever.

"Trust me, yeah?" I ask, eyes on hers. She nods, forehead rubbing against mine. I move to press my lips to hers as I slowly, torturously slowly, lower her down onto me until she's sitting in my lap, filled with me.

She's mine.

Nothing's between us, just Gabi and Vic, together in the way we were meant to me.

It sounds fucking flowery and ridiculous even to my own mind, but it's like the world has pushed her to me, and this is where I was always meant to end up.

She breathes in deep, the intake moving her curls into my face, her breasts into my chest.

"You good?" She doesn't answer, just another deep breath, this one shakier. "Gabi."

"I have never felt better in my life, Victor." I don't know if I've ever heard her call me that.

She knows.

It's not because she's sore; it's not because it feels good. Her breath has gone shaky, her mind has gone blank, and her voice has become low because the same part of me that recognizes her? There's a part of her that knows me as well.

I don't have any words.

So I just say, "Yeah," and then my hands move, rocking her back and forth, her clit moving on me. We're close, faces together, her chest on mine, lips brushing but not kissing, and all the while, I can't keep my eyes off of hers.

"Vic," she says. It's building in her, each grind of her clit on my pelvis.

"I know, baby, me too," I pant, a hand going to her back to pull her chest closer to me.

This is all I want right now. Her and me and us, together, reminded that life goes on, and it's our choice how we live it.

She tries to dig her knees in, lift herself, get movement, but I don't let her. So instead, I keep my hand on her hip, keeping her in place, continuing to rock her back and forth on me. "Like this, Gabi. Just like this." Her breathing is erratic as she keeps her eyes locked on mine, and when it builds, I know.

"Vic, I think—"

"I know, kitten. Go. Take me with you," I say, and I press my lips to hers as she clamps around me, moaning into our kiss. My orgasm follows close behind, spectacular in a different way than the night before, if not better, but that's not what I'll remember for the rest of my life about this night.

Not by a long shot.

THIRTY-ONE

-Vic-

"Have you eaten?" Her voice is soft, quiet. Gabi's curled up into me like a cat, like her namesake. She cleaned up long ago, returning to me in my tee shirt. Something about that was a comfort, her knowing I wasn't quite ready to move on, to recognize the world continued spinning. Knowing I wanted to sit in this little bubble where it was just the two of us for a few minutes longer.

"No," I say, moving hair to the other side of her neck, revealing the soft skin there. "You really are a kitten. Always curled into me."

"It's comfy. You're comfy."

"No complaints here."

"I like dogs better. Dogs are cuddly but also fun."

"Not a fan of dogs," I say, hand swiping down that expanse of neck. Her body tightens—ticklish, I think.

"You want food?" I want to say no. I want to stay here forever. But instead, my stomach growls. "You want food," she says with a giggle before getting up. I let her but grab her hand when she's standing, pulling her to me for a quick kiss. When I let go, she's smiling at me. "You stay there. I'll make sandwiches."

Again, part of me wants to argue, tell her no, stay, we'll order takeout, or I'll starve, or I'll just eat you until I'm full, but she has that look about her. She might be stubborn and goofy and spacy, but Gabi loves to take care of the people who are important to her.

The people she loves.

So instead, I reach over to the coffee table, grab one of her books covered with some dude half-naked, and flip. "So this is what you read when I'm not available?" I say with laughter in my voice. I laugh outright when her curls spin, her face looking at me and the book in my hand.

"That's... I..."

"No worries, babe. I know you like to read the fun stuff," I say, flipping until I reach what I can only assume is an intimate scene. "Jeez, Gabi—you read some filthy shit." A blush blooms on her face before she ignores me, opening the fridge door and hiding behind it.

"'You want my finger in your ass, baby,'" I quote, reading off the page. "Fuck, no wonder you like it when I talk to you." I keep flipping as she argues.

"Vic! Put that down! Stop... reading it!"

"Why? Are you embarrassed?"

"No." The word comes out quick, without thought. "Maybe. Yes? It's a little embarrassing."

"Does reading it make you happy?" She leans back from the fridge to look at me before nodding. "That's all that matters." I keep flipping, landing on another scene where he's fucking her on the kitchen floor. Fuck, I can see the appeal. "Does it turn you on?" I ask, genuinely curious, not even looking up at her as I continue to read.

A clatter has me looking up as she bends to grab a dropped bottle of mustard. I smile. Good to know I can still fluster her. I hope I never lose the touch, always able to do it. It's cute. It would be a shame to never see it again.

"I... uh..." The blush is a full-blown red running down her neck as she busies herself with condiments and lunch meat.

"Good to know, Gabi."

"This is so embarrassing," she says, grabbing bread from a high up shelf. The very bottom of her ass cheeks peek out and *fuck*.

For a split second, I think there's nothing in this life I wouldn't do to have this every day. To come home from a shit day to her, sit with her while the world stops shaking. Laugh with her while she walks around her kitchen in my shirt and go to bed holding her close.

We really need to talk. And soon.

"Nothing to be embarrassed about." She rolls her eyes as she spreads mayonnaise on bread. "You can see my search history. Watch what I do when you're not around." I don't tell her that search history has been lonely lately, my mind wandering to a film of her moaning my name, coming on my fingers, on my mouth, on my cock...

"What?!"

"If you want to, you can. Nothing to be ashamed of," I say, putting the book down to watch her.

"That's..."

"Or we could watch it together." My voice goes low even to my own ear, and looking at her body, I can see she doesn't hate that idea. "Noted," I say, smiling. She just rolls her eyes as if I didn't see her interest, continuing to make sandwiches and pull out chips.

She looks... nervous now, though. Like her mind is somewhere that she's trying to get the courage to say out loud.

I could push, but instead, I wait. She'll speak when she's ready.

And then she does, keeping her eyes and hands busy with our late dinner while she speaks.

"So I think... I think it's time for Cassie to match you. You've, uh, passed. With flying colors. In my opinion." My eyebrows come together as I watch her, confused, but she doesn't look my way.

I've passed.

Cassie can match me?

I play along still.

"You... think so? You think I'm a good enough man to set up? Think I pass the strict standards?" I say, joking, trying to get a smile to break her nerves. Why is she so nervous?

"Well yeah. You're a bit of a mess, but you mean well. And our.. arrangement is finished. You know." There it is. She thinks this is done, that we're done.

Not if I have anything to do with it.

But still, I need to see where she's going with this. I'm Gabi's first—and I'll be damned if I'm not her last—but she's inexperienced. She has set ideas for how this will go and no matter what happens, I don't want her to look back and wonder. For us to be celebrating our 20th wedding anniversary and her questioning if she just fell into this because it was comfortable, because it was what made sense.

And with the way her brain works, it would eat at her—at us.

"I guess," is all I say, leaving the ball in her court.

It's clear I need a better plan than just telling Gabi she's mine forever. I look around at the books around me, cheap, mismatched bookshelves stacked and stuffed with paperbacks and hardcovers, a rainbow of colors and textures but all containing a story. A story of a couple who was meant to be, who fell for each other, and, from what I know of what Vivi used to read, get their fairy tale ending.

This is what Gabi wants.

She wants the fairy tale ending.

She wants the lead chasing her at an airport and the boombox outside the window.

She might be rainbows and butterflies and chaos and, in a way, nonchalance. We might have jumped into this looking for casual and found forever. But regardless, she wants that big moment.

And she deserves it.

I just need to figure out how.

Her words interrupt my masterminding.

"And I think I might... have Cassie match me too. You know. Since I'm not... a virgin anymore."

I can almost hear a needle scratching a record.

I'm sorry, what the fuck?

She keeps talking, not taking in my shocked expression. "I told Cassie that if I vetted you, at the end she could match me. That was my deal with her. She was worried... about me getting attached."

The fuck she is. *You are attached, kitten. To me. You gotta work if you want to get rid of me.*

But then my mind drifts to my conversation with Vivian.

"Women need to date. It should be a prerequisite to marriage. You need to date around. How else are you going to know he's the one?"

Does Gabi need that? To date other men in order to know that we are the end game? I know she's dated before, but it has to be different. If I lock Gabi down and tell her we're it, will she one day look back and wonder if she made a mistake?

I know she's it for me, but I've had... others for comparison. I know to the bottom of my soul that Gabi is it for me. But does she know the same unshakable truth?

My own foundation is quaking as I watch this beautiful mess that is us waver before my eyes.

"Is, uh... Is that what you want?" My gut churns as she continues to stack sandwiches quietly, cutting them on an angle and placing the sandwiches onto the plates already piled with chips.

She's avoiding the question.

She's avoiding my eyes.

Maybe she's in Vivi's camp. Maybe she wants the freedom to explore. Maybe she needs this. To sate some kind of curiosity before coming back to me. But no matter how she answers, she will come back to me.

She's mine.

"I don't know. I think so?" Her eyes are still on the mess she's made as she tidies, putting away things in the fridge and cabinets. Anything to avoid looking at me. "Maybe... I don't know. Cassie's good at her job. Who knows what's out there, you know? She wants me to explore." Her words are both a balm and a burn, a comfort in that she seems to want to explore for Cassie's sake, and a burn because she's not instantly saying no, admitting she's mine.

Then her eyes meet mine.

And it's there.

My girl. She's my girl. She might think she can hide her true thoughts behind carefully curated words, lift and reinforce that filter she uses for everyone else, but I know the truth. I can see through it, tear it to shreds and see what she's too afraid to say.

She's mine.

She's also so fucking stubborn that I think if I tell her that, if I tell her she's mine and I'll cut the hands off any man who tried to change that with surgical precision, she'll go insane. I could lose her.

I need to make a plan. I need to make her see. She needs to know I'm all in. This was never just an arrangement.

She needs a grand gesture. Chicks love that shit.

I smile to myself, smile at her, smile at this jacked-up situation. But I also smile knowing I've got her. She's mine. I just have to convince her of it.

"You gonna come feed your man?" I say, and she smiles too, bringing two plates to the couch, my tee grazing the tops of her thighs.

It's all going to be just fine.

THIRTY-TWO

-Gabi-

THE DAY after Vic stayed at my place, I walk into work with two cups, both scribbled on the side with the orders Cassie and I have perfected to fit us after a million and seven orders over the past two years. But for the first time since that stomach bug last winter, I don't even want mine. My stomach churns, but I'm not sick.

Not traditionally so, at least.

Because Vic wasn't there when I woke up this morning.

It was just me, in my bed, with too many pillows. Alone.

No note, no text. Nothing.

My stomach is churning, not because I'm sick, but with the knowledge that it's over.

But Cassie would know instantly if I skipped getting our drinks, and I'd like to put off this conversation as long as I can.

This morning, I came into the office and dumped my bag, rushing out of the office with a shout to Cassie about grabbing coffees before she could interrogate me. That's the problem with a boss-slash-best friend who decodes people for a living. The chances of her not realizing I'm a mess are slim to none. I'm taking whatever measures I can to avoid it and also give myself time to get my mind in check.

Placing the cup on her desk, I'm relieved when she just waves a hand at the Bluetooth earbuds she's wearing and mouths a thank you. I have at least thirty minutes I note when I check her schedule. Thirty minutes to collect myself, to plan distractions or an excuse.

Losing myself in notes and spreadsheets, I make it an hour. An hour before a black wrapped ass is sitting on the edge of my desk. Cassie.

Cassie is in one of her classy mega-bitch outfits, as I call them.

She's staring at me.

Not in the way a boss stares at an employee.

In the way a friend stares at a friend she knows needs her.

Fuck, fuck, fuck.

I go over the plan in my head.

There's a chance—slim, but it's there—that I'll be able to get away without her noticing. That I'll be able to tell her my news, my decision, and she'll be so excited, she won't see...

"Hey, Gab," Cassie says, staring at me.

"Hey, did the call go well? Should I add her to the onboarding process?" She nods, but her eyes tell me she's not in the conversation.

Shit.

"Yeah, she's good. But... you."

Okay. It's game time. Let's go, Gabrielle. You can do this. You once convinced your mother that it was Gio's fault you dropped an entire platter of bruschetta in the pool, even though she watched you do it and he wasn't even outside.

"I'm ready."

"Ready?"

"To be matched." Her eyes widen, huge, shocked. "It's time."

"It's time?" Information only. Don't go any deeper than that. She doesn't need to know...

"Vic's and my arrangement is over. We've... well, you know. All is good. I'm... ready." She stares. She had to know this was coming.

Oh yeah? Then why did it take you so much by surprise? the voice in my head asks.

I don't dare speak while she stares at me. I don't know what will leave my mouth if I do, but after 28 years of living in this mind, I know it wouldn't help the cause.

"And you want to be... matched." I nod. "With a man," she says, clarifying further.

"Well, I'm not into women." The words fall out of my mouth, word vomit. "Not that I have a problem with women. I think they're beautiful! Way too beautiful. Women kind of scare me, to be honest. Plus, I just figured out how my own parts work. I don't think I'd be too good at—"

"Gabi, shut up." I shut up. "What's going on?" Her eyes have gone from confused to soft, and fuck, I hate it.

I hate having good friends.

Honestly, they advertise friends as these great things that you can drink with and have fun with and gossip with and share clothes with, but... for one, my boobs would never fit in any of Cassie's clothes. And her feet are bigger than mine. And my best friend since first grade, Paige, moved across the damn country, taking all of the clothes that *did* fit me with her, thanks a lot.

But they conveniently forget to tell you that friends—the good ones who know you and understand you—know when you're lying. They know when you're falling apart on the inside and don't know what to do with the pieces, even if all you want to do is ignore that fact...

Cassie is a good one.

And my pieces are falling apart.

"It's over."

It's all I say.

I could elaborate.

Our arrangement is over.

Our fun times are over.

We had sex and I'm not a virgin and then we had sex again, even though I wasn't a virgin anymore and there wasn't a real reason to do it, but we did, and it wasn't rough and amazing, but sweet and intimate and life-changing and then I pushed him too far by testing him.

And when I told him it was time, when I put it out there to get his reaction, he said... okay.

I could tell her that my brain understood this was temporary. My stupid, broken brain—*no, not broken, I remind myself. My brain is...*

Beautiful. The word isn't in my voice, not in the voice of inner me. Instead, it's Vic's voice saying it. It accompanies the memory of him brushing my bangs aside and getting mad when I called myself broken.

And now I really am, but not in the way I initially thought.

I'm broken, and I'm the only person to blame.

"It's over, Cassie," is all I say, and then I fall apart.

We don't work that day. Instead, Cassie calls in reinforcements in the form of Luke bringing ice cream cake and forks and wine and leaving with our keys and a promise to come pick us up when Cassie calls him.

Sure, we could have gone to one of our apartments.

But sometimes you want a change in scenery for your mental breakdowns, you know?

Cassie digs her fork into one of the creamy blue swirls of frosting on the side of the cake. "Okay. Let's have it." I sigh.

"I don't—"

"Shut up. Start from sex. How was it?" I can practically feel my eyes glaze over. "Did he take care of you?"

"What does that... mean?"

"I assume you came. That look on your face..." I blush. "Jesus, Gabi. So it was good." I nod.

"It was good."

"And he took care of you after? Did it hurt?"

"Yes and no, not really."

"I've heard the longer you wait, the less it hurts. Could also have been the lack of a fumbling 16-year-old boy. Plus, you'd been... primed... over the last month." And then I laugh, a feeling my body is dying for. It feels good. Good to laugh and not want to cry. "So it was good, and he took care of you. What happened after? That was it? You had the talk and shook hands?"

I eat cake to avoid her.

Ice cream cake really is superior to normal cake. The chocolate crunchies? The creamy frosting? The ice cream? Perfect combo.

"Gabi..."

"We had sex on Sunday. After family dinner." She stares at me, stunned. I spent Monday at her place, doing wedding prep stuff with her, and didn't bring it up once.

"Why didn't you say anything?" My gut drops. I didn't tell her because...

"Because I thought if I spoke it out, that would make it real. If I told you we'd had sex, that our arrangement was complete, it would be over. And I... I didn't like how that made me feel. Then he called me last night and... well. You know. I left."

"Yeah, what happened with that?"

"He had a shitty day in the ER. Tragedy. It was... intense. He was upset." She nods, understanding.

"Okay, so you comforted him and then..."

"Well, uh... Well..." God, why is this so embarrassing?

"You had sex again."

I avoid her eyes.

"Gabi..." Her voice is soft, no longer digging as her hand goes to my wrist.

"We had sex again. And it was... different. The first time I told him I wanted rough, and I wanted good. I didn't want delicate feelings. But..." My voice cracks, the sound reflecting how I feel inside.

"Oh, Gabi." But I've started. The words roll like a rock tumbling down a mountain. My only option is to let it go and stay out of its way before it crushes me.

"It was... slow. And sweet. And it... it meant more."

"Honey..."

"To me."

"But not to Vic?" I shrug.

"I didn't... I didn't want to be a pain. I don't want to be a clingy girl. The one who loses her virginity and then gets attached. We were... a hook up when you boil it down. There was more, of course... but... I'm not stupid to not understand that's what we were."

"I saw you guys, though. You weren't just that. You were..."

"I brought up us ending to feel him out."

"Oh, Gabi..." Cassie says, and it's almost annoyed, disappointed. "Men don't take well to games."

"I wasn't playing games! I just... I wanted to know..."

"If he'd try to keep you?" My eyes snap to her.

"Luke did everything under the sun to try and convince you to stay."

"Vic isn't Luke, babe."

"Yeah, but—"

"No. No buts. One thing I've learned over the years is no two men are the same—for better or worse." I open my mouth to speak but she keeps going. "I have two things to say. You're going to listen." I widen my eyes because Cassie is bossy, but not usually like this. And not usually with me. "One, and it kills me to give any man other than Luke props, but the way that man looks at you? It is not 'taking someone's virginity and calling it a day.' I'd know. That's the look my high school boyfriend gave me when he took mine." She rolls her eyes, and I try not to laugh. "It's more. Two, when you set a man up to force him to give you an answer you want to hear but you lead him to the wrong one? *He will give you the wrong answer*, babe. Men are simple, stupid creatures." I try to speak, but she cuts me off.

"As women, we're taught never to ask questions." I start to interrupt because has she met me? All I do is ask questions. "Not questions like why does gum lose its flavor so fast." She rolls her eyes at me, exasperated. "Questions like, 'What is our relationship and where is it going?' We're taught that if we ask these questions, if we ask for too much or demand too quickly, we'll lose the man. He'll become the one who got away and then we'll end up buying Meow Mix in bulk when we're 80." I laugh, but then I think about how cat fur would totally mess with my velvet couch and frown.

"But do you know what happens when we don't ask what's on our mind?" She raises an eyebrow as I run my spork through the puddle of melted chocolate ice cream. "You lose the man. Or you lose yourself. You become my mother, who knew all along my father was cheating on her but was scared that if she mentioned it, if she asked, if she demanded what she deserved, she'd lose him. And you know what? She lost him in the end, anyway. But along the way, she lost herself. And now she has nothing."

"I thought... I thought if I was subtle, I could ask without putting the pressure on. I just... I don't want to lose him. "

"But you did, didn't you?" My gut sinks.

"I guess."

"Gabi, honey, if you lose him... No, if he lets you go, with your beautiful soul and happy energy and fucking amazing, crazy brain, it's his loss."

"He liked my brain." The words are so soft, and I almost think I didn't say them, but then there's a warm hand on my shoulder, Cassie's.

"What?"

No one gets it.

"He liked my mind. Or he pretended to. All of those weird things I say. The way my mind goes off on tangents and my mouth follows suit. It's annoying. I know it is. But... he liked it. He... encouraged it."

"Babe, you're not annoying. You're... Gabi."

"Great, thanks."

"No, I mean... that's why we're friends. I'm boring and straight-laced." I laugh, remembering the escapade on the side of the road with Luke. Somehow, she reads my mind. Good friends... "Shut up. That was all you!" It was. I totally dared her to do it. "Anyway. I'm boring and by the book. I'm hot girl armor and decoding people. You're Gabi. You're color and fun and excitement. You're questioning everything and laughing and making people feel comfortable. God, look at us. I avoided people forever, and your tiny ass came in and forced yourself on me."

"I didn't "

"In a good way, Gabs," She looks around for the plastic cups in the corner and grabs them along with the bottle of wine. "He liked your mind because you are your mind. He likes you, babe." I grab the wine and drink straight from the bottle, ignoring the cup in her hand. Cassie laughs. "But Gabi?" She stops until I meet her eyes. "If he took what you said and ran with it, accepted that you're over and nothing more than friends, that's on him. You deserve someone who will break into your office and demand you listen to him. You deserve a Luke." She pauses. "Not my Luke. You'd drive him nuts." We laugh. It's true. "But you deserve someone who takes the random shit you spew to try and protect yourself with, even if it's leading him in the wrong direction, and fights for you. You deserve your raunchy romance book ending."

I think of the dozens of books on my shelves, of how my mind took a mental snapshot of Vic in my messy apartment flipping through pages and pointing out parts he thought were funny. I think about how everyone gets their happily ever after, how they fight through the red flags to find their white knight.

Cassie's right. I do.

I deserve that.

So what if I fell for a red flag.

I guess it has to happen to everyone once, right? And shit, Cassie's right. If he was it, if he felt what I feel, then when I said that we were done because we'd finished our arrangement together, he'd have fought me on it.

It kills me to say it, but he didn't. He didn't fight. The realization has a choked sound coming from deep inside of me.

"Oh, honey."

"I fell, Cass. I should have listened to you," I say, the words scratching my throat. Recognition goes through her face as she moves the cake aside and pulls me in.

"Oh, honey. I know. I know."

And I sit on the floor in a puddle of melted cake and cry on my best friend's shoulder because no matter how many warnings I had, how much training, I fell for a walking red flag.

And shit, it hurts.

THIRTY THREE

-Vic-

Tuesday morning, hours before I was even planning to wake up, my cell rings.

I have two sounds for my phone—one is for normal people. That one I can sleep through easily.

The other is the hospital.

That one haunts my dreams.

As an ER doctor, I don't have specific patients I need to be on call for, like an obstetrician or a surgeon, but after a day like Monday, I asked Pam to call me if there was any update.

The child woke up.

Vitals were weak, but it looked like she'd survive. Her father was asking for me.

After everything that family has gone through and will go through, I couldn't not come in. So I rolled out of bed, kissed a sleepy Gabi, and told her I was taking her spare key to lock the door behind me before heading out to the hospital.

The whole day I waited for Gabi to reach out to me.

At first, I'm talking with my patients, unable to check my phone except for quick glances. Nothing.

Then again, the hospital can have unreliable service. When I got off though, I expected a missed call or a text or... something from Gabi. After everything yesterday, after our conversation before bed, I just assumed....

But nothing.

Strange.

I know she said our arrangement was over, but I didn't think she meant it for real. After a month and a half of daily calls and texts, I find my day empty without them. Without *her*.

It's then I realize I fucked up.

Who the fuck cares if one day down the road Gabi might wonder if we rushed things, if she should have explored more? I could have a lifetime to prove to her she made the right choice, that we were always end game. There's no way I'm letting Gabi play the field now that I've had her. Not a single part of me is letting go of Gabrielle Mancini.

I've spent 34 years living free, dating and not feeling the slightest whim to settle down, dodging my mother's disappointment at every turn. But a month with Gabi has me making plans I wasn't sure I'd ever feel the urge to make.

When she said that we were done, our agreement completed, I froze.

I spent a full month dragging things out, spending time with her, learning her body. Learning her. I could have fucked her that first day. I could have done that, made it good, and gone on my way. But there was no way I would let her go that quickly. That first time making her come, I knew I needed more. I needed everything.

But it was more than just sex with her. It's talking to her. Watching her thoughts move behind her eyes and then her inability to stop them from coming out. She makes me wonder about everything, question everything. For a man who was raised to be straight-laced, to excel and do things by the book but was dying for chaos and unpredictability, she's a dream.

She's my dream.

She's my adventure, the chaos I've been looking for my entire life. It turns out I didn't need constant change or the lack of knowing. I didn't need to avoid staying in one place or with one person for too long.

No, what I needed was Gabrielle Nicolette Mancini. Chaos personified. I know that with her by my side, my life will be filled with what I've always craved.

I will never be bored, never suffer from the monotony of life.

I was certain she realized this as well. In fact, I was pretty sure she'd last a few hours, maybe. Once she let her mind run through all the excuses, once she got over the fact this isn't what it was originally, she'd call with some silly question, some crazy theory. She'd ask if I could come over, if we could get coffee, if I wanted to finish that *Supernatural* show she got me watching. I figured on her own time, she'd come to the realization I'm already at.

I would have said something then. I would have laughed at her, told her there was no way in hell things were ending like that. Or ever, if I have anything to say about it.

And honestly, I thought my patience would also last longer, giving me more time before I have to make my move. Because at the same time, though I hate that she decided our arrangement was over, for some reason, I wanted one concrete end to it before we got our solid beginning to the rest of our lives. Something that Gabi couldn't question in any way, nothing she could read into.

In six months, two years, or 40 years, I don't want her to look back and wonder if she somehow conned me into something I don't want, if I felt obligated to continue regardless of the fact that I'm a grown-ass man who doesn't do things if I don't want to.

I've gotten to know this woman well enough to know she has the potential to overthink this to death.

But I've gotten nothing from her. Nothing at all. In fact, I'm so confused by this that if it weren't for a text from my mother demanding she meet my "young lady," I'd take my phone in to get it looked at and make sure it was still working.

I'm thinking I made a big fuckin' mistake in not telling Gabi right there that this wasn't ending.

Being with her was... groundbreaking. That second time was world shifting, game-changing, earth-shattering—all the cliches needed, cliches Gabi would probably pick apart and organize based on credibility, red flag status, and realism if she were here.

Despite that, it was different, and I could see in her face she knew it too. Different from the first time where I was worried about hurting her and then I was getting my fill, a month of pent-up energy and want and need releasing at once.

The second time was soft and sweet. The second time brought feelings I'd been hiding for weeks into clear vision.

I'm crazy in love with this crazy woman.

Somehow, after a month of teaching her about herself, her body, and her mind, teaching her to learn it and love it and appreciate it—it just led to me doing the same.

A part of me wonders if I ever had a chance. If it really was a case of being together and growing together that made me fall for her slowly.

But then I remember checking her chart to see her results from her six-week check up. So I remember six weeks of thinking of her, despite only having talked to her for five minutes, at most.

I remember seeing her on that dance floor, one in a million, in a black outfit that should have blended in, but instead, I was drawn to her.

I remember fighting with her friends that night, forcing them to let me take her home. And, embarrassingly enough, I remember that any other woman, virgin or not, I would have tried to get out of my system earlier.

Not Gabi.

Gabi, I let in, let her leech her way into my veins, into the sinew of my muscle, seep into my bones until I can't discern myself from her. And I don't want to.

Now, sitting in the apartment we spent so much time in—an apartment I've never taken another woman besides my sister back to, I realize I should have told her that. That she was the only one here.

The only woman I've made dinner for.

The only woman I bought expensive art for.

The only woman to show me what life was missing and crave it.

I should have told her the ways she is special.

That we were special.

That there would be no matching. That it was us, her and me, from now on. For real.

I fucked up.

I need my plan.

But I also can't rush it.

When I'm cleaning up my room and find her little pajama pants with dogs wearing heart-shaped sunglasses, that thought gets heavier.

And when there's that nasty hazelnut creamer in the fridge, the one that made her squeal when she saw I'd bought it, I reach for my phone.

I need to call her.

So I do.

Fuck rushing and big grand gestures and plans.

Swiping until I reach her name. Above her name is the only photo contact on my phone. Her eyes are crossed and her lips are pursed in some weird fish face that makes me laugh because I haven't seen it yet. I have no idea when she would have done it, but there it is. I smile. Smile at her face. *At my girl.*

Shit, my girl.

I hit send before putting the phone to my ear.

It rings.

And rings.

And rings.

But just when I think I missed her, the line clicks. There's the sound of a television then muffling, like a hand on the receiver as the phone is moved to another location.

"What do you want?" a voice asks.

It's not Gabi.

It's a man's voice.

A fucking man's voice.

It takes everything in me not to go ballistic.

"Where's Gabi?" I pull the phone from my ear, checking to make sure I hit send on the right contact. Maybe I called someone else.

"What do you want?"

"Look, man, I called my girl and some fuckin' guy answered. I deserve for you to tell me where the fuck she is. Or at the very least, who the fuck you are."

"This is Luke." Luke, Luke... Cassie's fiancé? Ben's friend.

"Why are you answering Gabi's phone?"

"Why are you callin' her?" This guy is still a fucking dick.

"Is she at your place?"

"Yes." We're both silent. He's clearly waiting for me to say more. I'm waiting for him to explain why he's answering Gabi's phone. "What do you want, Vic?"

"I want to talk to Gabi."

"Why?"

"This isn't something I want to discuss with a relative stranger."

"Too bad."

"What?"

"I said, too bad. You get me. Talk to me." What in the actual fuck?

"Man. I don't know you, and you don't know me. But I'm pretty sure you can get why it would not be great for me to call my girl and another man answer." There's silence for a few moments before he speaks.

"Is she your girl?"

"What?"

"I said, is she your girl?" I don't answer. "Are you deaf, man?"

"You know sure as fuck she's my girl." I really don't like this guy.

"Do I?"

"I don't like games, man."

"She's sitting in my living room, eating from a 5-gallon tub of cheese balls and watching *Titanic* with my girl." This sounds like a very normal Gabi-thing to do. Maybe he doesn't actually know his fiancé's best friend that well? Maybe— "And she's crying." That shuts up my train of thought. "And it's not because of the movie."

"What happened?" *Is Nico okay? Gino? Sammy? Did something happen to her sister or her brothers?*

"Aren't you, like, a doctor or something?"

"Yes." Has something happened where someone needs medical attention?

"Didn't you have to go to a lot of schooling?" Where the fuck is he going with this?

"Yes."

"So you're telling me a mechanic is smarter than an ER doctor?"

"Look, man, I don't know what game you're playing, but I'm not having fun. What is going on with Gabi?" He's silent for a few moments, long moments, and I wonder what the fuck he's thinking. I like to read people, but that's near impossible through a phone.

"You really are clueless, aren't you?"

"About what?"

"Holy shit, you are, aren't you? You're both completely clueless." He's laughing now, like something about this whole situation is humorous. I disagree completely.

"Man, if you don't—"

"She's crying over you." That silences me. That definitely silences me. It also adds a rock to the pile in my gut.

'What do you mean, she's crying over me?"

"You two ended things?"

"I mean..." Shit. I fucked up. "Fuck. Unintentionally."

And then he laughs.

The man laughs.

He laughs like the thought of my girl sitting on his couch eating cheeseballs and crying while watching *Titanic* is funny.

And okay, the visual isn't *not* funny, but in context...

"Can I talk to Gabi?" His laugh stops, his voice changing.

"Absolutely not."

"What?"

"You just gave that girl her first real heartbreak. She's a wreck. No way you're talking to her, not right now."

"Excuse me?" Who the fuck does this guy think he is?

"Look, I'm sure you know—I've heard all about your dumb as fuck deal. But Gabi is... she's sweet. Innocent. She's—"

"She's not innocent."

"I know you went and fucked her, but—"

"No. I mean, in that way, yeah. But she's not innocent and soft and in need of protection. Yeah, I'm gonna do that regardless, but she's not innocent; she's not weak." I remember the conversation we had, her losing her mind because everyone her whole life has made her feel innocent and precious and delicate. She hates it. "She's strong as fuck."

He's quiet on the other end.

I wonder if I went too far.

Then I wonder if I give a fuck.

Then I wonder if Ben would tell me where his buddy lives so I can drive there and talk to Gabi.

"Meet me at Tommy's in an hour."

"What?"

"Tommy's Tavern. On the boardwalk. Meet me there, and we'll talk."

"Talk?" I ask, but the line is already dead.

And shit, I guess I gotta go to Tommy's.

THIRTY-FOUR

-Vic-

When I walk into the dark tavern on the boardwalk, I instantly see Luke sitting in the corner.

My phone vibrates in my pocket, and I check it. Ben. I had texted him earlier.

> Pretty sure I'm about to be interrogated by your friend Luke.

> You fuck over Gabi?

The reply is simple.
I shake my head. Why does everyone jump there?
Oh, because I haven't had a single steady girlfriend in years. Got it. Really set myself up for that one.
And because it seems like I may have been an actual moron at reading the signs she was giving me.

> Not intentionally. Trying to fix it.

He replies almost instantly.

> Well, he'll probably call me if he needs to hide a body. I'll make sure we put you somewhere your mom can find you.

I laugh as I approach the table, stuffing my phone in my pocket.

"That some woman you're texting?" Luke asks as I sit, his arms crossed on his chest.

"I'll be sure to let Ben know you think he's a woman."

"You were texting Ben?" he asks.

I nod. He glares at me. We're both silent for a long moment.

"Look, man, I—"

"Why is Gabi crying?" His words hit my gut.

"I didn't mean—"

"I'm not playing games. I have questions. There is a sweet girl in my house crying her eyes out over you. You're some hot shot doctor and I'm just a lowly mechanic, but I know how to put two and two together. You were with Gabi, now you're not for some unknown reason and she's a mess. You're calling her, for what? A booty call? Because that's—"

"Shut up," I say, frustration rolling off me in waves. He stops and looks at me, an eyebrow raised. "You don't know anything."

"That's what I'm trying to find out."

"Why should I explain anything to you?"

"Because Gabi is sweet. Gabi works with my woman, and I love my woman. Cassie loves Gabi, thinks of her like a sister. That, in a way, makes her my sister."

"She has enough brothers."

"Well, she's got another." I stare at him. "You want me to call up her brothers, have them sit down with us? You can explain to one of them what's going on?" I think about the chaos that is the Mancini brothers.

"No."

"That's what I thought." And through his frustration, I see a smile. He knows the brothers too, I remember. "Okay, so here's your chance. Tell me everything. I like what I hear, you're moving on to Cassie."

"What?"

"Tell me what happened. Give me a single good reason I should let you through to Cassie. Cassie's going to interview you, vet you. And let me tell you this: I'm the easy one. Cassie will somehow weasel her way into finding out about the lie you told your mother in fifth grade."

"You lost me."

"Jesus, man. Are you sure you're a doctor?" He's smiling.

Honestly, he's kind of a dick, but he's a dick in the way that I could see how he'd be fun to have a beer with.

And I like how he's protecting Gabi, even if it means I don't get to see her right now.

Fuck.

Do I maybe like this guy?

"Cassie's gonna interview me?"

"You wanna be Gabi's match, you need to pass her test."

Then I remember Gabi's words. *"And I think I might... have Cassie match me too."*

Gabi is going to get matched, and this is my chance to make things right.

And to possibly get my grand gesture.

Alright, let's do this.

Then I let Luke Dawson vet me.

THIRTY-FIVE

-Gabi-

Today is the day.

I should be excited. "Should be" being the operative phrase.

Instead, I'm anxious and nauseous, overthinking every single moment.

I miss the quiet that I've only felt a handful of times, all of which were with the same person.

Sunday, Vic and I had sex for the first time.

Monday, we had sex for the last time.

Tuesday, I spent the day crying at Cassie's, Luke popping in and out with essentials to keep the marathon going—wine, sugar, and carbs. Occasionally he'd throw a water bottle at us and run, like it was some kind of grenade and he was nervous for the blowback.

Today is Thursday and, as per Cassie's rule number 789 (exaggeration—I don't have the energy to number all of her rules), I am going on a date.

The best way to get over a man is to get with another, right? Or something like that... I feel like when she initially told me it, I blushed and scribbled it down.

So I'm on my first date, perfectly curated to be a brilliant match by my best friend who is a matchmaker for a living. Technically, I'm in the bathroom hyping myself up while I wait for that date to appear.

How do people do this? Go on random dates, no idea if the person they'll be meeting will be the love of their life or a total douche?

But Cassie wouldn't steer me wrong. When I handed her my notes on Vic—notes I wrote up when I was back in my apartment, painstakingly laying out each pro and con as if it didn't kill me to know that another woman would benefit from the fact that he's protective but also has a soft spot and needs to be protected—Cassie smiled sadly and told me she'd take it from there and that I'd done a great job.

And really, I should feel relief. With my first official matching assignment under my belt, I can take on more and know that maybe Vic will find what he needs too. My plan has been completed, has ended. I should be... happy. I should feel fulfilled. I am now open for business, free to find Mr. Right. Someone who won't remember me as awkward, fumbling, anxious, and overthinking.

But I also remember the hope in my chest when I told Vic it was time to be matched.

And he just said yes.

Didn't fight me.

Didn't try to stop me.

I keep reminding myself that Luke did. When Cassie told Luke their arrangement was over, he fought for her. He broke into the office and got mad. He never stopped believing that they would be more, that they would be everything.

I want that.

You deserve that, I tell myself.

You could have had that, a smaller, quieter voice whispers.

Could I? Could I have had that with Vic if I were open and honest from the beginning? Honest about what I wanted, or at least when that changed? If I'd been honest about ending our arrangement instead of setting him up to answer, like Cassie said?

I didn't mean to play games, but...

I shake my head, curls bouncing in the mirror of the women's restroom as I do. That doesn't matter. None of it matters.

In fact, all that matters is going back to that table and waiting for my match, the match Cassie promised me up and down she was sure would be perfect. The start of something beautiful.

"Romance book-worthy, Gabs."

And if Cassie says this date is perfect for me, it must be right. So I nod at myself, inspecting the light pink lipstick once more before straightening the tight red dress and heading out to the table to wait for my dream man.

Except, when I get to the table that Maria sat me at when I arrived, there's someone already sitting there, across from the seat I placed my purse on before heading to the bathroom.

I know this person.

I know him well.

Vic.

Vic is sitting at the table with a big, shit-eating grin, eyes locked to mine.

That's actually a lie.

His eyes lock to mine then travel down my body, scorching a path before they meet my eyes again. I would roll my eyes and call him an idiot or a cliche, but I'm way too shocked to do that right now.

"What are you... What are you doing here?" I ask, staring at him. He's decked out in a white shirt, the top few buttons undone, and a black suit jacket, sitting in front of a perfectly laid place setting at a fancy restaurant with that grin like he has something up his sleeve.

It's straight from some kind of early 2000s Jennifer Lopez rom-com movie.

Except, I think this is my real life.

Probably.

This could all be some kind of an elaborate work of imagination. I might be still asleep on Cassie's couch, bright orange cheese dust staining my fingers, my hair slowly becoming one giant mat on top of my head.

But I remember brushing out that mat. I remember getting dressed and the nerves that accompanied it. I look down at my fingers. Not orange. What makes that dust so radioactive, anyway?

My mind wanders as I stare at him, his white teeth gleaming at me and reminding me I never asked him if he gets his teeth whitened or if he just has really, really good genetics.

God, Gabi. Focus. If there is one moment in your life you should be focusing, it's this one. This is not the time for pondering teeth whitening regimens or cheese ball dust.

Especially when he opens his mouth to speak, words falling out.

"I'm your match." Those words circle the drain in my mind.

I'm your match.

I'm your match,

I'm your match.

I watch them go round and round, slowly getting to the center, my mouth working them, repeating them silently as I try to figure out what he's saying, to decode his words.

He waits.

Ding.

Match. I'm here to be matched.

He's my match?

There's no way.

"Match? But Cassie…"

"Cassie set it up."

"No way. Cassie wouldn't talk to you. She saw me have a full-on meltdown and thinks you're a giant jerk. Girl code, and all. If a man makes your best friend rub cheese dust into your couch while letting her hair turn into one giant mat, you hate them for life." He ignores the important part of what I'm saying.

"Cheese dust?"

"It's a long story. One I don't really want to relive, but at this rate, I will nightly." He laughs.

He is not allowed to laugh.

"You're not allowed to laugh."

"Why?" He's smiling. That happy smile, the one he gives me when my mind is reeling and I can't catch up to it.

"Because my life is in chaos. I'm supposed to go on a date. You... You can't be—"

"I'm your date, Gabi."

"But Cassie—"

"I spoke with Luke, who cleared my talking with Cassie."

"You talked to Luke?"

"He's very protective of you." A mixture of warmth and annoyance runs through me. Warmth because I love Luke. Annoyed because I need another brother like I need to break my wrist again and meet a sexy doctor who will break my heart at no true fault of his own.

"Okay, so you talked to Luke, and he... what? Vetted you?" Vic nods. "And once he did that, he let you talk to Cassie?" Honestly, that sounds on brand for Luke. "Why did you talk with Cassie?"

"Because if I found out you were going on a date with any man other than myself, I would have gone fucking feral, Gabrielle." My eyes widen.

"Oh." It's the only thing that comes to my lips. A million words come to my mind, but all I can say is "oh."

Why am I like this?

"Yeah, oh." He stares at me, that smile still playing on his face, but his eyes are serious. He's saying something. I just can't quite...

"But..."

"But what, kitten?" His words are soft and they run through me, familiar and warm, and I have missed that sound so much. It's been three days.

It shouldn't be like this.

It was never supposed to be like this.

It was supposed to be easy. Fun. It was supposed to be losing my virginity, learning about myself. A couple of nights together. And it turned into thinking about him every waking moment and building some abstract future in my mind I had no place to build.

It became spending nights together and sleeping better with the weight of his arm on me. It became confidence and freedom. It became him researching the dumb shit I wonder, not thinking I was crazy for wondering it. It became him sticking up for me to my insane family. It became... more.

It became everything.

But...

"But you said it was time?"

"*You* said it was time." His face goes to a mask of frustration. "Think about it, Gabi. Did I ever say it was time?" I go back over that night, running the tape like a film in my mind. I did, didn't I? I brought it up. Not him. In my head, we were good, mission accomplished.

I was no longer a virgin.

I could come.

"But you agreed." He waits, pausing, the same way I do sometimes when I'm sifting through my thoughts, trying to decide how to phrase something.

"Yes. That's true. You... caught me off guard. You do that often." He smiles.

I don't find it funny.

That must have come across my face.

"Look, Gabi. I was your first. Initially, when you told me that, I figured I should give you space. I should..." He stops, eyes going over my crossed arms, then down my body to my feet still planted on the gaudy restaurant carpeting before shifting his eyes to the empty chair to my right.

"Can you please sit, Gabi? You're making this weird." I don't. I stay standing, staring at him, lost and confused and trying to figure out what this all means. "If you don't want to sit, we can leave. Go for a walk and talk. Would that... Would that be better?" He looks... nervous. It's strange on him. He's usually so confident and self-assured. But even so, his words remind me of what it's like to be with him, of him being understanding of my quirks and always trying to help in any way he can. His constant efforts to make me comfortable. He works to make the world fit me instead of asking me to fit into the world.

I sit.

"Thank you," he says, his smile hypnotizing. We stare at each other then. Stare. And god, it's been three freaking days, but I missed this man. I missed this smile.

I am so utterly fucked.

How am I supposed to survive a lifetime without that smile if I can't handle three freaking days?

"What were you saying?" I ask.

"What?"

"You were going on some grand tirade. This is the grand gesture part, right?" He smiles.

"You read too many books."

"Fuck off." The words come out before I can even stop them, even think about them.

"I love it." I want to say fuck off again, but that seems harsh. "I love lots of things about you, Gabi." My breathing stops. "In your books, what happens next?"

"What?"

"You love those books. What happens next? They get together, things end because they're both too stupid to stop it—what happens next?"

"I'm not stupid."

"Gabi."

"I'm protecting myself."

"Kitten." This time his words are softer, sadder.

"You could break me into a million pieces, Vic."

"What happens next, Gabi?" His words are pushy but not angry. Like he's trying to get me where he wants me.

"Things end."

"And then?" I sigh. He's going to make me keep doing this until he makes his point.

"And then one of them realizes what a shitty idea that was."

"And then?"

"And then that one makes a... a grand gesture. Something to prove they mean it. Running through an airport to stop her from leaving. Which, unfortunately, isn't realistic anymore. It's kind of crazy that's still the go-to of romance in the normal brain, you know? Because you can't even get past security without a boarding pass. No way in hell would the TSA let some random, potential stalker just run through the airport looking for a woman. Or a man. Equal opportunities and all." He's smiling at me, but I'm somewhere else. "Now that I think of it, so many of those big moments are major red flag stalker shit. Like Lloyd Dobbler? The boombox? Creepy. Super creepy. If a man came to my apartment holding a boombox in the middle of the night, first off, my neighbors would call the cops. And if he was wearing a trench coat, I'd think he was some kind of weird flasher." I shiver.

"Come back to me," he says softly, and I do, looking at him and seeing him again. "Then what?" he asks when he knows I'm here.

"What?"

"They break up, they realize it was dumb, and one of them creates some kind of grand gesture. What happens after that?" I blink.

"There's a confession. Some kind of confession that changes everything."

My breath catches.

His smile widens like he was waiting for that answer.

I keep staring, the world around me going quiet, the way only he can make happen.

My mind only sees him.

"You're it for me, Gabi."

Again, the words circle. They're too much to understand, so far beyond anything I know to be true.

You're it for me, Gabi.
You're it for me, Gabi.
You're it for me, Gabi.

It clicks in my mind, like a LEGO in my brain, staying there. Cemented forever.

You're it for me, Gabi.

He sees it and goes forward.

"I want you to be mine. And I want to be yours. Not temporarily to teach you things or to get my mom off my ass, which was a bullshit excuse, by the way. But because I've fallen head over heels for you." My breathing stops, frozen in my lungs. "How's that for a confession?"

I gloss right on over the "bullshit excuse" part and move right on.

"But... but..." I stop stuttering. "That's impossible." He laughs, the sound deep, the smile easy.

"Not impossible. I'm very much in love with you, Gabrielle Nicolette Mancini."

In love with me.

The world swirls around me, a confusion of colors and noises and feelings and... I'm overwhelmed.

Nothing makes sense.

Up is down and left is right and red is green and Victor Brandt loves me.

"You can't."

"Why's that?"

"Because you're... Vic."

"Yeah." The words are a laugh and it's starting to get annoying. How dare he laugh when I am having a mental crisis.

"But... you're..." Should I say it? Would that be offensive? I mean, it's true, but...

"What am I, Gabi?"

"You're a fucking walking red flag!" I shout, the words flying from my mouth. I clap my hands there as if I can drag them back in.

"What?" he says, the smile on his face telling me he finds this entertaining. Me, entertaining, I suppose. I stare.

I ponder for a moment how to put it, but the reality is my filter is already in shreds. There is no chance I'm holding this back, no matter how much I would love to.

It's a crumbled mess on the ground, right alongside my dignity.

"You're a red flag! Everything about you screams red flag, Vic."

He sits back with that stupid cocky smile (red flag) and crosses his arms on his chest like he knows he's going to come out on top regardless of what I say. (Red flag!) "Like what?"

"Well, you're classically handsome, for one. And you know it. The whole tall, dark, and handsome thing is basically the ultimate red flag." Cocky smile. Lord. "Except for being blonde, everyone knows that tall, dark, and handsome is the biggest red flag. No one person can handle the responsibility of being all three."

"Would you rather I be short, pale, and ugly?"

He's got me there.

I move on without commentary.

"And you get weird when I wear what I want out."

"You're gorgeous, Gabi. Men are pigs. I want to keep you safe. You're also mine." His eyes dip down my body, X-ray vision burning my curves through the table. "We'll talk about what you're wearing to meet who you assumed was a stranger later." A thrill runs through me.

Stop it, body! Stop!

I move on down my list.

"You don't like dogs," I say. It feels dumb, an excuse. Which I suppose it is...

"I'm allergic." Good answer. Too good. How is he answering all of these questions right? Is that also a red flag?

"You have women's clothes in your house!"

"I told you, those are my sister's. You want me to call her, have her confirm?" He reaches in his pocket to do so and I shake my head. "I've never had a woman who wasn't my sister in my apartment." That has me pausing.

"What?"

"Never. You can ask the lobby. They'll confirm." I shake my head. I can't dwell too long on that bomb or I might lose my mind, lose all nerve.

"You've dated, like, a million girls."

"Okay? You're learning to date men for a living." I shake my head.

"No. I'm not. I told Cassie I wanted to stay as administrative. She's bringing someone new on." After that disastrous co-interview and then my clear inability to date someone without getting attached, I decided I like the role I'm in now. Vic smiles a triumphant smile I've never seen before and shit, I hate that I like it. Like that something I did, a decision I made, made him smile like that.

"You're mean to your mom. That's a big red flag. Huge."

"When?" he says the words instantly, his brow furrowing in confusion.

"You said she's crazy and annoying."

"She is." I roll my eyes.

"That's mean. You're mean to your mom."

"You said the same thing about your own mother. Your entire family, actually." Valid. "You also haven't met my mother or seen how I am with her. I love my mom. I'd never call her annoying to her face. She'd probably slap me, for one."

"You've never taken me to meet your family." That one digs. God, I hate to admit it, but that one burns in me.

"Baby, that's because your family is amazing and fun and crazy and mine is uptight and frustrating. I need to get you to fall for me and get in there deep before I risk scaring you off with them."

"But..." I start my final reason, my final argument. I have a list in my office filled with red flags. Tons I could probably use as an argument against Vic, but the truth is, the only one that matters isn't even on that list. "This was... This was temporary."

"And it's not anymore." He's no longer smiling. "And, kitten, tell me when this ever actually felt temporary. When this ever felt like we were just together to help you lose your virginity. Shit, my 'end' of the deal was for you to get my mom off my back, but I didn't even tell her I was working with a matchmaker until last weekend. Wasn't that strange to you?"

It was.

It was very strange.

I just didn't think it was my place to ask.

Part of me feared that if I pushed too hard, questioned too much, this would end. That he'd get tired of my questions, realize he wasn't getting anything from this, and move on. I wouldn't have blamed him either—the scales haven't been even during this arrangement, not in the least. Not, unless...

"But—"

"Is that all?"

"What?"

"My red flags. Is that all of them?" I glare.

"No."

"What else, baby?" My mind goes blank. I know there is more. An entire college-ruled sheet of red flags to keep me up late at night, chinks in his armor for me to overthink and dissect. But I can't think of a single one now that he's sitting across from me, saying these words.

He smiles at my hesitance.

There.

There's one.

"You have a panty-dropping smile!" His head goes back, a laugh rumbling from his chest, and my stupid, stupid, stupid fucking body. It responds exactly like it always does when he does that, when I see his Adam's apple bobbing with his laughter and his strong chin tipping back, and when I hear the noise that makes everything inside of me quiet.

Peace.

That's what he gives me.

But I learned that he also has the power to take that peace away, whether he means to wield it or not.

When his head tips back to me, he runs a hand through his thick hair, long fingers getting lost in the black strands momentarily before he leans forward on the table, that exact panty-dropping smile on his lips.

"Does my smile make you drop your panties, kitten?"

Jesus Christ.

Well, yes.

Yes, it does, actually.

I don't reply, instead crossing my arms on my chest like a child.

He laughs again, knowing.

He always knows.

The asshole.

The smile melts into a look of introspection.

"What are you doing here, kitten?"

What *am* I doing here?

"Cassie set me up."

"Why?" I don't want to answer this. I don't want him to know that I'm here because I was hoping it would stop me from shattering. That moving on was what I needed. I'm here because when I'm home, the quiet suffocates me and all I can think of is what could have been.

"It's... time," is what I say instead.

"It's time."

"You agreed. I should... date."

"We already went over that part. I was dumb. I was scared that if I didn't let you decide to be with me on your own, you'd always question it. I was sure that as soon as I left and you thought on it, you'd see that all I want is you—and that you're mine. I thought you'd get that and reach out, ready to try this for real. I should have known better than to expect you to come to me first." My nose wrinkles in confusion. "You're stubborn, kitten. You're also protective of yourself and your pride. Coming to me first, admitting you want more than we agreed to, especially after my dumb ass told you that you could date? Fuck, if I didn't make that first move, you never would have."

"I'm not stubborn." He stares at me. "Maybe a little."

"That aside, what are you doing here, Gabi?"

"I told you, Cassie set me—"

"How long have you been working for Cassie?"

"About two years. "

"In those two years, has she ever set you up?" I stare at him. "Have you been single in those two years?" The entirety of them, I don't say. "Has she ever made it seem like she would frown upon it if you wanted to get matched? Or that she couldn't do it for you?"

Quite the opposite. My mind flashes over the dozens of times she dropped hints—new clients she thought would be a good match for me. Quiet moments where we were together when she'd tell me to let her know when it was time.

"Why now, Gabi?"

I don't answer.

"Why now?" His voice is firmer, more insistent, but I continue to stare at him.

Which version do I tell him? The version I've been telling myself for days? The reason I told Cassie?

Or do I tell him the truth about why I finally gave in, finally asked for her to match me? And why I insisted on it happening as soon as possible.

"I'm not a virgin." I go with the easy answer, eyes drifting left to right as I do to see if anyone can hear. The restaurant isn't loud, but everyone nearby is too engrossed in their own conversations to worry about ours. He looks at me, one thick eyebrow raised. Shit. He's not buying it.

I need to sell it better, then.

"I didn't want her to match me and get it right the first time." Still nothing. "I was a virgin. I didn't want... whoever I end up with to remember me like that. Nervous and awkward and no idea what I'm doing. Whoever I end up with... I don't want them remembering me like that." He's staring at me still with a small smile. "Cassie's good at her job. Gets it right a lot of the time. We're friends. She'd work hard to make sure whoever she picks is a good match."

"Okay?"

"So if he was a match, I wanted to be free of that... burden. Not to mention, I have brothers. I've heard them talking. They don't mess with virgins. Too clingy. They expect.. more. Too much." Part of me was afraid that if I asked Vic for more, that's how I'd seem.

"I want you clingy."

"What?"

"I want you clingy," he repeats, slower this time.

"I—"

"I want you to expect too much."

"I don't—"

"I want you to expect everything."

"Vic, I—"

"I'm your match, Gabi."

"What?"

"Cassie interviewed me." I'm silent. Confused and silent, and deep in there is a tiny kernel of something beautiful and fragile.

Hope.

"What?"

"She called it untraditional. No dates, because she said that would be weird, you being mine and all. Two interviews instead." I mouth the word *what?*

I am so confused. More confused than normal, which says a lot because I'm pretty much always in some state of confusion.

"The first interview was with Luke."

"Luke?" Now that shocks me.

"Yeah. I called you on Tuesday."

"Tuesday?" I sound like a parrot. He gives me the smile. Confusion kicks up a notch, partly because that smile always makes my mind scramble a bit.

"Yeah. Made the mistake of thinking you'd call me, tell me you were being Gabi and definitely didn't want to end us." I blink. My belly drops.

"I was at Cassie's."

"Crying into a container of cheese balls and watching *Titanic*, yeah, I heard." Instantly my face burns.

"How did you know that?!"

"I told you. Luke interviewed me." My patience snaps.

"Victor, you need to talk in complete freaking sentences because I have no fucking clue what is going on." He laughs again. It brings me down from the ledge of panic, but it honestly ratchets my annoyance a bit more.

"Stop interrupting me and I can."

I glare.

He smiles.

And fuck, but my glare starts to break, drifting into a small smile as well.

Shit, shit, shit, the hold that smile has on me.

"Tell your story." I grumble the words under my breath, but still he hears me.

"Thank you." I stare, waiting for him to continue. "I called you on Tuesday to meet up. To talk. I realized I was an idiot. You're not innocent, but you're not experienced in dating."

"I work for a matchmaker!"

"I thought you weren't going to interrupt?" I glare again. "You might work for a matchmaker, baby, but your head is in those books.

In your books, things just work, even when the woman does something dumb that means the man has to chase her down."

"Excuse me, you didn't put up much of a fight either, did you, Vic?" If I'm honest with myself, that's the part that hurts the most. I was an idiot and put the thought out there, setting him up to give me an answer. It was childish. I was playing games. He's right there. But he also failed the test.

"I'm not used to falling, Gabi." My heart stops. "It's never happened to me. I'm an idiot man who works on a temporary basis when it comes to women. I've never felt the need to fight for a woman to stay, for something to last longer." I scrunch my nose, lifting my lip like I smell something gross.

He is the gross thing, to be clear.

"Stop. You know what I mean. In college and med school, I fucked around. But the past two years? Casual dating but the same women. You know that." I do, unfortunately. He'd told me this already. The thought still roils my stomach. "I never had to fight to make it continue. It was also basically whenever one of us was done with it, we said so and that was it. And Gabi, when you said so, my initial reaction, regardless of the fact that I found it frustrating and annoying, was to agree." I open my mouth but close it so he can speak.

"Who was I to tell you you can't explore, can't date? In the same way you wanted to lose it before you met your match, I didn't want you to feel stuck with me because you lost your virginity to me. I know you treated it like it was nothing, but it's not. Not to me. And that first time? There was something there. You know it. I know it. I just... I agreed partially because you caught me off guard, but also partly because if you want to go off and date and experience men before you settle down, who the fuck am I to tell you no?"

"You'd be the man who wanted to be with me."

"I am that man, Gabi. For me? This is it. You can go off and date, but I'll be here, waiting for you. This is it. Get that through your chaotic mind now. As soon as you say yes, it's me and you."

"Are you proposing?" Panic floods me.

"No, Gabi," he says with a laugh. "For one, I want to date you for real for a while. Date and fuck around with you and have time to introduce you to everyone I've ever met as my girlfriend. Have them feel jealous but also let those fuckers think on some far-off planet, there's a chance if I fuck it up. Then I want to put a ring on your finger and take away that hope."

"You're fucked up."

"I'm yours."

"What's the second part?"

"Your father would kill me. And your brothers. I think there's at least seven people I need to ask for your hand before I can propose. It's going to take at least a century to get them all on my side." I recount my brothers, confused.

"Seven?"

"Luke. I might have won him over, but I'm pretty sure I still need to run any permanent plans by him." That reminds me.

"What was the interview?"

"When I called your phone, he answered."

"What?!" I instantly start to dig in my bag to pull out my phone and rage on him or Cassie or possibly both of them because it's becoming clearer that she had a hand in this ridiculous mess.

"Stop. Let me at least finish this freaking story." I put my hand back on the table begrudgingly and he grabs it.

Jesus.

That jolt of energy.

It burns from his hand to mine, up my arm.

How could I ever, for a moment, have thought another man could do that to me?

He just smiles.

Goddammit, he feels it too.

Is that good or bad?

"I called your phone. Luke answered, was mad at me. Said I broke your heart." That's true, but not fair. I broke my own heart, in a way. I think about telling him that, but we might be here until midnight if I don't stop interrupting. "I had no idea what was going on." I roll my eyes. "Stupid man, yeah, yeah, I get it. Trust me, your boss reamed me good." That's both funny and heartwarming to me. "I told him I needed to talk to you, and he said I needed to talk to him first. I met him for dinner and we talked. He yelled at me. I explained I was an idiot.

"I thought that would be it, that once I explained myself to Luke, I could go talk to you, but apparently your friends gatekeep you like crazy. Once Luke okayed it, I had to go meet with Cassie. Wednesday night, I was her date."

My mind wanders over her schedule and the random name that popped up that I didn't recognize and definitely didn't schedule. She told me he was a last-minute addition.

"A friend of a friend."

"Like a Luke situation?" I'd asked, referring to the fact that Luke bypassed our screening process since his sister was a friend of a previous client. She'd smiled huge like I had told a funny joke.

"Yeah, something like that."

I was too far into my own head to notice the sarcasm.

Shit.

"Yeah. That was me, kitten." He sees the recognition in my face. "I met with her. We talked. She asked me more questions than they asked when I was interviewed to be a damn doctor." I blink.

"Cassie interviewed you?"

"You have good friends, Gabi. Annoying, but good." I blink. Again. "Luke was my first interview. I had to pass that in order to talk to Cassie. Cassie was harder to impress. I needed to get past her in order to meet with you. She made me realize what a moron I'd been."

My head is spinning. Cassie... and Luke... they... vetted Vic? And he's my match.

He's here for me. Intentionally.

And I think he loves me?

Panic starts to settle in as I try to decode this situation, separate daydream from reality.

It turns out it's all real. This beautiful dream is my life. I know this when Vic's face gets serious, taking me in, eyes flitting over me. He sees the panic.

He knows.

He *always* freaking knows

"Let's get out of here," he says, standing up.

"What?" Words are fuzzy in my brain.

"You need air. We need to talk. This isn't the place." He stands, taking money from his wallet and tossing it on to the table. Then he's standing next to me, towering over me with that face that tells me he'd do absolutely anything to make me feel better.

"Come on, Gabi." He puts a hand out, waiting for me to grab it. I stare at it.

"I don't know… I need…" I don't know what I need. But I do know that if I take Vic's hand, everything will change. Maybe forever. I also know that if I take that step, he can absolutely demolish me, body and soul. His next words make the decision for me. They're low and throaty and *desperate*.

"I need to hold you, Gabi. I need that right now more than I need to breathe. Not a part of me thinks we won't figure this out, eventually. I can wait for you to process and come to terms with the fact that this is it. But I'm not doing it without you in my arms. Please. Let's go."

It's then I know.

He feels it too.

The quiet, the peace. It's different for him—a comfort rather than a quiet, but a peace all the same. I should have known when he called after that bad day at the hospital. I should have known when I opened the door and he pulled me into him, breathing me in. When I felt his finger tapping out the beat of my heart, a reassurance, a grounding.

I give him what he gives me.

Something about that playing field being even helps make the decision. I place my hand in his that's outstretched, that jolt running through me, that smile hitting me because he knows I feel it. I let him lift me from my seat and lead me out into the cool night air, waving at Maria in a Vic-induced haze as we do.

The second we're out of the restaurant, he tugs me out of the way of the door and pulls me into his arms.

And he's right.

All is right with the world.

But he's also wrong.

I don't need time. I don't need to process. All I need in this world is right in front of me.

Wrapping my arms around his neck, letting that feeling, that knowledge sink deep, I stare into his eyes.

"You're mine?" He smiles my favorite smile.

"If you'll have me."

And then I kiss him and my world quiets and settles, and that's when I know he's right. We'll figure it out eventually, but at the end of it all, it will be us.

There's only one thing left to do.

Breaking our kiss, I run my hand through his thick hair, tilting my head to look in his eyes, and I say the words I see reflected in them.

"I love you, Vic."

THIRTY SIX

-Gabi-

"This is going to be a train wreck, isn't it?" I say, twisting my fingers in my lap as Vic drives us to my parents'.

It's Sunday.

My mom is throwing a backyard barbeque in lieu of the normal Sunday dinner. That's fine. This will be the third Vic has attended, only missing one since that first Sunday dinner when he was on call. He's come to understand the dynamics and the intricacies, and the stress of going has bubbled down. Ever since he faced down Enzo to stick up for me, it's been smooth sailing with the Mancini brothers.

Unfortunately, it seems Vic's sweet sister has a mouth like Gia, unable to keep a single bit of information from their mother. So when Vic let it slip to his sister that we go to my parents' every weekend, and then Vivian let it slip to their mom, she decided she wanted in on that action.

Don't ask me how, but somehow Mrs. Brandt got my mother's number and, according to *my mom*, who called me very excited in the morning, the two of them chatted until late into the night about everything under the sun, including having sons who refuse to settle down regardless of their "harmless" prodding (my mother's words).

Unfortunately, this means I'll be meeting Vic's parents for the first time, not in a controlled, regulated environment like a restaurant or dinner at Vic's, but at my parents'.

During Sunday dinner.

With my entire family there to witness my downfall.

Kill me now.

Which explains why we're sitting in front of my childhood home in Vic's car (he hasn't let me drive since that first time which is utter bullshit, but right now, I'm not complaining because my hands are shaking) and I now get the, ahem, privilege of meeting my boyfriend's overbearing, reserved mother for the first time with an audience of my own large, obnoxious family who will never let me live down what a shit show this is going to be.

"We can leave," I say.

"No, we can't, babe."

"We can. We have passports. We can leave and run to Mexico. I'm sure they need doctors there. I took Spanish in high school. I could manage." I don't mention that I barely scraped by with a C minus because I cheated and wrote vocab words on my hand.

My brain can barely function in English.

"We're not running away to Mexico."

"Fine. Let's go to Florida. Get lost there. Change our names, become cast members at Disney World. I'm short. Maybe I could be Minnie Mouse." My head tips from left to right, contemplating. "That sounds like fun."

"You don't like confined spaces."

"I bet it would be fine if I got to be in the happiest place on earth." I stop and think. "Do they call Disney*land* the happiest place on earth too? Or just World. What about Paris, or Hong Kong? Seems like a poor marketing strategy, you know? Make one the best? Like, 'once you come here, you'll never be happier, not even if you go to any of our other, just as expensive locations.' Who thought that was—"

"Gabi."

"What?" I look over at him and the smile playing on his lips. The smile he gets when I run on, when he just sits there listening to me like he thinks I'm the most interesting person he knows.

It's crazy.

I love it.

I love *him*.

"I love you, Gabi." The words still make my heart flutter, my belly flop, and my mind settle.

That *feeling*.

That's the one I'd follow him to the ends of the earth to keep. That feeling I've gotten nowhere else in my entire life but when I'm with Vic.

"Love you, but we gotta go inside." My peace shatters. I open my mouth to argue, but his hand is on my chin, pulling it to him where he plants a soft kiss on my lips.

"I don't wanna."

"She's going to love you."

"I'm nothing special for her perfect boy."

"You're everything special, and if she doesn't see that, it's her loss." That should be comforting, but it's not. It's so not. "But she will, Gab." I scrunch my nose, not quite believing him. "Now, we gotta go. Gotta go inside, okay?" Silence. "The kids are standing at the door." Damn the man for knowing my weakness. I turn my head to see Nicky, Gino, and Sammy all standing at the door, smiling. They start to wave. I sigh.

"Okay, let's go."

———

We walk in and greet everyone—all of my brothers, my sister, my brother-in-law. My niece and my nephews. Dad is sitting in his recliner and I bend over to kiss him on his head, the strong patchouli cologne he wears hitting my nose in a comforting waft of memory.

"Hey, beautiful."

"Hey, Daddy."

"You say hello to Doctor Brandt?" my dad says, tipping his head to a man sitting, ankles crossed, on the loveseat. He looks exactly like Vic, just older with salt and pepper hair. But when he smiles, I see it. All Vic.

"Hello, Doctor Brandt, how are you? It's so nice to meet you. Vic's told me all about you, I—" I start rambling, but his dad just laughs, head tipping back just like Vic's does.

"You're right, Vincent. She's a rambler." My mouth drops and I turn my face back to my dad, the traitor, while Vic pulls me in with a thick arm until I hit his chest that's also rumbling with laughter. My brothers are also chiming in.

I hate it here.

"But gorgeous, Victor. You were right," he says, smiling once the laughter settles. "Pleasure to finally meet you, Gabrielle." I don't open my mouth, just smile tightly for fear more word vomit will spew out.

"All good, kitten. One down," Vic says as he moves to shake his dad's hand in greeting.

"Your mom and Vic's ma are on the back deck," my dad says. I want to barf. "Nice lady. Think we scared her off, you know, all the chaos. Ma took her out back to set up the table." Well, at least when I go out there, there won't be many witnesses to my ultimate downfall. Vic told me his dad would be easy. His mom... "She told me to send you and Vic out as soon as you got here. Hey, son," my dad says, sitting up with a grunt and reaching out to greet Vic. Vic shakes his hand and my dad smiles that smile that tells me he's squeezed every drop of blood from Vic's hand and he's proud of it.

"Dad, he's a doctor. Please stop that."

"Man can handle a bit of a squeeze, right, Vic?" I roll my eyes, but Vic just laughs. No one makes the mistake of calling me annoying in front of him anymore, but to my horror, Vic has been ushered in by my brothers and dad to poke fun at and irritate me.

Lovely.

"Come on. Let's get this over with," I say with a mumble, low enough so only Vic can hear, eyes to the deck where I see an enormous table and my mom fluttering over a smaller table, groaning with food.

"Good luck," I hear Gia say from behind me. I look at her with a glare and flip her off, making Dom and Gio laugh when they see it.

"Don't let Bruiser out!" my dad shouts, and I close the doors on the snuggly lab Dom just bought Sammy as a birthday gift before he can make a break for the food.

"Hey, Mom," I say as we step out onto the deck. The weather is warm, late spring in full force.

"Gabrielle! My gorgeous girl! About time you finally got here! Poor Mrs. Brandt has had to deal with your brothers and your cranky father. I had to bring her out here to get some fresh air and away from them."

It takes everything in me not to remind her she is the ringleader of the crazy.

"Vic, darling. How was the drive? Tell me you didn't let Gabs drive again. I told her father we needed to have someone outside the family teach her how to drive. But no, he never listens to me when it comes to his baby girl, does he, Gabi? He had to teach her. Heavy foot on the break, way too fast, reckless, I tell you." She turns to who I can only assume is Mrs. Brandt. "I refuse to get into a car with her. Refuse. Terrifies me!" Vic laughs and my mother pulls him in for a kiss on both cheeks.

"Oh, well, never get into a car with Vic either. Gives me a heart attack!" Mrs. Brandt says.

"Mom, I'm an incredibly safe driver."

"What about the time you almost *killed me?*"

"I was seventeen."

"So?"

"I'm 34 now."

"And?"

"I'm literally double the age I was when I perfectly swerved to avoid a *deer* that had lept out into the road when I was *seventeen*." Honestly, that's kind of impressive.

"You should have seen it coming."

"It was night and it came out of the woods!"

"I'm not having this argument again, Victor." It seems Mrs. Brandt might have more in common with my mother than I thought. "Gabrielle! I've heard so much about you!" she says, turning to me. Her face goes from stern and annoyed to pleasant and enjoyable.

"Hi, Mrs. Brandt. It's wonderful to meet you."

"Oh, no. Call me Vera!" I hesitate. This feels like a trap. "Or Mom!"

"Yes! Let's do Mom!" my mother says. "Vic, you call me Mom from now on too!"

Oh, no. No, no, no. This is... too much. Way too soon. They are going to scare off this perfect man. Cassie has told me *all* about this, about expecting too much too soon and how it screws everything up.

"While we were waiting for you to arrive, Mrs. Mancini and I were talking about *grandbabies*."

Oh, fuck no.

"Mom—" Vic starts, but I see it already. My mom's eyes have gone gooey and dreamy.

Shit.

"Mom—" I start, trying to cut my mother off. It seems Vic and I are having the same internal crisis. I know his mom has been dying for him to settle down, but he has no idea how my mom can be with this topic.

Brutal.

Brutal is the only word I've got.

"You two would have the most beautiful *babies!*"

"Vic's coloring and Gabrielle's hair!" Mrs. Brandt says.

"Gabrielle's build on a girl with Vic's eyes!" my mother shouts. Her voice is creeping up in volume.

"Mom, this is—"

"I want at least three," Mrs. Brandt says.

"At *least!*" my mom agrees. They're staring at us, me held protectively in the crook of Vic's arm, like we're a science experiment, like they're going to run off and make Punnett squares to figure out the highest probability of what our collective children will look like. "Need to start soon, though," my mom says.

"Mom!"

"Vic isn't getting any younger," his mom agrees.

"Mom, this is—"

But they aren't listening to Vic or me. They keep going. Looking over us and then confirming with each other.

New best friends.

A nightmare.

"Mexico is looking pretty good right now," Vic says, looking down at me with a laugh.

"Mexico? Hear it's nice there. Need a passport, though," my dad says, walking out the back door with his paper rolled up under his arm, Mr. Brandt not far behind.

My father has never left the East Coast his entire life. The furthest he has gone from home was Orlando to take us to Disney. Otherwise, it was a life of Jersey shore trips and nothing else.

"Can't go to Mexico when you're pregnant, Gabi. I think the water would be bad for a baby," my mother states, Mrs. Brandt nodding like she agrees.

"Honestly, you should stay close; you never know when you'll need family!" his mother says, but my father has stopped dead, looking back at us.

"Somethin' you wanna tell me, Victor?" His face is fury and aggression and simmering dad rage.

"I don't think Mexico is far enough," I whisper.

"Oh, hush, Vin," my mom says, pouring an iced tea for Vic's

father, who is quietly taking in the sideshow. Vic is his father's son for sure.

"Hush? *Hush?!*" His face is going red.

"He's going to give himself a heart attack," I say in a whisper to Vic, tipping my head to him but keeping my eyes on my dad.

"You can't give yourself a heart attack. There would be pre-existing conditions."

"He'd be the first case. Congrats, you get to be here for it. You could write some kind of groundbreaking medical journal on it," I say.

"Downside, though, your dad would have a heart attack."

This is going on while my mom and dad argue about my mom telling Dad to hush.

"What's going on?" Dom asks, walking out.

Great.

This is only getting worse.

Nico comes out on his heels, followed by Sammy.

Yes, let's just bring the children out into this chaos. Great. Awesome.

"Your sister is pregnant. Her boy hasn't even manned up and talked to me about it, definitely hasn't asked me to marry her. "

"Dad, I'm—"

"I'll get to you next, *polpetta*." I shut up.

Why? I'm not sure. But when my dad's got that voice on and his eyes are directed at me and frustrated, my lips seal.

"You're *pregnant?*" Dom says, eyes wide. Nico laughs, knowing the chaos that's unfolding.

Gia comes walking out. "Who's pregnant?"

"Auntie *Gabi!*" Sammy shrieks, jumping up and down. "I hope it's a girl!" Gia's mouth drops open as she looks at me. I try to shake my head, but before I can, Dario comes out.

"Did someone just say Gabi's pregnant?"

"Jesus Christ," I say, looking to the sky like it will give me an answer. Maybe one of those skywriters or a plane holding a sign will tell me what the fuck to do.

It will probably say, "Run away to Mexico."

"It's all good, kitten," Vic says in my ear. I look at him.

"I'm not pregnant." Voices around us are yelling, chaos continuing and rising to new levels. "And the neighbors are going to call the cops."

"All good, babe."

"We should have gone to Mexico."

"Ask Cassie for vacation time. We'll go." I melt. "We'd have to come back, though." I scrunch my nose. "I wouldn't mind, by the way."

"What?"

"If you were pregnant." I say nothing, that rare shock and quiet coming over me. "I'd like to go the traditional order. But you and me? This is it, Gabi." Silence in my mind. "But I also think if I knock you up before I put a ring on it, your dad will kill me."

"Cement blocks," a voice says from behind us. Enzo. "He knows people." I punch my brother.

"I'm not pregnant."

"Oh, I know."

"Why haven't you tried to stop it?"

"It's entertaining."

"You're a shitty brother."

"I'm your favorite brother."

"Wrong. Dom's my favorite brother."

"Dom!?" He looks genuinely taken aback.

"He's nice. And he's got a cute daughter."

"Fuck that." Enzo lifts his head, ready to stir the pot. "I get to be the godfather to Gab's baby!"

I fucking hate my family.

"No fucking way, I'm Gabi's favorite," Dom yells from across the deck.

"All of you, shut the fuck up!" I yell.

Everyone listens.

Silence takes over the deck, and I can *breathe*. Vic laughs. I shoot him a look.

"Gabi isn't pregnant," he says, staring at my dad. In the corner, Vic's dad is laughing hysterically, wiping tears. Good lord.

"Jesus, Vin, give us two seconds to tell you before you go off the rails," my mother says, and I shoot a look at *her* now because she started this chaos.

"Gem and I were just talking about how much we can't wait for Vic and your daughter to marry and have babies." Gem. Only my mom's closest friends call her that. Is this a good thing or a bad thing?

And like always, Vic can read my mind, dipping to my ear as the chaos of my dad arguing with my mom starts again. "It's a good thing, kitten. Calm down. All good."

"This is chaos."

"The good kind. Good chaos."

And with that, there's a slam from the table as Bruiser, let out by someone leaving the door open, jumps onto the picnic table of food, sending it crashing to the ground as he attacks a bowl of potato salad.

Chaos.

We order pizza.

THIRTY-SEVEN

-Vic-

I ALWAYS KNOW when Gabs has had just a tiny bit beyond her standard one glass of wine because the filter goes first. That filter that holds back her menagerie of thoughts shreds, and she reveals her every whim.

I love it.

Except, of course, when I'm driving on the Parkway and it comes out in a much different way than I'd ever expect.

"What's squirting?"

I nearly swerve into the next lane.

"Jesus, Vic, what the fuck?"

"What did you just say?" I look over at her on the passenger seat, her feet up on the dash, her face on me, eyes wide.

"Stop looking at me! Look at the road, you psycho!" I obey, but I have questions. "And you say I'm the bad driver."

"What did you just say, Gabi?" She hesitates. I look over at her again.

"Vic!"

"Did you just ask about squirting?"

"Look at the road and we'll talk!" She's sitting up straight now, hand reaching for the wheel like I'm going to kill us both and she can stop it. Still, I put my eyes to the road and say a little prayer that this woman said what I hope she said.

"Gabi."

"I said, what is squirting." She's embarrassed now. Shit. *I need to play this cool. Don't seem too eager.*

"Gabrielle. What's my rule?" She sighs.

"I can ask questions, but I can't be embarrassed. Questions are healthy." I smile. This is not her first... question.

"Where'd you hear about squirting?" She looks from me to the window, and I know I'll get my answer. Then, in true Gabi fashion, she starts talking.

"Okay, so I was reading this book, right? And they kept talking about it—talking about squirting. And, like, I thought it was just another way to say wet. Like really, really wet, you know? That happens sometimes and, I guess, you could describe it as that. Not what *I'd* call it, but, to each their own." She looks at me for confirmation and I nod, fighting a smile.

"Okay, so I kept reading and then he's like... really working for it. And he's saying some dirty stuff, like... ya know." She tries to gloss over *that* one.

"Like what, kitten?" Silence. "Gabi?"

"Like the kind of stuff you say," she says in an annoyed rush. She rolls her eyes, but her voice gets quiet. "The stuff I like." *Fuck yeah. My girl loves dirty talk.* It's the surefire way to keep her on this planet when I'm fucking her.

"Got it. Carry on," I say with a smile, flicking my blinker and turning at the exit for Ocean View.

"You like that, don't you?" she says, her voice exasperated.

"Like what?"

"Making me uncomfortable."

"I like making you feel a lot of things, kitten. I just find you adorable when you're uncomfortable." Again, she rolls her eyes and this time I don't hide the smile. "Okay, continue your story." Her frustrated sigh comes again, but she hesitates like she doesn't want to keep going. I move my eyes from the road to her, a vague threat.

"Fine," she says, and my eyes go back to the road. The smile that rarely leaves my lips when I'm with her widens. "So, like, then he's really going at it, you know?"

"No, explain." She looks at me and sees the smirk.

"Don't be a dick or I'm not finishing my story." I laugh.

"Fine."

"So he's... doing it, and basically he says there's a ... gush. And she's screaming, apparently, and he's like, really into it."

"Any man would be."

"So that's a thing!?" Her voice squeaks a bit with her question.

"Yeah, kitten, that's a thing."

"And like... it's hot?" Her voice has gone low, inquisitive. Shit. I'm going to get hard, aren't I?

"I've never done it with a woman. But thinkin' of you doing it? Shit." I move a hand from the steering wheel to readjust myself. Her eyes follow the movement and I hear her breaths go shallow.

"Do you... do you know how?" She's interested. Fuck. Yes. This is a dream. *She* is a dream.

But also, my manhood has been brought into question.

"I'm a doctor," I answer.

"So?"

"So I'm a doctor. I know bodies."

"You're an ER doctor. You can't do a triple bypass."

"A triple bypass is very different from squirting, babe."

"Just because you took an anatomy class—" she starts, using my excuse that got us in this position all those months ago.

"I could make you squirt, Gabi." She stares at me as I put the car in park in the parking garage of her apartment. Her eyes are hot and fuck if we're not trying this. "Let's go, Gabi."

Once the door is locked behind Gabi, she turns to me with a smile, hands on her hips. "So?" she says. Good to see she still has that happy, no filter buzz going. I don't say a word. Instead, I dip, putting a shoulder into her belly and lifting her giggling body, carrying her to her room. Then I toss her onto her bed.

"Get naked," I say, hands going to my belt.

"What?"

"You heard me, Gabi. Take your clothes off. I have an assignment." She stares at me with wide eyes for a few moments. There was a time when that face would mean I was tiptoeing into dangerous territory, where I might lose her.

Not any more.

It's interesting to see how we've both evolved—Gabi rarely needs my help coming back to earth anymore, both of us to in tune with each other.

I'm still talkative with her though, just because she really fucking likes it.

Instead of losing her, she smiles a cat-like smile and starts to do as I ask, crossing her arms over her front and tugging up her shirt. I follow, removing my clothes with a precision she'll probably mock later but I'm formulating my plan.

When she's naked, she lies back and stares at me with a raised eyebrow, waiting for me to crawl up the bed between her legs.

But I don't do as she expects.

Instead, I walk around to her nightstand.

"What are you doing?" She looks equal parts confused and paranoid.

Which makes sense.

This is a drawer filled with sex toys that I still can't figure out if she bought in an effort to make herself come before she met me, or after.

Either way, since that first day I discovered them three weeks ago, I've been lying in wait to use them. Tonight is the perfect time.

"Vic?" Her eyes are wide as I reach for the handle. She tries to roll, to stop me, but too late. It's open. Inside lies a collection, mostly small vibrators with various purposes I'm happy to try on her later, but there's one that caught my eye instantly. I grab it.

"Have you ever used this? I ask, pressing the button on the purple G-spot vibrator, bringing it to life.

"What? I-I don't—"

"No embarrassment, Gabi, remember." I sit on the edge of the bed next to her and move the vibrator towards her. Her eyes are wide, nervous, and locked to the purple silicone.

"What are you doing with that?"

"We're going to use this."

"For what?!" I love her frantic look that is quickly morphing into something warmer. I take the end of the vibrator that will be inside her in not much time and start to move it around her nipples, already peaked. Her back moves off the bed at the sensation. "Oh, god," she says, a whisper.

"I'm going to use this to make you squirt, Gabi." Confusion wars with the pleasure on her face.

"What, why?" I move on to the other nipple, circling it, not quite touching the peak, drawing circles on her skin while she writhes.

"Because this will make you come."

"I thought you were going to make me squirt. I want to squirt." Sometimes it's a shock to my system to remember that there was a time when Gabi was shy, a virgin, and never had come before. That time wasn't even that far back, but she's come a long way.

I smile, knowing she didn't mean to admit that she wants to come in that way. This is supposed to be some kind of test of my abilities, not her desire. But, in a way, it feels like those first times when I needed to get past her barriers and prove that she could do what she saw as the impossible.

"You need to come first, then you'll come a second time. The second time will be your squirt, kitten. And then you'll come a third time because I'm already hard as fuck just thinking about this." Her eyes move to my hand that strokes my cock, a small, suffering squeak coming from her.

I start to move the vibrator down her belly.

"First, I'm going to put this in you. Then I'm going to suck your clit, fuck you with it until you come that first time. Then I'm going to keep working you through that one, and baby? I'm gonna make you gush for me." Her eyes go hooded and dazed. Down the vibrator goes, circling her belly button which makes her giggle, but that sound stops when I reach right above her clit.

"You ready?" I ask, smiling. She nods and I watch her chest rise and fall with her heavy breaths. Gorgeous.

And then I do as promised. I move the head of the vibrator to her clit and her back bows.

"Oh, shit! Oh god, Vic!" I love that sound: my name on her lips when she's like this. The vibrator moves from its direct assault to circle the edges of her clit, her hips moving to get me where she wants me. Instead, I dip down, running the vibrator through her wet, pressing just barely into her entrance before moving back up, circling. Teasing. "Oh, fuck, oh fuck!" I move over her clit again, repeating the circuit until her back falls, her hands going to her hair as she continues her frustrated rambling.

Finally, I give her what she wants.

Slowly, watching it disappear inside of her in the sexiest show I'll never forget, I push the vibrator all the way in. The way it's angled means it's right against her G-spot and I tip it down to press harder there.

"Holy shit!" she yells, eyes snapping open and locking with mine.

"The prettiest pussy I've ever seen, baby." She moans, and then I move down to get face to face with my prize. My tongue dips out, tasting her clit, vibrations from inside just a whisper on me. She groans again, a deeper sound.

She's close.

Fuck, this is going to be quick.

Locking my eyes to hers again as I continue to move the vibrator in slow circles, her hips moving to try and fuck herself on it, I lower my head and latch on.

"Vic!" she shouts. I keep sucking, my tongue moving to flick over her swollen clit, nipping as her hips continue to move, demanding more.

I love this woman.

I love the *change* in this woman.

But possibly more, I love the sound she makes when I circle her clit completely and suck hard, moving the vibrator to press on her G-spot, and she explodes. I have to work to keep the vibrator in place, and all I can think about is her clamping on my cock the same way.

She screams my name, coming hard and quick as I slowly stop licking, but don't remove the vibrator. Face wet, I sit up on my knees to watch the rest of the show as I move into phase two.

Her breathing is going, ratcheting higher and higher as I continue moving the toy in her. My eyes move from her pussy to her face and back again. When she tries to close her legs, just seconds after coming down from her first orgasm, I use my free hand to push one leg back, opening her up to me.

"Vic, I— It's too much. Oh, god, fuck!" she says, hips bucking, trying to get away from the overwhelming sensation.

This is the hottest thing I've ever seen and I've witnessed Gabi make herself come on her own fingers while sucking me off.

That was hot, but this? Gabi squirming, panting, squealing?

Amazing.

"That's it, baby. You got it. You're so fucking wet for me," I say, watching her drip down the purple vibrator I keep moving in her, slow, small circles pressed against the spot.

"Vic," she mewls, her head thrashing.

"Is that all for me? Are you wet for me, Gabi?" I ask, my voice low. Her hand is moving up her body, frantic, unsure of what to do. She grabs her tit nearly too hard, pinching her nipple, and I groan at the sight. "Answer me," I say, slapping her inner thigh. Her moan is loud, deep, and I start to hear a quiet sloshing where the vibrator is moving.

Fuck yeah.

"Yes, yes, it's for you," she moans through her pants, and I keep going, fucking her with the vibrator, trying to get to the promised land.

I have a reputation to uphold, anyway.

"God your pussy is so pretty Gabi. Is it going to gush for me? I think you're gonna, baby. You're gonna squirt for me, aren't you?"

"Vic, I—oh god. Oh *god. Vic you need to stop!*" Her voice is frantic, but I don't stop. I know what this is. Her hand is slapping the bed, the other hand trailing to her belly and pressing there, adding pressure. *Instinct.*

"Why, baby, why should I stop?"

"Oh my god, Vic, I'm gonna pee. I need you to—"

"Good, baby. Do it. Fuck yeah, Gabi. Holy fuck this is the sexiest thing. I'm gonna fuck you so hard after, you're going to be fucking sore tomorrow. Push through it, kitten. You're gonna squirt for me." I encourage her, and she keeps moaning, those moans moving to deep, visceral grunts as the feeling builds.

"Vic!" she moans, eyes locked to mine, half panic, half intrigue.

"That's it baby, let go," I say, then my eyes move to her pussy, and holy fuck, it happens. An absolutely primal sound falls from Gabi's lips as her pussy gushes liquid, more than I've ever seen from a normal orgasm, as she continues to buck her hips, riding the vibrator still deep in her cunt.

I leave it there, pushing deep and dipping forward, latching my mouth around her clit and swallowing the last of it, glorying in the fact that this just happened, something I will have fucking amazing daydreams about for the rest of my life.

When I release her, I instantly move up her body, lining my cock up with her.

Her eyes are shut, far off on another planet.

"Don't leave just yet, baby. I gotta get my fill of you." Her eyes open, glazed with lust and satisfaction as I slide into her. "Fucking perfect fit every time," I groan. "Never seen a more perfect woman than you. Made for me, Gabrielle."

The passion has moved from frantic to somehow sweet as her lazy eyes meet mine.

"I'm yours, Vic," she says.

"Yeah, you are," I reply, pumping in as I kiss her.

And she is.

She always will be.

I will spend a lifetime exploring and learning and teaching this woman. Her body, her mind, her soul.

And when I move my hand to her clit, rubbing until she comes one last time around me before I pump into her, I know she knows it too.

"Always," she says.

EPILOGUE

-Gabi-
Eight years later

"Let's go, Antonia!" I yell up the stairs to my daughter. "We're going to be late for the party!"

An explosion of pink comes running down the stairs.

"Are you kidding me?" I say, looking her over: sparkly tee shirt, giant pink tutu that was the pièce de résistance of her ballet uniform last month, neon green leggings.

Antonia.

My girl.

In so many ways. Not only does she look almost identical to me, just with gorgeous, darker skin, the spitting image of what my mind created all those years ago, but her mind works the same as mine. Always working, always pondering. Always getting into trouble, if I'm being honest. My mother-in-law wants me to bring her to a doctor and get her tested, but until it starts to impact her, starts to become something she isn't proud of, I want to nurture it.

Make her proud of the way she's different.

The way her father made me feel.

I want to teach her ways to work around it, work *with* her mind so she can function in a world of "normal" people when she is so far from that in the best way possible.

It's strange how becoming a mother can help you love the parts about yourself you never liked, seeing them in a tinier version of you that you love to pieces.

"What?" she asks, hands on her little hips.

The attitude isn't me though.

No way.

No matter what Vic or my brothers or my father say, that attitude did not come from me.

Gia, maybe. That must be where she got it. Or maybe Vic's sister, Vivian.

"What?" I parrot in response, the mom eyebrow raised.

"Are we ready to go yet?" my husband says, walking in, eyes to his wrist as he adjusts the watch there. His temples are sprinkled with gray, the crinkles at his eyes more profound, but his broad shoulders haven't changed. Neither has his panty-dropping smile, the one he gives me when he catches my eyes running up and down him.

Black fitted slacks, a white, crisp button-up.

This man is gorgeous.

"You gotta wait another 6 months, kitten." That snaps me out of my haze.

"Absolutely fucking not."

"Two years between babies. Not healthy for your body if you go any sooner."

"You can wait an eternity. No more children are coming out of this body."

"Are you having another kid!?" The voice is in the living room, coming closer.

Cassie.

Cassie with my beautiful baby boy on her hip.

He's not a baby any more but moving into toddlerdom, in a tiny boy's outfit that matches his daddy's. I put my arms out to grab him, to snuggle him and smell his head as if he's still a newborn.

God, I miss that smell.

No, Gabi. No more babies. Childbirth sucks. Newborns suck.

Vic's arm comes around my waist, his voice in my ear, breath on my neck.

"But I love seeing you pregnant," he says, voice low.

That doesn't suck. The way Vic dotes on me even more when I'm carrying his child? Yeah, that part I like. A lot.

"I just lost the baby weight," I complain.

"Every time you get pregnant, your tits are magical. I like the baby weight. More to grab when I'm—"

"Oh my god, ew!" Vivi, my sister-in-law says, wearing a pristine red dress, the perfect politician's wife. "I'm gonna barf."

"Why are you even here?" Vic asks his little sister, stepping back from me with a glare on his face.

"I need to borrow a pair of earrings," she says, walking up the stairs in the foyer towards our bedroom. "You don't mind, right, Gab? V gets you the nicest shit."

"Why not have your own husband buy you jewelry?" Vic yells up the stairs, but Vivi just laughs her tinkling laugh, ignoring him.

"Gabi!" my brother shouts as he walks through my door. "Can you talk to Paige? I swear to god she's losing her mind!"

Paige stomps in behind him, slamming the door shut, blond hair flying behind her in a perfect sheet.

"Don't you run off to your little sister to try and get out of this. We need to talk about it!" She stops, heels clicking on tile, and looks at me. "Oh, look at you, my handsome man!" Her tone changes, and she grabs Vinnie from my arms, named after my father. She takes her position as godmother very seriously and doesn't even flinch when he tugs hard on her hoop earring. "See! Look at this! I want one!!" she shouts as she walks toward the kitchen where my brother disappeared.

I just roll my eyes.

I have no idea why everyone is here at my house when we all are headed to our parents' anniversary party, but I love it.

I love this chaos.

A small, warm hand slips in mine, the other hand going up my wrist.

"Mommy, how did you get this booboo?" Antonia asks, touching the faded scar on my wrist.

Cassie laughs hysterically as Vic looks on, a smile on his lips.

"That scar is how I met your father, baby. That's all you have to know."

CASSIE'S LIST OF RED FLAGS:

- Tall, dark, and handsome.
- Panty-dropping smile.
- A good dancer—why can he move that well?
- He doesn't like his mom.
- He calls his exes crazy.
- You never meet his family.
- He doesn't like dogs—only jerks don't like dogs.
- He knows what he's doing in bed way more than any man should.
- He has women's clothing in his home.
- He takes calls in another room.
- He gets mad when you dress hot.

ABOUT THE AUTHOR

Morgan is a born and raised Jersey girl, living there with her two boys, toddler daughter, and mechanic husband. She's addicted to iced espresso, chips, and Starburst jellybeans.

Writing has been her calling for as long as she can remember. There's a framed 'page one' of a book she wrote at seven hanging in her childhood home to prove the point. Her entire life she's crafted stories in her mind, begging to be released but it wasn't until recently she finally gave them the reigns.

I'm so grateful you've agreed to take this journey with me.

Stay up to date with future stories, get sneak peeks and bonus chapters by signing up for my newsletter here.

Stay up to date via TikTok and Instagram

Stay up to date with future stories, get sneak peeks and bonus chapters by joining the Reader Group on Facebook!

HAVE YOU VISITED SPRINGBROOK HILLS?

If you're looking for spicy small town romance, Morgan Elizabeth has you covered! Check out these releases:

Get book one, The Distraction, on Kindle Unlimited here!

The last thing he needs is a distraction.

Hunter Hutchin's success is due to one thing, and one thing only: his unerring focus on Beaten Path, the outdoor recreation company he built from the ground up after his first business was an utter failure.

When his dad gets sick, Hunter is forced to go back to his hometown and prove once and for all that his father's belief in him wasn't for nothing. With illness looming, distractions are unacceptable.

Staying with his sister, he meets Hannah, the sexy nanny who has had his head in a frenzy since they met.

When Hunter's dad gets sick, he's forced to leave the city and move back into the small town he grew up in at his sister's house. Ever since he watched Hannah dance into his life, he's finding himself drifting from his goals and purpose - or is he drifting closer to them?

She refuses to make the same mistakes as her mother.

Hannah Keller grew up watching what happens when a family falls apart and lived through those consequences. When it's time, she won't make the same mistake by settling for anyone.

But when the uncle of the kids she nannies comes to stay for the summer, she can't help but find herself drawn to the handsome, standoffish man who is definitely not for her.

Can she get through the summer while protecting her heart? Or will he breakthrough and leave her broken?

Out now in the Kindle Store and on Kindle Unlimited

He was her first love.

Luna Davidson has been in love with Tony since she was ten years old. As her older brother's best friend, he was always off-limits, but that doesn't mean she didn't try. But years after he turned her down, she's found herself needing his help, whether she wants it or not.

She's his best friend's little sister.

When he learns that Luna has had someone stalking her for months, he's furious that she didn't tell anyone. As a detective on the Springbrook Hills PD, it's his job to serve and protect. But can he use this as an excuse to find out what really happened all those years ago?

Can Luna overcome her own insecurities to see what's right in front of her? Can Tony figure out who is stalking her before it goes too far?

Out now in the Kindle Store and on Kindle Unlimited

She was always the fill-in.

Jordan Daniels always knew she had a brother and sister her mom left behind. Heck, her mom never let her forget she didn't live up to their standards. But when she disappears from the limelight after her country star boyfriend proposes, the only place she knows to go to is to the town her mother fled and the family who doesn't know she exists.

He won't fall for another wild child.

Tanner Coleman was left in the dust once before when his high school sweetheart ran off to follow a rockstar around the world. He loves his roots, runs the family business, and will never leave Springbrook Hills. But when Jordan, with her lifetime spent traveling the world and mysterious history comes to work for him, he can't help but feel drawn to her.

Can Jordan open up to him about her past and stay in one place? Can Tanner trust his heart with her, or will she just hurt him like his ex?

ALSO BY MORGAN ELIZABETH

The Springbrook Hills Series

The Distraction

The Protector

The Substitution

The Connection

The Playlist, coming March '23

Holiday Standalone, interconnected with SBH:

Tis the Season for Revenge

The Ocean View Series

The Ex Files

Walking Red Flag

Bittersweet

The Mastermind Duet

Ivory Tower

Diamond Fortress

Printed in Great Britain
by Amazon